CASSIE EDWARDS

THE SAVAGE SERIES
Winner of the *Romantic Times* Lifetime Achievement Award for Best Indian Series!

"Cassie Edwards writes action-packed, sexy reads! Romance fans will be more than satisfied!"
—*Romantic Times*

THE HAND OF DESTINY

"I came to Louisiana thinking that I might find a new start here, and then I discovered that I had been won in a game of poker as though I were some inanimate object, a poker chip," she said.

She fought the urge to cry, for now she was feeling more hurt than angry over what had happened.

"I am a person . . . a person with feelings," she said, her voice breaking. Tears fell from her eyes as her defenses crumbled.

"Now will you please let me pass? Or do I have to ride around you?"

Feeling so much for the woman, and touched by her vulnerability, loneliness, and loveliness, Red Feather inched his horse closer to hers.

"If you will not flee . . . if you will stay, I will make you feel like anything but a person who was won in a game of cards," he said thickly. "I will see to it that you have a good life. You came to Louisiana thinking that you were to be married. Well, that can still happen. *I* will marry you."

CASSIE EDWARDS

SAVAGE DESTINY

LEISURE BOOKS **NEW YORK CITY**

To Mirl Cruse, a very special person
from the lovely state of Louisiana.

A LEISURE BOOK®

February 2003

Published by

Dorchester Publishing Co., Inc.
276 Fifth Avenue
New York, NY 10001

Cover art by John Ennis.
www.ennisart.com

ISBN 0-8439-5051-X

Printed in the United States of America.

Visit us on the web at www.dorchesterpub.com.

ACKNOWLEDGMENTS

A special thank you goes to Debbie Melancon and Melanie Aymond, the research coordinator for the Chitimacha tribe in Louisiana.

And in memory of Ralph Darden, past chief of the Chitimacha tribe.

SAVAGE
DESTINY

Forbidden Love

Forbidden was the love they made last night,
Powered as one, they made it right.
Fear filled their hearts from lifetimes before,
Now together in one another's embrace,
Peace is evermore.
The pleasure of his hands giving their soft
   touch,
She never knew rapture could bring her this
   much.
Thunder sent from God above was all they
   needed to hear to know
God had blessed this forbidden love.
In lifetimes to come, they will always know,
Though forbidden is the love, it will always
   grow.

—By Angela Dawn Reinhardt,
poet and friend

Chapter One

Sweet Babe, in thy face,
Soft desires I can trace,
Secret joys and secret smiles,
Little pretty infant wiles.
　　　　　—William Blake

Jamestown, Louisiana, 1821

As she lay in her soft feather bed wearing a lacy, white satin nightgown, Jewel Ratcliffe looked lovingly at the naked newborn baby lying at her right side. His copper-colored skin contrasted with the fine white linen sheet upon which he lay.

Although the child's skin and eyes were the

1

same color as Jewel's, instead of pale like his father's, and she was filled with maternal protectiveness, she still could not feel the same connection to him as she had to her firstborn.

She loved her newborn, but he was not the child of her soul her firstborn had been, for this second son was born of a man she had not chosen for a husband.

He had chosen . . . had *stolen* her . . . from her Chitimacha people . . . and had made her his wife.

He had given her the name Jewel and forbidden her ever again to call herself Soft Flower, which was her true name.

Although he had been good to her, had given her all the luxuries enjoyed by his neighbors' white wives, Jewel had not been able to love him as a woman should love her husband. She could never shake the feeling of being a prisoner, even though her white husband doted on her like the person she truly was . . . a princess.

Yes, before her abduction, while she lived among her true people, she had been a Chitimacha princess . . . Princess Soft Flower.

She turned her gaze to her left where her ten-month-old baby lay asleep, seemingly unaware that his world had changed . . . that he had a brother, although one that shared only his mother's blood, not his father's.

"Yes, son, you have a new baby brother today,

but not one you can ever call a full-blood brother, for his father is different from yours," Jewel whispered so that her voice would carry no farther than the child to whom she spoke. "But you both will be labeled half-breed by those who enjoy belittling our people."

She placed a gentle hand on her son's soft cheek. "No one will know until it is time for them to know," she whispered. "You are a full-blood Chitimacha whose father is . . ."

She swallowed hard as tears rushed to her eyes. Her son's father was a beloved chief. A chief who had lost his princess when Soft Flower was abducted.

She had strayed too far from her village that day, enjoying the peace of the woods, digging roots, and talking to Mother Earth and the birds who sang to her in the trees overhead.

She would never forget how silent those birds had suddenly become. Moments later, a rough hand reached out and covered her mouth so that she could not scream. A strong, muscled arm had swept around her waist and dragged her away. She was gagged and hidden beneath blankets, then thrown over the back of a pack horse, so that no one would suspect she was a person, not part of a packet of newly acquired pelts.

After she was taken from the horse and unwrapped, she found herself standing before an expensively dressed white man in a type of house

3

she had never known could exist. The riches surrounding her were astonishing to a woman who had lived her entire eighteen years in a buffalo-hide-wrapped tepee.

Although she had heard that some white people were richer than others—she had even seen white people's dwellings standing taller than the live oak trees that were so plentiful in the forests of this land—she had never been inside one of their mansions.

She had known then that no Indian woman could imagine anything as big and beautiful as this house was.

"Ratcliffe Manor," she whispered.

When she had been told that it would be her home after a white man's preacher married her to the expensively dressed white man, she had still not accepted that she would live in it.

And how could she?

She was already married!

She was married to a wonderful man, a chief who was revered by all who knew him.

But the white man had told her that it did not matter to him that she had been married in some—as he had mockingly called it—hocus-pocus way by some strange sort of Indian medicine man, for to him that was not a true marriage.

He had told her that no one was officially married unless the ceremony was conducted by a white preacher.

Shortly after that, he had brought a man dressed in black to his mansion. Holding a white man's "talking leaves" Bible, the preacher had spoken words over them and pronounced her the wife of the rich white man.

"The man I was forced to marry that day did not know I was already carrying you in my womb," Jewel whispered to Red Feather, the secret name she called her firstborn when she was not in the presence of her white husband.

Otherwise, he was called . . . Troy.

Yes, she had been pregnant at the time of her abduction, and after learning the white man's intentions for her, she had not told him about the pregnancy right away. She had been too afraid that he would find a way to make her abort the child. It was terrible enough to have been swept from the life she loved, the *man* she loved. She could not also lose her true husband's child. Her unborn baby would be the heir to a chieftainship should she ever find a way to return him to her true home and people.

"Red Feather, one day I still hope to take you to your true people, to your father," Jewel whispered, even though she doubted she would ever be given that chance. Day and night she was watched to prevent just such an escape.

She knew now that she would never be given

a chance to flee, and she had finally accepted the changes fate had brought to her life on that day she'd ventured out alone.

Tired from the birthing only a few hours earlier, Jewel turned to her newborn and drew a soft blanket up around him so that only his face was left uncovered.

She then turned again to Red Feather and covered him, as well. "I love you both so much," she whispered.

But she knew that there would always be a difference in her feelings for them, because she had plans for her firstborn that her second son could never know about.

"I will make it so, Red Feather," she whispered. She brushed a soft kiss across his copper brow. "Somehow, son, someday, when you are older and understand who you are, and who your true father is, I will find a way to lead you back to your true people."

Chapter Two

The counter our lovers staked was lost
As surely as if it were lawful coin:
And the sin I impute to each frustrate ghost.
                                —Robert Browning

Twenty-five years later—Autumn 1845
Jamestown, Louisiana

Smoke swirled throughout the room and hung low over cigar-smoking men who sat around several tables, gambling.

The tinkling of piano music blared in the background.

Scantily dressed women, their faces gaudy with

paint, laughed and teased the men drinking at the long bar. At the tables some even sat on the laps of the gamblers, helping them toss out their coins, hoping to rake some in for themselves if that particular man won a hand.

Two of the gamblers who sat opposite each other at a table ignored both the women and the cigars, as well as the patrons. They were completely focused on besting each other, as brother challenged brother in a game of cards.

"Big brother, there's now only the two of us left in this game. Do you think you're going to be the winner, or do you think it'll be me?" Larry Ratcliffe said, his midnight dark eyes narrowed as he smiled almost cynically at his brother.

Troy, dressed expensively in a dark suit, the white collar of his fancy shirt contrasting with his copper-skinned face, gave his brother a half smile.

He shuffled the cards and gave the men who had left the table a glance over his shoulder. The other gamblers stood back, waiting to see which brother would take home all that *they* had lost this evening to the brothers.

Some had hate etched on their faces, placed there not only because they had lost a week's wages to the brothers, but also because they had lost to Indians, whom they quietly despised.

They knew that most Indians would not dare

enter a tavern for a game of cards. Most of them knew they were not welcome.

But these two were of a different breed than the others. They had been born into the wealthiest of families; Jon Paul Ratcliffe, their white father, owned most of the town, and controlled those who dwelled there in one way or another.

No one would dare to mention the fact that Jon Paul Ratcliffe had an Indian wife, although most did whisper about it.

No one would dare to taunt Jon Paul Ratcliffe's boys.

And no one could outplay them in cards, although all the gamblers persisted in trying.

Tonight was no different from other nights, not even so far as the individual brothers' skill at gambling was concerned.

As usual, Troy had outplayed Larry, who was close to losing all the money he had brought. Larry's last available possession lay in the middle of the table.

If Troy won that . . .

"Why don't we call it a night, little brother?" Troy asked as he gathered the cards and placed them in a stack in the center of the table. "You know you don't want to lose that pocket watch to me. It was a present from Father and Mother on your last birthday."

"I don't intend to lose it," Larry grumbled. He nervously stroked his long, lean fingers through his thick coal-black hair, then shook his head so that his hair fell down his back, almost to his waist. His hair was the only thing he wore in the manner of his Indian ancestors.

He behaved like a white man in all other respects.

Larry frowned and leaned his face closer to Troy's. "Damn it, Troy, shuffle those cards again, then deal them," he said tightly. "Like I said, I don't plan on losing. The night has just begun, and my luck just changed for the better."

"And what has caused this change in your luck?" Troy said.

Troy sighed heavily, for he had heard it all before. Every time he outplayed his younger brother, Larry would insist on continuing, saying that his luck had just changed for the better.

But it never did.

And Troy knew that Larry resented him for this, as well as for other things. Upon first meeting Larry and Troy, most people noticed right away that there was quite a difference between the brothers.

Troy was stoic, thoughtful, intelligent, warm, and caring, especially to his mother, while Larry was cold, sometimes to the point of being heartless. He was snobbish, calculating, a liar, and lazy.

But both young men shared one weakness.

Gambling.

The only difference was that Troy knew when to stop.

Larry didn't.

"Troy, damn it, let's get on with it," Larry said. His eyes flashed angrily at his brother. "I'm ready to prove which of us is the better gambler tonight."

Troy gazed at his brother, then looked over his shoulder. Everything had gone quiet in the tavern.

Even the women had grown quiet, their eyes now on Troy, watching and admiring him.

Then Troy focused on the game of cards.

If his brother wanted to make a fool of himself again, so be it.

Troy shuffled, then dealt out two hands of five card stud.

When the game was finished, it was as Troy had known it would be.

Again he had won.

"No, I don't want the watch," Troy said as Larry shoved it across the table toward him. He straightened the cards, placed them in their wooden box, and started to rise from the table.

"Damn it, Troy, take the watch, and deal those cards again," Larry said, his eyes almost wild with envious anger.

"Why should I deal the cards when you've nothing else to gamble with?" Troy said, again shoving the watch back toward his brother. "And take the watch. It's yours. I do not want it."

"Alright, I'll take it back, but I am *not* finished gambling tonight," Larry said. He took the watch and slid it back inside his vest pocket. "Deal another hand, Troy. I've got something special to ante this time."

Troy's eyes narrowed as he gazed intently at his brother. "What are you talking about?" he asked. "The watch is all you have left to ante tonight, and you surely won't use it again, will you?"

"No, not the watch," Larry said, his eyes gleaming. "Deal. While you're dealing, I'll explain what my ante is."

"I'm going home, Larry," Troy said, rising from his chair.

When Larry rose so quickly from his chair that it tumbled over onto the floor behind him, his eyes flashing angrily, Troy stopped and stared in disbelief at his brother. This was the first time he had gotten so out of hand; he looked as though he was ready to have a fistfight if Troy didn't sit back down and continue gambling with him.

"What's got into you?" Troy asked, his eyes locking with his brother's. "You usually know when you've had enough. But tonight? It's as though you are possessed."

"I have something important to offer you as my ante, so it is only fair that you give me one more chance at the cards, Troy," Larry said, his chest heaving as his frustration with his brother grew. "One . . . last chance?"

Troy studied his brother a moment longer. There was a look of pleading in Larry's eyes. Troy breathed in a heavy sigh, then eased back down onto the chair.

"Alright, one more hand," he said, taking the cards from the box and shuffling them again. He cocked an eyebrow as he gazed at Larry. "What have you got to lay on the table, little brother? What is it that you are so eager to ante?"

"What do I have?" Larry said. He chuckled. "A woman, that's what."

Troy stopped shuffling. He gazed in disbelief at his brother. "A woman?" he said tightly. "What woman?"

"I've sent for a mail-order bride," Larry said, his eyes gleaming. "I will use *her* as my ante. If I win, I will take all the money and I will keep the woman, but if I lose, you will have not only all the money, but also the woman, who should be arriving soon on a stagecoach from Saint Louis."

"A . . . mail-order . . . bride?" Troy gasped. "I've heard of such a thing. It is mainly being done out West where men outnumber women. But here? In Louisiana? No. You've got to be jesting, brother. And why would you contract with a mail-order bride when you can have your pick of women in Jamestown?"

"It's true alright," Larry said. He smiled dev-

13

ilishly. "I'm bored with Jamestown women. I want a change. So when I saw a poster the other day in the bank, a poster advertising a mail-order bride, I went over her description and liked what I read. I decided that if she fits the bill, I'll marry her and settle down, whereas if she isn't what I expect, I'll just gamble her away to someone else."

Larry chuckled. "But tonight?" he said, his eyes gleaming. "You have a chance to win her first." He shrugged. "And, anyway, I probably *wouldn't* marry her. She is probably some toothless, ugly hag who gave a false description on the poster just to lure someone like me into sending for her. She must be homely, or why isn't she married? Why would she have to lower herself to do something like this if she is worth anything at all?"

Troy was disgusted by what his brother had done. "I don't want the woman," he said firmly. "And that's it for tonight, Larry. I'm through. Leave the table like a gentleman, Larry. There will come another time. But I suggest that you bring more coins with you next time so that you will have a better a chance of winning against me."

Larry glared at Troy resentfully. It made Larry's blood boil to know that everyone admired his brother more than him. It infuriated him that his older brother was more skilled at gambling, and everything else.

And there was one thing Larry resented most of all. He had spied on his mother and Troy and knew about the secret times they spent together, times when Larry had not been invited to join them.

He had no idea what they did during those times, for he had not dared get close enough to the closed door to listen.

He didn't want to be caught.

But he did know that his mother had made a distinction between the brothers, and it hurt Larry deep within his soul.

That was why he wanted to win tonight, to prove that he was as good as Troy in at least this one thing.

Just as Troy started to rise from the table again, Larry slammed a fist on it, startling Troy into sitting back down, his gaze wary as he studied his brother.

"Troy, you *must* give me this one last try tonight," Larry said thickly. "Deal just one more hand. If I lose, then I'll step aside and accept it. But you must give me at least this one last chance. The woman, Troy. I vow that the woman will be yours, to do with as you wish."

Tired of arguing, Troy nodded, then dealt. "This will be a game of seven card stud," he said evenly. "Play it carefully, Larry. I truly do not want that woman."

In a matter of minutes, the game was over and Troy had won again.

Larry grabbed a piece of paper from his inside coat pocket. He slammed it on the table.

"This will give you all the particulars about the woman," he said brusquely. "It has her description and her time of arrival."

Roughly he pushed his chair aside and stormed from the tavern.

Troy picked up the paper and read it. The description said the woman was beautiful. But perhaps Larry was right. She might have made herself sound pretty so she would be chosen as a mail-order bride.

No matter why she had done this, Troy could not help feeling a deep empathy for anyone so desperate that she would resort to such a ploy.

He made a quick choice: when the woman arrived in Jamestown, he would pay her well for her trouble, and then tell her that he had changed his mind, that he couldn't marry her after all.

He would not tell her that he had won her in a game of cards.

That would be humiliating, and surely she was humiliated enough by having to sell herself in such a way in order to gain a husband.

He gathered up his winnings from the table, slid the coins into his front coat pockets, then left the tavern and rode from the town on his black steed.

When he arrived at Ratcliffe Manor, his mother was waiting for him in the dark corridor.

"Son, I must talk with you," Jewel said in a voice only loud enough for Troy to hear. "I've got to speak with you alone. I have many truths to tell you about your Indian heritage. It's time, son. I have perhaps waited too long already."

Troy gazed at her questioningly. His mother had never before been so somber during their private talks.

He nodded and went with her into the library, where she closed and locked the door behind them.

When his mother turned to him, her eyes were wet with tears.

"My son, you are, oh, so much like him . . ." she murmured as she reached a hand to his face.

"*Who*, Mother?" Troy asked, raising his eyebrows.

"Tonight I shall start from the very beginning, son," Jewel murmured. She gestured toward two chairs before the fireplace. "Come. Let's sit."

He went with her and sat in one chair, she in another.

He waited for her to begin speaking, his heart strangely anxious.

Chapter Three

Love is not love which alters
When it alteration finds;
Or bends with the remover to remove:
O, no! It is an ever-fixed mark!
　　　　　　　—William Shakespeare

The stagecoach ride was a rough one for Angela Dawn Cutright, and lonely. Since she had left Saint Louis, there had only been one other passenger to keep her company on her long journey to Jamestown, Louisiana, and that had been a lady who truly did not fit Angela Dawn's description of a "lady." She had been a dance hall girl who had left the stagecoach several hours ago in a town filled with saloons and whorehouses.

Angela Dawn hated to think of what that woman was doing to keep herself in money. She, herself, had tried everything decent since her parents' deaths to keep herself alive.

In order to arrive at her destination looking respectable and refined enough for the man she would soon marry, she had spent hard-earned money to purchase the dress she now wore. It was a pale green, fully gathered velveteen dress with a lacy white collar.

She knew how important it was that the first impression people had of her now was a good one. She had even splurged a bit more and purchased a lovely hat which matched the dress, and her auburn hair flowed long and free beneath it.

On her hands were beautiful white gloves, and she carried a purse of the same fabric as her dress; it was decorated with beads of various colors sewn in the shapes of flowers.

As the stagecoach bounced in and out of potholes in the dirt road, Angela Dawn held on to the seat to steady herself. She leaned this way and that, her bottom aching from the long ride.

Her heart was empty and sad, yet she was filled with a determination that kept her chin high, as well as her hopes.

She stared out the window. The sky was blue, the sun high and bright, the autumn breeze cool and refreshing as it blew in through the opened window.

As far as her eyes could see, she saw pines, oaks, pin oaks, and muscadine vines.

Then the stagecoach ambled past a hillside covered with live oaks and briars.

She caught an occasional glimpse of deer, fox, and even a wild hog standing beneath the trees.

When she saw a persimmon tree heavy with fruit, she thought back to Missouri, where she had gone persimmon-picking with her mother more than once. There was nothing like the aroma of a persimmon pie in the oven.

Ah, that seemed so long ago. . . .

She became lost in thoughts of what had brought her to this place in her life. Her emerald-green eyes filled with tears when she recalled how she had found her mother sprawled out on the bedroom floor only a few short months ago.

The investigation had revealed that she'd died from an overdose of some sort of medicine prescribed by her doctor to counteract the depression she had been fighting since the death of her husband, Virgil Cutright.

Her mother, Dorothy, had truly fought hard to understand and accept her husband's sudden death, but in the end she had given up trying. It seemed death was the only way she could escape her despair and loneliness.

Angela Dawn wiped the tears from her eyes

and set her jaw firmly. Her parents' deaths had reminded her of the mission she was on.

She was on a mission of vengeance!

Her father, a gambler who had made life sweet and comfortable for his wife and daughter, had been killed in a duel.

And now that Dorothy Cutright was also dead, Angela Dawn was all alone in the world at the age of eighteen.

She had sold what she could of her own and her parents' belongings before creditors had swarmed around her and taken the rest.

Since then, Angela Dawn had been forced to fend for herself for the first time in her life. She had vowed to be stronger than her mother. She had taken any reputable job she could find, having mainly worked as a housekeeper.

One goal drove her now: taking revenge on the one who'd murdered her father.

But no matter how many places she worked, she had not been able to accumulate enough money to pay her way south, where she planned to search for the murderer.

And it *was* murder.

The man had pulled the trigger before the countdown had been finished. Afterward, he had fled the authorities. No one knew his name; only that he was from a rich family in Louisiana.

She didn't even have a description of the man, but she hoped that when she arrived in Jamestown, where the duel had taken place, someone would remember the murderer.

She was going to search until she found him.

But to find her father's killer, she had to first find a way to travel south and live among those who might eventually lead her to him.

She had decided that the only way she would be able to afford to do this was to advertise herself in Jamestown as a mail-order bride.

Once there, she could begin her investigation.

If she ever did find the guilty party, she had her father's dueling pistols, which had been returned to her with his body. She planned to use one of them on the murderer. She had kept the pistols, and would only part with them if the man she was to marry turned out to be a scoundrel. In that case, she would sell them in order to pay her way elsewhere.

"Yes, I must, I *will* marry a stranger," she whispered determinedly.

She was willing to make this sacrifice if it meant that she had even the slightest chance of finding her father's murderer.

The search was on. And if she succeeded in avenging her father's death, she would be avenging her mother's as well, for her mother would not be dead now if Angela Dawn's father had not died at the hands of a murdering, cold-hearted man.

"Father, Mother, I *will* avenge your deaths," she whispered.

When her father had first shown his pair of dueling pistols to Angela Dawn, he had told her that a duel was called an "affair of honor."

In no way had the duel in which her father had participated been an "affair of honor." There had been nothing honorable in the way he had died!

Chapter Four

In all external grace,
You have some part,
But you like none,
None you,
For constant heart.
    —William Shakespeare

"Son, what I am about to tell you must remain between you and me," Jewel said softly. "And listen with an open heart. You will have a decision to make that might change your life forever. Possibly . . . even mine."

"Mother, again you are excluding my brother Larry," Troy murmured. "Is that fair?"

"Always before, you have shown an uneasiness over leaving your brother out of our talks," Jewel said, her voice drawn. "And I have not felt at ease, myself, doing this to your brother. But you are the only one affected by what I have told you. And . . . if anyone else were told, it might go farther . . . to your *father*. I am so proud that you have kept silent about what we discussed. Were your father to know . . ."

"Mother, thus far all you have told me is that you wanted me to know about my Indian side, yet when I asked why it was so important, you never answered," Troy said. "Are you going to disclose all of it tonight . . . the reason you have never told me before?"

"I will tell you everything tonight . . . who I truly am, how I came to be with the only father you have ever known, and why it was so important never to allow him to know that we discussed your Indian heritage," Jewel murmured. She lowered her eyes, inhaled a nervous breath, then gazed again at Troy.

"As you know, you have been given a secret Indian name, which we use when you and I are together like this," she went on. "Son, Red Feather, I also told you my Indian name, which is Soft Flower. But today I will tell you so much more, it will, I am sure, stun you. But then I hope you will understand that you have an important decision to make. You must make it soon, for time is running out."

Troy leaned closer to his mother. "Running out for whom?" he asked, cocking an eyebrow.

"Your true father," Jewel said warily.

"Father?" Troy said, taken aback. "Father is ill? He . . . he . . . seems well enough to me."

"I am not speaking of the man who raised you, the man you have always addressed as 'Father,' but someone else you have had no knowledge of until today," Jewel said, swallowing hard. "Son, oh, son, how can I say it? I . . . I . . . had thought it would be much easier. I had even looked forward to this moment, yet I . . ."

"Mother, you are confusing me more by the minute," Troy said. He slowly rose from the chair. He walked across the room, then came and stood over his mother. "Mother, if Father isn't my father, then . . . who . . . is? And why haven't I ever been told?"

"Please sit," Jewel said. She gestured with a hand toward the chair. "Just listen and then I shall answer all your questions."

Troy paused, gazed in wonder down at his mother, then sat down. He was stiff, for he knew that his mother would not have told him something so unbelievable unless it was true.

"Is my brother not my true brother?" he blurted out. "There is so much difference between us. I mean . . . our behavior . . . our passions . . . our purpose in life."

"He is your blood brother, but you have different fathers," Jewel said softly. "Son, Jon Paul Ratcliffe is Larry's father. *Your* father is . . ."

She paused, rose quickly from the chair, then went to the door and slowly opened it.

She stepped out into the corridor to be certain no one was there to hear as the truth was finally told.

She only hoped that Troy would accept her revelation. It was so important that he get to know his true father, and even his true people. If he refused to go to the Chitimacha village, she would be terribly disappointed.

She closed the door and sat down beside Troy again. "I shall begin, and please do not interrupt me until I have said all that I have waited so many years to say," she murmured.

Troy nodded, but he could not stop the rapid beat of his heart, or his building curiosity about who his true father was, and why he had not been told until now.

"Jon Paul Ratcliffe was a rich Englishman who came to Louisiana to establish himself in the sugarcane business, as well as the tobacco industry," Jewel began. "He had heard about Indian slavery years ago in the lower Louisiana territory, which accommodated the needs of the early French settlers, but died with the original French trading families. He heard that the Indian women were not used so much in the sugarcane, cotton, and tobacco fields as they were for concubines, prostitutes, and wives."

"Slaves . . . concubines . . . prostitutes?" Troy gasped out. "Please don't tell me that you were—"

"No, I was not a slave, concubine, or prostitute, but . . . I did become a wife to a man not of my choice," Jewel said. "That man was Jon Paul Ratcliffe."

"He forced you . . . ?"

"He abducted me and then forced me," Jewel said, her spine stiffening at the remembrance of that day when her whole world had come tumbling around her.

Troy leaped to his feet. He curled his hands into tight fists at his sides. "He abducted you?" he said tightly. "He forced you to marry him?"

"Red Feather, please sit down and listen to the rest, and then I shall answer your questions," Jewel murmured.

Troy's pulse was racing, as were his thoughts.

He had never felt a close bond to his father. Now he understood why.

Somehow, deep inside himself, he had known that this man was not as he tried to portray himself to the community, or to his sons.

He was a man who had many sins on his soul.

The thought sickened Troy.

He leaned closer to his mother. "Please continue," he said earnestly. "I shall not interrupt again."

She reached over and took one of his hands. Resting it on her lap, she covered his hand with hers.

"One day, oh, so long ago, I was at a trading post outside Jamestown," Jewel said. "Jon Paul was there. He saw me. He was taken with me. As he described it later to me, he said that he had never seen such loveliness, such a statuesque build, such flawless copper skin. He had never seen such a beautiful woman, so poised, proud, and unafraid, when I caught him staring at me."

She sighed, then continued.

"He questioned a companion about me. He discovered that I was a princess, and that I was of the Chitimacha tribe, whose village was located not far from Jamestown where his mansion stood tall on the outskirts of town. Jon Paul's fascination with me built in his mind when he discovered that I was the wife of a Chitimacha chief ... Chief Straight Arrow. He went as far as to inquire whether or not I had any children with the chief, and found out that we had none, and that I was a new bride."

Again she paused, sucked in a nervous breath, licked her lips, then continued as Troy sat quietly, absorbing it all.

"Jon Paul concluded that I was around eighteen winters of age," Jewel murmured. "He was thirty, and although there was a large age difference between us, he still vowed to have me, not as a concubine or prostitute, but as his wife. His wife Charlene had died during childbirth in England. At that time he had vowed never to marry again. But seeing me changed his mind."

"And so he did have you," Troy said thickly.

"Yes. His plot to abduct me was successful," Jewel said softly. "Against my will, he married me. Then . . . then . . . a few weeks into the marriage, I had to confess something to him . . . that I was with child. I had no choice but to tell him, because my pregnancy had begun to show."

She lowered her eyes, then gazed again at Troy. "He knew immediately that the child was not his because I was too far along," she murmured. "He knew then that when he married me, I . . . I . . . was pregnant with my true husband's child. I had not told him earlier, because I was afraid that he would make me abort the baby. I hoped that if I got farther along, he would not be as cruel as that." She lowered her eyes again. "I was wrong."

"He forced you to abort the child?" Troy said, his eyebrows narrowing angrily. "I had another brother or sister that I will never know?"

Her eyes lifted quickly. She squeezed his hand reassuringly. "No, it is nothing like that," she murmured. "That child . . . that child . . . was *you*, Red Feather."

"Me?" he said, his eyes widening. "My father is a Chitimacha chief? Jon Paul . . . Father . . . allowed you to carry me within your womb even knowing the child was not his own?"

"After I begged him, over and over again, he allowed me to keep the child within my womb," Jewel said. "But not until I told him that I would kill myself if I was not allowed to carry my child full term. I even begged him to allow me to return to my true husband . . . to the true father of my child, but . . . but . . . he refused. But he did agree to let me keep my child, and at that time, I was so grateful, I accepted that I must stay with Jon Paul."

"That child was me," Troy said thickly. "My true father is a proud Indian chief!"

"Yes, but, son, listen to the rest of what I tell you, for it must be said," Jewel said. "Jon Paul said something more that day. He told me that if I ever told anyone who the true father of this baby was, he would not hesitate to kill me, *and* the child. He never wanted anyone to know that he allowed me to give birth to a child that wasn't his. He said he would not be able to live with the humiliation of people knowing that the child was a full-blooded Indian."

"He threatened you?" Troy said, his voice drawn. "He actually threatened not only you, but

31

also your baby . . . the baby that was, in truth, me?"

"Yes, and I had to learn to live with this threat for the rest of my life," she said, swallowing hard. "I was a prisoner, guarded so that I would not escape, and so that none of my people would come for me should they somehow discover where I had been taken. Jon Paul forced me to play the role of his wife. He had me wear expensive dresses; he showered me with riches, especially jewelry."

"But you have seemed so content with . . . with your situation," Troy said, recalling the times when he had seen his mother laughing with Jon Paul. "Was it all fake?"

"No, not all of it," Jewel murmured. "Slowly my feelings toward Jon Paul softened. He treated me gently. If I asked for anything, it was instantly mine. Anything except . . . my freedom. Although a part of me had softened, deep within me was a resentment that I could not get past, especially a year later when I heard that my Chitimacha husband had remarried and that he became the father of a son. My hopes of ever escaping and returning to my true husband and people were truly dashed, for there was no place in his life for me now, nor you, my son, who was also his."

"And now?" Troy asked, his voice drawn and tight.

"Red Feather, I never allowed myself to lose

all faith that sometime in the future you and your father could meet," she said. "That is why I secretly taught you of your true heritage. I planned to choose when the time was right to tell you the full truth. It would be when I knew you were a man in your own right who would be strong enough to fend off the threat you and I would always have over our heads. Then you would make your own choices, choices that I would have prepared you to make. And I always wondered, would you choose your true people? Or those you had known since your birth?"

"*This* is why Larry was never included in our secret talks," Troy said. "He is only *part* Chitimacha. I am full-blood. And my father is not Larry's father."

"Yes, that is why," Jewel said. "And when you disclose to everyone your true Indian name, you will wear that name well and with pride. As I told you, Red Feather was the name of my father, your grandfather, a name befitting a man who might one day be chief, for you, my son, are truly next in line to be chief of our people. Your name, Troy, was given to you by your father . . . a nickname Jon Paul had been called in England. It was a name that had nothing to do with your true heritage. That was why Jon Paul chose it, and I had no choice but to agree."

She brought his hand to her lips, kissed it, then released it. "Son, you will in time decide for yourself which name you prefer . . . Red Feather or Troy . . . and even which father."

"I . . . am . . . next chief in line?" Troy said, kneading his brow. "But you said there was another son. Would not he be chief?"

"You were the true firstborn son of Chief Straight Arrow, not the one born to him of his second wife," Jewel said softly. "And, son, your true father does not even know that you exist . . . or that I do. He surely thought I died long ago. It hurts so that he knows not of either you or me."

"And now he will know?" Troy said. "You want me to go to him?"

"It must be your own choice. But, Red Feather, I have more to tell you," Jewel said, tears springing to her eyes.

"What more *is* there?" Troy said, swallowing hard. "You have already told me so much."

"Not enough," Jewel said. She sighed. "I chose tonight to tell you the full truth about your past and mine, because . . . because . . . I managed to discover that your true father is ill. He might even be dying. I'm not that sure about his illness, but I do believe that you must return to your true home, to your true people, and reveal your identity to your true father before Chief Straight Arrow dies."

She anxiously awaited his decision. For so long

she had secretly fantasized about her son being chief.

He *was* the firstborn to Chief Straight Arrow.

He *must* be given the chance to be chief and to know his people!

"My true father is . . . is . . . possibly dying?" Troy gulped out. He found it hard to believe that after only just learning his father's true identity, he would not have much time with him.

"It is rumored that he is ill, but I am not certain how sick he is. That is why I had to tell you the truth now, not later," Jewel murmured. "Your brother is called Gray Fox. His mother, your father's second wife, died a few years ago."

"So I not only have a father I have never known, I also have a brother," Troy said, almost numb from today's discoveries.

"It is time that you know now," Jewel said with determination. "I ache to return with you to our true people, for as I age, that part of me that will always be Chitimacha wants to be among them again. In my dreams I am with them. I am with my beloved first husband, his wife again. I ache for the simpler life that was mine as Chief Straight Arrow's wife. I ache to sit with the other women and sew and talk and laugh among them."

"I now know why those secret moments with you were so special to me," Troy said. "My true self was trying to reveal to me that I had another life, another father, another people."

"I waited for you to become your own man, for you to be old enough to make your own decisions, and strong enough to stand up to this husband who forced himself on me so many years ago, who forced me to call you *his* son," Jewel said. "I no longer fear your father and what he might do when he discovers my deceit. You are all that is important. My son, I urge you to go to Chief Straight Arrow. Let him know that you are his son, and that you have been taught the ways of the Chitimacha by your mother, who has never forgotten her first love."

She framed Troy's face between her soft, gentle hands. "Straight Arrow will be proud of such a son," she murmured. "He might even enjoy knowing that his first wife is still alive and well."

When she moved her hands away, Troy rose from his chair and began slowly pacing.

He was torn in two directions.

Although an appreciation of his Chitimacha heritage had been awakened in him long ago by his mother's teachings and he wanted to know his true father and people, so much of him was of the white world.

How could he go among the Chitimacha and profess that he was one of them and be accepted by them?

"My son," Jewel said as she rose and went to Troy. She took him gently by the hand, stopping his pacing. "As soon as you reveal who you are to your true father, you will be accepted with open arms."

She clutched his hands. "Son, I beg of you to go," she said. "Go and take your true place among the Chitimacha. Take your father the news of a wife who never stopped loving him."

Troy gazed into his mother's eyes. "What of my loyalty to my white father?" he asked uncertainly. "I have been treated well by him."

"I understand your feelings, but your true loyalty is to a father who was denied not only his wife, but also his son . . . his firstborn," Jewel said forcefully. "It is only right that at least he should know this son before he dies, and hear that his wife lived through her abduction."

Again she stretched her hands to his face. "My son, through the years I have prepared you to eventually meet and know your true father," she said. "It must be done now, for if Straight Arrow dies before getting to know you, I would go to my grave a liar; a woman of deceit. You have been robbed of your true birthright, your people, your father. Now is the time to take them back."

She lowered her hands again. "But," she said, "I warn you that this might cause enmity between you and Gray Fox. He may resent a brother who shows up just before his father dies, fearing you are there to fight for the right to be the next chief."

She firmed her jaw. "But you must chance anything in order to meet your true father and know him before his health worsens," she said. "I am so glad you have not cut your hair. I urged you to grow it down your back to your waist, even fought my white husband to allow it, so that when the time came for you to return to your true people, you would fit in with them."

"But Larry wears his long, too," Troy said.

"Only because he was jealous of how handsome you were with your hair this way," Jewel said, laughing softly. "But you are the one who is truly Chitimacha. You even look like Straight Arrow when he was your age. He will see that when you reveal to him you are his son."

"But what of Father . . . of Jon Paul?" Troy asked. "The threat . . . ?"

"He would not harm either you or me now, for his love for both of us is too strong," Jewel said. "And even if he does resent that I told you, the telling is done and what can he do to take it back?"

"Then I would very much like to meet my true father," Troy said, his eyes brightening. "I am also anxious to know my true people after hearing so much about them through the years."

Jewel took him by the hand. "Come with me to my room," she murmured. "And we must hurry. Your father, or perhaps even your brother, might return home at any moment. I have something to show you . . . to give you . . . before they come home."

Troy went with his mother to the attic. He watched her fall to her knees before an old trunk.

His eyes grew wide with wonder when she lifted the lid, reached down beneath a pile of folded clothes, and took from it a buckskin outfit.

She took it in her arms, then stood before Troy. "This is yours," she said, her voice breaking with emotion. "I bought the tanned hide and beads some time ago while shopping in Jamestown. I secretly made you this fringed outfit for your eventual return to your true people, for all along I had planned it this way."

She handed the clothing to him, then sank her hands deep within the trunk again.

This time she brought out a pair of moccasins and a loincloth, and then a beaded headband.

"These are also yours," she said, giving them to him.

She smiled. "But there is one other thing," she said, again bending before the trunk and digging down.

She took something from the very bottom of the trunk, then stood before Troy and held it out toward him. It was an eagle feather that she had dyed red for this very day, the day when she would reveal to her son his true identity . . . his true savage destiny!

"A red feather for my son Red Feather," she

murmured, delighted when she saw the pride in his eyes as he gazed at it.

Then he looked into her eyes. "Thank you," he murmured. "Thank you for revealing this to me. I will go to my father. I will!"

He paused, then said proudly, "And in time, after everyone knows my true identity, I shall be called by nothing but Red Feather."

Chapter Five

Betwixt mine eye and heart,
A League is took,
And each doth good turns,
Now unto the other.
      —William Shakespeare

Troy—who did not see himself as Troy today,
but instead as Red Feather—was dressed in the
full Indian attire that his mother had given to
him. It was a garment of finely tanned deerskins
which extended from the shoulders to midway
between knee and ankle, its sleeves reaching
nearly to the wrist and tied at intervals on the
underside.

The garment was fringed at its bottom and at the sleeves, and finely decorated at the shoulders and arms with beads and shells.

Red Feather felt strangely comfortable in these clothes. It was as though he had worn buckskin all his life.

Reassuring himself that what he was doing today was right, he rode slowly into the Chitimacha Indian village on his magnificent black horse.

He had seen the village often as he rode past, but had never actually been inside it. He was especially curious to see it now that he knew he truly belonged there. He was a full-blood Chitimacha whose father was a proud chief.

As he rode farther into the village, he saw that the homes were a mixture of log cabins and tepees situated uphill from a gentle, meandering stream.

Warriors were coming and going, some on horses, some on foot, some burdened with deer.

Women were everywhere doing various chores. Some were stretching the drying hides and filling great drying racks with long, thin strips of rich, red deer meat. Others were tanning skins. Still others worked at making baskets.

But soon everyone stopped.

They were aware of a stranger in their midst.

They stared at him as he moved onward at a slow trot, his own eyes guardedly gazing back at first one and then another.

Although he looked like them, with his long black hair and copper skin, and wore the same fringed outfits as the warriors, he could see the lack of trust in their eyes.

And he understood.

He was a total stranger to them, as they were to him.

All that he knew about them was what his mother had taught him.

That had been enough for him to feel a bond with them. He only hoped they would feel the same once they heard who he was, and to whom he was related.

He looked cautiously from side to side in an attempt to spot his brother Gray Fox. Wasn't it possible he would recognize him?

Might there not be some resemblance to Red Feather?

Yes, Red Feather, he thought to himself. He was identifying himself by that name today.

He even carried the red feather that his mother had dyed for him tucked beneath his shirt, where it lay against his chest.

Although this was all so new to him, he felt right to be there, to approach his father, to introduce himself to him.

He would not concern himself over how Gray Fox might feel.

But then there was the chance that he would not even be believed. What would he do then?

He straightened his shoulders and firmed his chin. He would not ponder the negative side of introducing himself to his father.

No, he was who he was, and he *would* find a way to make those who were related to him understand, and believe. Especially his father. He was the one who was important to him today.

His heart pounded now as he found his eyes stopping and resting on a larger tepee at the far end of the long row of lodges. This was surely the lodge of the village chief.

Suddenly several warriors stepped forward and blocked Red Feather's further approach.

He drew a tight rein and looked slowly from one to the other as he waited to hear why they had stopped him.

"Who are you and why are you here?" asked one of the taller, leaner warriors, his dark eyes narrowed suspiciously.

When Red Feather's eyes went to him and lingered, he recognized his own facial features in the stranger.

Surely this was his half-brother!

"I am Red Feather. I have come today to have council with Chief Straight Arrow," he said, keeping his eyes on the warrior. The other man resembled him, oh, so very much . . . except for one difference. There was a streak of gray in his long, thick black hair. Red Feather knew that it could not be from age . . . but something born with him.

"I am not familiar with anyone who goes by the name Red Feather," Gray Fox said tightly. "Which tribe is yours? Where do you make your home?"

"Like you, I am Chitimacha," Red Feather said.

He was not sure just how much he should say in identifying himself before he faced his father with the truth.

He was not sure if he would even be allowed to go to his father if he openly told everyone that he was Chief Straight Arrow's son and was kin to Gray Fox as well.

"I know most clans of Chitimacha and warriors from them, for we have occasional councils and celebrations with them, and I do not remember you, or your name," Gray Fox said. He stepped closer to Red Feather.

Red Feather could see that Gray Fox was studying him closely. Surely he saw the same resemblance between them that Red Feather did.

"Again, why are you here?" Gray Fox asked. "Why have you arrived alone for council with my father, Straight Arrow?"

Red Feather's heart leaped with joy to know that, yes, he *was* facing his half-brother for the first time in his life.

It stirred many feelings within him, most of

which he must keep at bay, for he still had much persuading to do before this warrior would accept him into his heart.

Being so absorbed in studying his brother, and trying to figure out what his next move must be, Red Feather had not noticed a hefty, bent, gray-headed man approaching him, his chest heaving with each heavy step.

"And who do we have here?" the newcomer said in a gruff, deep voice. "Gray Fox, son, who is this warrior? What does he want here among our people?"

Gray Fox dutifully rushed to his father's side and lovingly placed a supporting arm around his waist. "This man calls himself Red Feather," he said, glancing over at Red Feather. "He has come for council with you."

"Red Feather?" Straight Arrow repeated, arching an eyebrow. His faded old eyes, which did not see all that clearly anymore, tried to study Red Feather's face. "I once knew a Red Feather. It was the father of the woman who was my first wife."

"Yes, I know of him, but never met him face to face," Red Feather said, nodding.

"And how would you know Red Feather?" Straight Arrow asked, squinting his eyes as he attempted to get a better look at Red Feather's face. "He has been dead for many long moons now."

"I know of him because my mother told me about him," Red Feather said thickly. "*She* named me after him. I am named in his memory."

"And why would she do that?" Straight Arrow asked. Then he stepped away from Gray Fox and took a slow step closer to Red Feather. "And who is your mother?"

Red Feather swallowed hard.

He looked cautiously from side to side, aware of many eyes on him as the whole village gathered around, listening and watching.

He then turned slow eyes back to his father, whom he was glad to see was not all that ill, after all.

He was not sure whether to reveal his true heritage now, with so many listening to him. He wanted to tell his father in private.

But how could he?

It seemed that he was cornered, and had no choice but to say what he had come to say as he sat on his horse, not in the privacy of the chief's lodge.

"My mother is Soft Flower, who was a princess to your people before she was abducted and taken from her home," Red Feather said cautiously.

At these words, his father suddenly gasped and grabbed at his heart. Was it his heart that was bad?

Was Red Feather's presence going to make him go into a seizure?

47

Red Feather was not sure how much more to say, yet now that he had begun, he knew that he would have no choice but to say it all. The chief would demand it.

"My mother was your first wife," Red Feather rushed out. "She is alive and well but was never able to let you know that. She was watched. And . . . when she had her firstborn, it was not of the union with the white man who forced her to marry him. She was with child when she was abducted. That child was me. You are the father . . . *my* father."

"What . . . ?" Straight Arrow gasped.

He clutched his head.

Gray Fox rushed to him and grabbed him as he started to collapse.

Gray Fox glared at Red Feather. "How dare you come here with such lies! See what you have done to my father?" he hissed out. "Leave. Take your lies with you. And should you ever come again, I shall see that it will be the last time."

Straight Arrow composed himself.

He inhaled deeply, then stepped away from Gray Fox.

"Young man, I will hear all that you have to say, and *then* you will leave," Straight Arrow said in a drawn voice. "Come. You will have council with me. Gray Fox, come with us to my lodge."

"Father, this man is an impostor," Gray Fox

said, glowering at Red Feather. "Please, just send him away."

"Somehow he knows much about my first wife, and I want to know how. Gray Fox, do as you are told." Straight Arrow motioned toward Red Feather with a shaky hand. "Dismount. Leave the horse with one of the young braves; he will keep it for you until you are ready to leave. Accompany me to my lodge."

Relieved that his father was at least going to hear him out, Red Feather dismounted.

He handed his reins to a young brave, then followed Straight Arrow to his lodge, which was a tepee instead of a cabin like the dwellings where many others lived.

He looked to his left and saw a tepee that was discolored and shaggy with age. He could not help wondering who might live there.

"Come inside," Straight Arrow said, lifting his buckskin entrance flap and gesturing with his free hand for Red Feather to enter ahead of him.

Soon Red Feather was sitting on thick pelts beside his father's lodge fire. Straight Arrow sat across the fire from him, his eyes studying Red Feather, his arms folded defensively across his chest, which was covered by a blanket that he now wore around his shoulders. Gray Fox sat stiffly at his father's side.

Red Feather glanced quickly around, familiarizing himself with his father's belongings. He saw a magnificent chief's headdress of many feathers hanging in a prominent place at the rear, opposite the entrance.

He also saw an aged buffalo-skin shield that hung from one of the lodge poles, an eagle wing fan, and deerskin accoutrements for the chief's horse.

Before he could view anything else, his father spoke, drawing Red Feather's eyes back to him.

"Speak now, and I will listen," Straight Arrow said gruffly.

Red Feather paused before speaking, knowing that it was up to him to convince his father he was speaking the truth.

He finally found the courage to begin. He told his father everything he could remember his mother ever telling him, especially the latest of her revelations.

He watched his father's expression, yet could not tell whether or not he believed what he was hearing. He seemed practiced at hiding his feelings. No doubt that was an advantage to a great chief who had had many people to deal with during his lifetime.

"And that is it?" Straight Arrow said as soon as Red Feather went quiet, his story told. "And you think that I will believe you? Why have you come to tell me such a story as that? What is the reason for your trickery?"

Red Feather's heart seemed to fall to his feet.

At first he was too stunned to speak, but then he made himself look directly into his father's eyes.

"What I have told you is true. Your first wife, my mother, sent me to you with the truth," he insisted. "She taught me the ways of my heritage secretly. When she heard that you were ill, she urged me to go to you with the truth. Through the years, there was a threat held over both our heads. But I am an adult now and can fend for myself should the man who calls himself my father hear what has been told me and act upon his anger over it."

"It is quite an intriguing tale and cleverly thought up and told," Straight Arrow said. "But I cannot believe any of it. You see, I have learned not to trust easily."

"It is truth," Red Feather said. "I speak no lies. I am a man of morals. Those morals were taught to me by the woman who was once your people's princess, who was once your *wife*, who still is your wife. She is not the sort of woman to make up stories for any reason."

"I believe your tale must be a new sort of trick that the white people have thought up to get something from the Chitimacha," Straight Arrow said. "They find a man who resembles the Chitimacha and pay him well to come seduce this old man with tales that they hope he will believe. What is it? What do they want now? It was their greed for the valuable Chitimacha lands that fanned the original flames of hatred years ago. First, the Chitimacha's vast holdings of rich delta land were bargained away to wealthy Creoles for a fraction of their worth. Then the English came. Shady lawyers brazenly stole some of the land, while a great deal more was lost for non-payment of taxes, which according to Indian lawyers were not owed in the first place."

Straight Arrow sighed heavily. He drew the blanket more closely around his shoulders. "My people are content now on our small parcel of land," he said. "I will not stand for anyone saying he is of Chitimacha blood, telling lies in order to get himself involved with my people, only to take from them in the end."

Red Feather's heart ached to know that he had come in vain today, that neither his father nor his brother believed him.

He wanted to plead his case with his brother, yet knew that any more words spoken today would only be wasted.

Straight Arrow stood shakily. He pointed toward the entranceway. "Leave and take your tricks with you," he ordered. "My people are a people of peace, but if anyone else tries to take from us, he will suffer the consequences. The shame is even worse today, because you, a man whose skin is the same color as those you came to trick, would come among us with such lies, with such deceit."

"My mother has never forgotten her people, especially her husband," Red Feather said, slowly rising. "Please remember that she was forced away from her land, her people, her home, her husband. She had no choices in life. Despite all that, she made certain that I knew who my true people were and waited for the proper time to send me home to you. When she heard that you were ill, she knew that the time had come for my return."

"Any wife of mine would have found a way to escape and return to me," Straight Arrow said, his voice breaking. "She never would have mated with a white man."

He folded his arms across his chest again. "No, I will never believe that this woman was my wife, nor that you are my son," he said. "Leave. Now. *Leave.*"

Red Feather gazed intently into his father's eyes for a moment longer, then turned and found himself facing his brother. It was Gray Fox's glare that said it all. Red Feather was not welcome there. And he might never be.

He nodded toward Gray Fox, then walked past him and went outside, where he mounted his steed.

He held his chin high as he rode from the village, then urged his horse into a hard gallop, his heart aching for what he had not achieved today.

But he had sat with his father.

He knew him now.

And he knew that he was not as ill as his mother had thought him to be.

At least he had seen his brother and spoken with him.

For now, that had to be enough.

After riding a short distance, he stopped and changed from his buckskins back into the expensive clothes he'd stored in his saddlebags. Then he set out again toward the mansion he had thought was his true home, until recently.

But now he felt something new inside his heart . . . a resentment toward the mother who had kept the full truth from him for far too long, so long that it might now be impossible for him ever to become a part of the lives of those who were kin to him.

Chapter Six

What is your substance,
Whereof are you made,
That millions of strange shadows on you tend?
Since everyone hath, everyone, one shade,
And you, but one, can every shadow lend.
                    —William Shakespeare

As the stagecoach stopped in front of a hotel in the city of Jamestown, Angela Dawn's heart raced with a mixture of fear and anticipation. She had no idea what she was walking into. If the man who awaited her was a cad, or cruel, or ugly, could she go through with this?

Yet she knew that she must. She had made up

her mind to achieve vengeance against the man who'd killed her father.

She glanced from the window of the stagecoach as the driver stepped down and came to open the door for her.

Her pulse raced when she saw only one man standing on the platform, gazing at the stagecoach as though he was waiting for someone to alight from it.

Was this the man who had sent for her?

Her eyebrows rose when she saw that he was an Indian dressed in white man's clothes.

He had all the appearance of a rich white person, yet his skin was copper-colored, and he wore his coal-black hair hanging free to his waist.

"Step on out, ma'am, and be careful while doin' it," the driver said as he threw back the door and reached a hand out for Angela Dawn. "The steps can be mighty slippery at times for women in tiny, delicate shoes like you are wearing."

She nodded a thank you and picked up her reticule, her eyes still on the man who waited below.

She took the driver's hand and stepped from the stagecoach, then waited for him to get her bags from the top . . . one small, the other large.

She glanced past the Indian, waiting for someone else to arrive.

Surely, oh, surely the Indian was not the one who had sent for her.

She was not prejudiced in any way, but still, she could not imagine this man being the one who'd sent for her. He had described himself as being from a wealthy family, who lived in a mansion.

She had never known of any Indian being wealthy and living in a mansion . . . unless . . .

She looked quickly at the Indian again. He *did* wear the clothes of a white man. Expensive clothes. Could he possibly have an Indian mother and a wealthy white father? Was he a half-breed?

Yes, that had to be the way it was, or else why would he be dressed as he was?

Could *he* be . . . ?

Larry saw how the woman was studying him, and gazed back at her openly. When he had seen Troy mysteriously disappear just when the stage-coach was to arrive with Angela Dawn, he'd been certain that Troy had forgotten that she was now his responsibility, not Larry's. Curious to know what she would look like, Larry had gone to meet the stagecoach.

Now that he had seen a woman step from the stagecoach alone, he was sure this was Angela Dawn.

He raised an eyebrow.

She was not anything like he had expected her to be.

She was beautiful, almost in a fragile way.

He was instantly drawn to her in a way he had

never been to another woman. He had sent for her out of boredom, but who could get bored of *this* woman? Her bewitching green eyes . . . her auburn hair, flowing down from the pretty hat perched on her head . . . her tininess—all made it almost impossible for him to stop staring at her.

He now regretted having gambled her away to his brother.

Well, by damn, Larry thought to himself, he would make sure that this woman would still be his, not Troy's.

Here was a woman he could settle down with.

He could hardly wait to taste her lips, to touch her body, to hear her speak his name and tell him that she loved him.

He was so caught up in this fantasy, he stood frozen for a moment longer. Then, when he saw a worried look on the woman's face as she continued looking around for the man who had sent for her, he straightened his shoulders and hurried toward her.

When he stepped up to her, he bowed slightly, then smiled and spoke to her. "Ma'am, might you be Angela Dawn?" he asked. "I am the man who sent for you. I am Larry Ratcliffe. Was your trip tiring?"

He noticed that she looked shocked to learn who he was, and realized that his race had disturbed her.

Even though he was dressed in velvet, with a

fine linen ascot that revealed a sparkling diamond in its folds, to her he was just an Indian!

Larry shuffled his feet nervously and waited for her to say something.

Angela Dawn was stunned to see that this man was the one who had sent for her. She wasn't sure how to react. But she had no choice except to ignore her surprise. She had come a long way, and for a definite purpose. She had a killer to find.

As the stagecoach driver set her bags on the ground, Angela Dawn reached a hand out to Larry. "Yes, I am Angela Dawn," she murmured. "And I'm sorry for my hesitation. I am truly pleased to meet you."

Hearing her voice, its softness, and her regret for her momentary rudeness, Larry felt his knees almost buckle with a passion he had never known before.

He reached out a hand and took hers in his. "The meeting is truly my pleasure, ma'am," he said, smiling. He did not care that this woman was not truly his to claim as his future wife, but instead his brother's. All he could see was her loveliness. Somehow, he would make sure that she *was* his, no matter what his brother said about it.

Chapter Seven

Another time mine eye is my heart's guest,
And in his thoughts of love doth share a part.
　　　　　　　　　　　—William Shakespeare

As the horse and carriage drove down the narrow gravel lane approaching a three-storied home which displayed many tall, graceful columns along the front, Angela Dawn was stunned by its magnificence. She had heard of such Southern mansions, had even seen pictures of them in books, but never had she thought she would actually see one, much less enter one. Yet she would actually live here if she went through with this marriage to Larry Ratcliffe.

The closer she came to the estate, the more unbelievable it all seemed. In the distance, she could see a series of lagoons with stone bridges, and flower gardens that sat apart from the huge sugarcane and tobacco fields. Copses of pine and live oak trees extended from the river to the mansion.

All of these things—the bridges and flower gardens, the fields of sugarcane and tobacco, the mansion, and even the magnificent horse and carriage in which she rode—proved just how rich Larry Ratcliffe was. If she married him, she would be rich, as well.

She had never dreamed of such wealth when she decided to send her photograph and announcement to the bank in Jamestown in an attempt to find a husband.

Seeing it all now was more frightening than exciting, for now that she knew just how rich this man was, she could not help wondering why he had the need to send for a woman.

She glanced over at him when he wasn't looking. As he stared from the window, seemingly in deep thought, she again thought how different he was from the man she'd thought she would be meeting. She had expected a white man, not a half-breed.

Was that the reason this man had not yet married . . . the fact that his skin was different from the rich women of this area? Did most women shun him because he was part Indian?

She knew that in most places it was forbidden for a white woman to marry a red man.

She looked slowly over his attire, her eyes stopping on the diamond nestled in the cravat. It was picking up the rays of the sun and flashing a rainbow of colors back at Angela Dawn.

Yes, that alone spoke of his wealth. Why hadn't his wealth made women look past his skin color and accept the sort of life he could give them?

She slid her gaze upward. There was an odd coldness in his eyes, but aside from that, he was handsome.

Was it the coldness that kept women from him?

Because of his eyes, the lack of friendliness in them, Angela Dawn sensed that he might not be a loving, kind man.

"We are almost there," Larry said as he turned to Angela Dawn, interrupting her thoughts. "Are you comfortable about our situation? You know that you will soon be meeting my parents."

"Yes, I am comfortable enough," Angela Dawn said, smiling. "And I look forward to meeting your parents."

"And yours?" Larry asked, still in awe of this woman's loveliness, yet concerned about how he would get his brother to let her go.

To Larry, this woman was *his* property, not his

brother's. He had discovered her. He had paid and sent for her, not Troy.

And Troy had said that he did not approve of what Larry had done. Hadn't Troy said that he would not marry her?

Angela Dawn lowered her eyes. The sting of having lost both of her parents pierced her heart anew.

"I will tell you about them one day," she murmured. She gazed at him and hoped that he would not see the shine of tears in her eyes. "But please, not now."

"Can I at least ask you if they are alive?" Larry asked, lifting an eyebrow.

Again Angela Dawn lowered her eyes. She had not expected him to get right to the point with such a question so quickly.

"Both are dead," she breathed with a heavy sigh.

"I'm sorry," Larry said, uncomfortable at having made her sad at a time when she should be filled with happiness.

"That's alright," Angela Dawn said, forcing a smile. "You didn't know."

"No, I didn't. Please don't feel as though you have to tell me any more about them, ever, if it makes you sad or uncomfortable," he said.

Now he understood the desperation that had prompted her to offer herself as a mail-order bride.

She was totally alone in the world.

She was seeking solace in the company of a man, a man she would marry.

Well, he was about to make all her dreams come true.

The horse and carriage drew up in front of the mansion and stopped. The carriage driver came and opened the door beside Larry.

Larry stepped down to the ground, then offered Angela Dawn a hand. "Welcome to Ratcliffe Manor," he said, his eyes gleaming. "Come with me. I shall introduce you to my parents, and then you will be taken to your room so that you can freshen up before dinner."

"That sounds wonderful," Angela Dawn said. She took his hand and carefully stepped from the carriage.

He placed his arm around her waist and guided her up the many steps onto a wide, long porch which displayed many wicker rockers and tall-backed wooden chairs.

Beautiful potted plants had been placed along the front of the porch, between the tall pillars.

The wind sang through the leaves of the many tall live oaks that surrounded the house on three sides.

The smell of gardenias wafted through the air from plants that grew on each side of the house.

It was as though she was entering paradise. She only hoped she would still feel the same after meeting this man's parents, and after getting to know the man hidden behind his cold eyes and devilish smile.

Larry opened the huge door, then ushered Angela Dawn inside.

What she saw then was more unbelievably beautiful than she could ever have dreamed.

Clustered columns and pointed arches ornamented a double staircase that rose to the second floor on opposite sides of the entrance hall. Faded Pompeii-red wallpaper provided a warm background for the artwork that lined the walls along the staircase. Glowing wood and gleaming gilt added to the richness of the decor.

"Come into the drawing room," Larry said. He took her by the elbow and ushered her inside, where even more riches widened her eyes with awe.

She looked slowly around her.

A mirrored Russian console displayed a fragment of a 17th-century Venetian painting and silver Grecian compotes.

A pair of caned Regency armchairs flanked a table decorated with Sèvres porcelain, and a long, red velvet sofa sat before a roaring fire in the huge stone fireplace.

A table held French porcelain, hand-painted in faded flower tones, that reflected the pattern of the carpet below.

On another table sat a Bouillotte lamp, so

named after a French card game. She knew this because her father had won such a lamp while gambling one evening . . . a lamp she had sold to acquire money for her survival.

Seeing the lamp made her lonely all over again for her father, and she looked quickly elsewhere.

There was much more to look at, but footsteps behind her drew her around.

She found herself being scrutinized by a tall, gray-haired man dressed as expensively as Larry, but whose blue eyes were much more friendly. His expression was curious as he slowly studied her.

Uncomfortable, Angela Dawn moved her eyes to the woman standing beside him. She hoped that no one heard her slight gasp as she found herself gazing upon the most beautiful Indian woman she had ever seen. Her face was exquisite, her smile radiant, her dark eyes friendly, yet filled with surprise as she gazed back at Angela Dawn.

The woman was dressed nothing at all the way Angela Dawn believed most Indian women dressed. She wore a low-cut pale blue velvet dress which displayed a diamond necklace around the long, slender column of her throat. Her black hair was worn in a tight bun above her head, and although she was middle-aged, she was tiny and youthful in appearance.

"And who have we here?" Jon Paul asked, sliding his hands into his front breeches pockets.

"Mother, Father, may I introduce my future bride to you?" Larry said. He stepped away from Angela Dawn so that he could look at her, as well. "This is Angela Dawn Cutright."

He turned around and faced his parents again. "And how did we meet?" he said suavely. "Angela Dawn came to me as a mail-order bride. I hope that does not offend you."

"Mail . . . order . . . bride?" Jewel gasped, paling right before Angela Dawn's eyes. "Larry, I . . ."

Jewel couldn't say any more. She was too stunned by what this son of hers had done. Yet why should she be so shocked? She had thought she could not be surprised by anything he would do.

She glanced over at Jon Paul. She saw that he was amused, not horrified, by what Larry had done. And she knew why. She knew that Jon Paul was thinking the same as she . . . that this so-called engagement would never last, and that there would not be a marriage. The engagement was just something that Larry was amusing himself with, and Jewel was sorry, for it would be the woman who would be hurt by it all.

It would be up to Jewel to make certain that the pretty young thing was comfortable at least for the short while she would stay in Jamestown before Larry sent her on her way again.

Jewel glanced toward the window, her mind

suddenly elsewhere. She was wondering about Troy. She could hardly wait to know what had happened during his visit to his father's village.

She turned and looked guardedly at her husband. Surely one day soon he would find out what she and Troy had done. Then what would he do?

She could not help being afraid.

She was glad for this diversion that Larry had brought into their lives.

At least her husband would have something else on his mind besides his wife's exploits.

"Angela Dawn, this is my father, Jon Paul, and my mother, Jewel," Larry said, gesturing toward his parents with a hand.

"I am truly pleased to meet you," Angela Dawn murmured. "I'm sorry, though, that my arrival has obviously come as a shock to you. I hope that I can prove I am worthy of your son, and of being your daughter-in-law."

"Yes, I am sure that you can," Jewel said, reaching for Angela Dawn's hand. "Come. I will show you to your room. Your bags have already been taken there. I will have a tub and water brought to you. After your bath, you might want to take a nap, and then tonight we shall meet again around the dining table. Is that alright with you?"

"It sounds marvelous," Angela Dawn said,

looking over her shoulder at Larry as Jewel swept her from the room.

After she was upstairs, alone in the room that would be hers, she sighed heavily. She leaned against the closed door and looked slowly around her.

The bedroom was as lavish as all the other rooms she had seen. The four-poster bed had a graceful canopy that stretched out above a mattress covered by a beautiful lacy bedspread.

The floors were covered with thick, soft-looking throw rugs.

The furniture was made of warm-toned cherry wood.

Her father had kept Angela Dawn and her mother comfortable in pretty hotel rooms in Saint Louis, but never had she seen anything like this. She truly had never expected this family to have such riches.

The closer she had gotten to Jamestown in the stagecoach, the more she regretted having promised to marry a stranger. And why should she? She had achieved what she had wanted from the beginning. She had found a way to get to Jamestown and stay there long enough to find the man who'd murdered her father.

But then, wouldn't she be daft to turn her back on such riches as this?

Angela Dawn went to a table and bent low to inhale the fragrance of the gardenias in the vase.

Then she slowly strolled around the room, absorbing its beauty all over again.

Sighing, she stopped and placed her bags on the bed, opening the larger one.

She gazed at the clothes folded neatly in the bag. Some were hers, but most were her mother's dresses. They were far more beautiful than her own. She hoped they were beautiful enough. She wanted to look well for her first dinner with her "beau" and his family.

"I have to make this work, at least until I find my father's murderer," she whispered to herself.

Chapter Eight

Who ever loved that
Loved not at first sight?
              —Marlowe

Still in awe of the mansion and everything in it, Angela Dawn sat at the lavishly set dining table with Larry's family. Everyone was there except for a brother, whom they had apologized for; it seemed he had been detained by something.

Angela Dawn had noticed that Larry's mother looked nervous when her husband asked if she knew where their son Troy might be.

And Angela Dawn could tell that both Larry and Jon Paul had noticed Jewel's nervousness, though neither questioned her about it.

Angela Dawn thought their reticence might be because *she* was at the table, a stranger still to everyone.

She smiled nervously as she found herself being scrutinized from time to time by each of them. She did not believe it was because of what she wore. She had on one of her mother's prettiest dresses. It was a pale yellow silk gown that displayed delicate white lace at both the high collar and the cuffs of the long sleeves. She recalled how all men's eyes had turned to her mother when she had entered a room wearing this exact dress. She had been so beautiful, so softly sweet.

"And did you get enough rest?" Jewel asked, interrupting Angela Dawn's thoughts. Jewel rested her fork on her dinner plate. The silver of the fork picked up the gleam of the dozens of candles that burned brightly in the chandelier over the center of the table.

"Yes, and thank you for giving me the opportunity," Angela Dawn said. She only now realized that she had been toying with her food rather than eating it. Both Larry and Jon Paul were gazing at her meal, which was still scarcely touched.

Although she was starved, and the food wafted delicious aromas to her nose, her stomach was rebelling. She was too anxious to eat.

Her nervousness stemmed from the newness of this experience: she had made a commitment to a stranger . . . a man she truly did not have an appetite for.

And the longer she was around him, the less desirable he was to her.

She could feel a strain between him and his mother and wondered at its origin.

"Where on earth can Troy be?" Jon Paul asked. He glanced again toward the door, as he had often since sitting down at the table. He frowned at Larry. "I know you two were out late last night. Were you gambling again? I thought I warned you about that. Although I've been known to enjoy a game of poker myself, now and then, I do not appreciate my sons getting the sort of reputation that comes from gambling and whoring around in the saloons of Jamestown."

"Jon Paul . . ." Jewel gasped. Her face flooded with color as she gave Angela Dawn an embarrassed glance. "Please. We have a guest."

"A guest?" Jon Paul said. His eyes twinkled as he gave Angela Dawn a wicked smile. "Ah, yes, our guest."

He glanced quickly at Larry. "And when is the wedding, son?" he asked mockingly. "Tomorrow? The next day?"

Larry laid his fork down on the table. He gave his father an annoyed look, then picked the fork up and again proceeded to eat.

Sensing the tension that flowed around the table, Angela Dawn decided to eat, after all. At least that would busy her hands and make the time pass more quickly. She preferred the privacy of her bedroom to remaining in this room of strangers.

While she chewed the delicious chicken, she glanced around her again at the lavish decor.

What seemed to be a family portrait presided over the dining room, hanging at one end of the room. The walls on both sides of the dining table were covered with elaborate French wallpaper, which was a stunning backdrop for a Regency over-mantel mirror and the gilt and bronze chandelier. The satinwood dining table and sideboard added warm highlights to the room.

It was a huge room, and Angela Dawn could envision it as the scene of lavish feasts and parties.

She had attended such parties in Saint Louis with her mother and father when her father socialized from time to time with rich gamblers. But the scenes of those parties could not compare with these people's riches.

She was overwhelmed by everything, and truly wished that she could become a part of it. But she could not ignore her growing dislike of Larry Ratcliffe. Even when he remained silent, there was an arrogance about him.

"Troy!"

Jewel's outburst and her obvious happiness at her other son's arrival drew Angela Dawn's eyes quickly to the door. Angela Dawn saw that Troy, too, was Indian. And he was so handsome, the sight of him almost took her breath away. Larry was handsome, too, but in a different way. Troy's handsomeness seemed to come from deep within him. She saw no coldness in his eyes as she did in Larry's.

She smiled almost sheepishly at him when she found him gazing at her questioningly. Surely no one had yet told him about this possible new addition to the family. He had not been home when Larry had surprised the family with her arrival.

"Son, son, I'm so glad you are home," Jewel said as she rose from her chair and went to him. She gave him a hug. "I was beginning to worry about you."

"I'm fine, Mother," Red Feather said, returning her hug, yet all the while gazing at the stranger.

Jewel stepped away from him, but took his hand and led him to the table. "You are just in time," she said. She laughed softly. "Or else there would be no more food left for you."

Red Feather was only half listening to his mother; he was only half aware of sitting down at the table and placing a napkin on his lap as his mother returned to her chair.

The woman.

Who was the lovely woman?

Then he turned slowly to his brother. When he saw a guardedness about him as Larry returned his gaze, then gave the woman a quick look, Red Feather looked at the woman again. There was an obvious uneasiness about her, as well.

But now that he was looking at her, truly looking at her, he saw just how beautiful she was . . . her emerald-green eyes, her auburn hair, her exquisite face . . .

But there was something else about her that drew him as no other woman had drawn him before. She was so petite. There was a fragile quality about her, as though she was in need of protection. He did not understand why he should have such powerful feelings for this woman, yet he did have them just the same.

And he was very aware that she returned his gaze so that their eyes met for too long, until finally she lowered her eyes, almost timidly.

He started to ask who she was, but he was keenly aware of his mother's eyes on him. He understood her anxiousness. She wanted to know about the meeting between him and his true father, but knew she had no choice but to wait until later to ask.

Red Feather gazed hard at his mother as he tried to understand why she had kept the truth about his heritage from him for so long.

Yes, there had been the threat held over both their heads.

But he had been an adult for many years now.

He could have stood up to his father.

He could not help resenting his mother's silence. Why hadn't she tried harder to escape from her abductor those long years ago?

Chief Straight Arrow had said that a true wife would never have stayed with a white man, for *any* reason. She would have found her way home to him, and to her true people.

Jewel became uneasy at the hard look Red Feather was giving her. It was as though he was seeing her in a different light. Might Straight Arrow have said something about her that was making Red Feather think less of her?

But what could that be?

She had been a loyal wife to her husband until her abduction.

And then she had been forced to comply with the demands of her abductor . . . even to marry him.

But she had only done so to keep her son Red Feather alive.

All of it had been for Red Feather.

She had also seen the questioning look in Red Feather's eyes when he saw the woman, surely he had no idea that his brother had sent for a mail-order bride. Surely it would be as much a surprise to him as it had been to her and Jon Paul.

Red Feather saw his mother glance quickly at the woman. He gazed at her again, too.

"Is anyone going to introduce me to our guest?" he finally said.

"This is Angela Dawn, your brother's fiancée," Jewel explained, glad to have something to take Red Feather's mind off whatever might be troubling him. She saw an expression of surprise on Red Feather's face.

"Yes, Troy. Larry's fiancée," she quickly added, finding it difficult now to call him Troy, when she truly wanted to call him by his Indian name.

"Angela Dawn...?" Red Feather repeated, only now remembering that he was supposed to meet the stagecoach today.

Then he realized something else.

His mother had just introduced Angela Dawn as Larry's fiancée!

Red Feather was stunned, because by all rights the woman was *his* fiancée, not his brother's. He had won the right to claim her in a game of cards.

He glared at his brother as he tried to figure out what Larry's scheme was this time. He would not ask in front of their parents, for once he did start asking how his brother had decided to take what was not his, he was afraid they might come to blows.

He gazed again at Angela Dawn, and was captivated by her loveliness. He had, in truth, expected a "used woman," for why would anyone so beautiful have trouble finding a decent man to marry?

Red Feather had decided that when she arrived, he was going to pay her way to wherever she wanted to go, and give her a good amount of money for her trouble.

But now?

How could he send her away?

He felt a sudden need to protect her.

She had sought a husband because she was alone in the world.

How could anyone as fragile looking as Angela Dawn survive alone in a world that was somewhat crazy and cruel, especially to unprotected women?

He glared at Larry again. It was obvious that his brother was not ready to hand over the woman to anyone. He had even introduced her to their parents as his fiancée, when he knew that she was not free to marry anyone but Red Feather.

Then he noticed his mother gazing anxiously at him again, and he knew that look had nothing to do with the woman. She was obviously growing more eager by the minute to know how things had turned out at the Chitimacha village; how he had been received.

He knew that he must find a way to tell her as soon as possible. He had questions of his own for her.

He wanted to know where her courage had been those long years ago when she should have defied her white abductor in all ways possible.

Angela Dawn was glad when Troy looked elsewhere. She could not help being totally captivated by his handsomeness.

And she was attracted by more than his good looks. She could see a quiet respect in his eyes when he gazed at her.

It was as though he saw her as something more than a woman who had been bought by a man. Did he even know that she was a mail-order bride?

She had noticed right away that there was some hidden meaning in the look exchanged between brothers after she had been introduced.

There was a quiet, controlled anger in Troy's eyes, and a look of mischievous triumph in Larry's.

She could not help wondering why.

She felt that it might have something to do with her.

If so, what?

Chapter Nine

A woman's face,
with Nature's own hand painted,
Hast thou, the master-mistress,
Of my passion.
—William Shakespeare

Red Feather had found it hard to sit through the dinner without lashing out at Larry.

But dinner was now behind him. He had managed to get a moment alone with his mother to tell her that his father had not believed him, that he had sent him away.

He would never forget the despair in her eyes . . . a look that changed quickly to determination.

He wondered what her next move would be, for he knew she would not give up on her dream so easily.

He had not questioned her about why she had not done this or that all those years ago. When he was with her, it was obvious to him that she wanted to make things right for him, his father, and their people. He knew it was not right to make her feel guilty about the past when he knew just how hard she had worked to make the future happy.

His mother and father had retired to the library for the evening.

Red Feather had watched Angela Dawn go up the stairs and knew she must be in her assigned bedroom. He watched now as Larry ambled up the winding staircase, a smug look on his face.

Having waited long enough to set things straight with his brother, Red Feather went up the stairs behind Larry.

When they both reached the privacy of a corridor, where their voices could not be heard downstairs, or in Angela Dawn's room, Red Feather hurried up behind his brother and grabbed him by the nape of the neck.

"Whoa, there, little brother," Red Feather said, his voice tight with anger. "I think we have a thing or two to discuss, don't you?"

"Let go, Troy, or by God, I'll..." Larry growled as he pulled at Red Feather's hand in an attempt to get away from his firm grip.

"You will what?" Red Feather said, knowing that when it came to fighting, he always got the best of his brother.

"Just let go, damn it," Larry growled. He lurched forward clumsily when Red Feather released his hold on his neck.

Larry wove his fingers through his long hair, pushing it back from his face as he swung around and glared at Red Feather.

"Why the hell did you do that?" Larry grumbled, his eyes narrowed angrily.

"You know damn well why I stopped you. Fess up, brother. Why did you do it?"

"Do what?" Larry said, his eyes wavering as Red Feather gazed steadily at him.

"Alright, act innocent," Red Feather said. He glanced over his shoulder in the direction of Angela Dawn's room. It was far down the other corridor. He hoped she wouldn't hear the truth just yet, especially in this way. He would inform her soon enough, in a way that would be less disturbing than hearing two brothers arguing about a card game and what the winner came away with.

"Alright, so I went and met the stagecoach and brought her home," Larry snarled. "What of it?"

"What of it?" Red Feather said, his eyebrows rising. "You know damn well why I'm angry. You pretended to be her fiancé, when you know that you aren't."

"She is rightfully mine and you know it," Larry retorted. "It was *I* who read the poster about her, and it was *I* who forwarded her the money to bring her to Louisiana. If I hadn't responded to that poster, she'd still be floundering and alone."

Larry leaned his face closer to Red Feather's. "And winning a white woman by gambling cannot be legal," he said tightly. "It could be seen as buying a human being, like slaves are bought." He laughed. "Must I remind you of the indecency of slavery? We have a few, and you know how they've been treated at the hands of our father."

Larry stepped back slightly, nervously raked his fingers through his long black hair, and smiled ruefully again at his brother. "And Troy, you *cheated*," he said. "You didn't win that last hand of poker fairly, anyhow."

Those words hit Red Feather like a cold slap to his face. He had not intended to get so angry over what his brother had done, but as each moment passed and Larry added insult upon insult, it was just too much to take.

He was incensed that his brother could be so conniving, so cold, so . . . He could not even think of a word that fit his brother at this moment.

But worst of all was that his brother had accused Red Feather of being a cheater, a word that men killed over.

Everyone knew Red Feather was a decent, honest, warm, caring man, unlike his brother.

Red Feather took a quick step forward, grabbed Larry by the throat, and leaned his face into his. "You have just crossed a line . . . one that makes brothers enemies," he hissed. "No man calls me a cheat and gets away with it, and no man but I will lay claim to Angela Dawn. I *did* win her in a card game, fair and square. And I see her as vulnerable. I will not let *anyone* bring harm her way, especially not a lying, conniving brother such as you have proven to be, time and again."

The voices wafting down the corridor, first talking softly in hushed tones and then growing louder, so loud that she could hear every word, brought Angela Dawn to her door.

She carefully opened it and left it slightly ajar, then listened to voices she knew belonged to Troy Ratcliffe and his brother Larry.

She went pale and grew cold inside when she heard that she had been brought to Louisiana because of a card game.

Because of gambling!

The brothers had gambled for her as though she were an object, not a human being.

Anger seized her. She had always despised

gambling, even though her father had made a living doing it.

She now detested anything that had to do with gambling. It was the very reason her father was no longer alive.

She was bitter and angry and filled with a keen resentment at having been the center of a game of cards.

A pawn!

In a swish of skirt and petticoats, she turned and stamped to her larger travel bag.

Intending to leave this place immediately, she slammed it shut, then stopped and thought more clearly about the situation. She could not get far on foot with such a large, obtrusive bag.

She eyed the smaller case and knew it was the only baggage she could take, for she planned to steal a horse from the stable and flee on it.

She wasn't sure where she could go, but she now knew that she would have no choice but to part with her father's dueling pistols in order to have money enough to live on the next few days.

And not only that. She would also lose any chance of finding her father's killer, now that she had no choice but to leave this house of gamblers.

Gamblers? she thought. Could this mansion actually house the man who'd killed her father? No, it would be too much of a coincidence.

Not taking time to change her clothes, she

packed what she could in the smaller bag, including the pistols.

Devastated with emotion, feeling defeated, and oh, so alone in the world again, she went to the bedroom window.

She struggled until she got it up, then reached for her bag and lifted it out onto the second-floor porch that ran the length of the three-story mansion.

She climbed out, and with bag in hand tiptoed across the porch as she searched for a way to get down to the ground.

She smiled when she found a trellis at one end.

She dropped her bag to the ground, then praying that the trellis would hold her weight, climbed out onto it.

She sighed in relief when she reached the ground without mishap or being discovered.

She grabbed her bag, then stopped and looked cautiously around. The moon was high and full, which gave her a clear view of everything, but would also give anyone a full view of her as she made her escape.

Luckily, she saw no one. She sought the cover of the huge cypress trees that ran all along the edge of the lawn to the stable at the rear of the estate.

As she ran to the stable, she looked to her right and saw the slave quarters. There was dim lamplight in some windows, and she could hear someone singing softly from one of the cabins. It was a sad song, sung surely by a female slave. It was a melody that reached inside Angela Dawn's heart, making her feel her own loneliness more keenly.

Fighting back tears and the building ache of defeat, she ran on to the stable.

She was relieved not to see the stable boy. He had surely retired for the night. She hoped he did not sleep overhead in the loft, where he might hear her stealing a horse.

Praying that the stable boy was not anywhere near, Angela Dawn slipped inside the stable.

She felt her way around in the darkness until she found the stalls.

She opened the first one she came to.

She had learned how to ride in Saint Louis with friends who owned horses.

She had always dreamed of owning one herself. But never had she thought she would steal one to make that dream come true.

But tonight?

She would do anything in order to gain her freedom again. And somehow she felt the people in this huge house owed her recompense.

She had been brought here for all the wrong reasons. She felt belittled just knowing how she had come to Ratcliffe Manor. She would not feel guilty for stealing a horse to flee the circumstances in which she had found herself.

"Come on, boy," Angela Dawn whispered to the white horse as she led it from the stall.

She felt around and found a saddle and bridle, and soon had the horse ready for riding, with her travel bag secured at the right side of the saddle.

Filled with fear of the unknown, she rode off into the dark shadows of the night, leaving behind the huge mansion with its many lamp-lit windows . . . and all hopes of ever finding her father's murderer.

"Troy and Larry Ratcliffe, I hate you more than you will ever know," she whispered.

She reached down and touched the travel bag, the feel of her father's pistols the only thing that gave her comfort this night.

At least while she had them with her, she felt her father's presence, as well. He had loved those pistols, perhaps too well.

"Father, I had hoped to avenge your death, but now . . . but now . . ."

Tears fell from her eyes in silver rivulets.

Chapter Ten

Describe Adonis and the counterfeit
Is poorly imitated after you.
　　　　　　—William Shakespeare

Red Feather stopped yelling, suddenly realizing just how loud his and Larry's voices had gotten as they argued in the corridor. If their voices reached Angela Dawn's room, she would hear everything. No doubt she would be hurt to know that two men had gambled on her, the winner gaining the right to marry her.

Yes, she would surely feel wronged if she learned that she had been won in a game of cards.

Just in case she had heard their argument, Red

Feather turned quickly away from Larry and rushed to Angela Dawn's room to explain.

He found the door closed.

All was quiet inside the room.

Perhaps he was wrong.

Possibly after her long day she had gone to bed and fallen asleep.

But he had to know.

He would not want to hurt her for the world. She had reached into his heart with her quiet sweetness.

And although he knew that she would have to find out the truth eventually, since he was not about to allow Larry to get away with double-crossing him, Red Feather wanted to be the one to explain things to her.

And if she wasn't asleep, now was as good a time as any, before Larry got the chance to tell her his skewed version of the events.

He knocked on the door and softly spoke her name.

When there was no response, he started to leave. But he just couldn't take the chance that Larry would get to her first when she awakened.

If he had to awaken her to get a few private moments with her, so be it. Again he knocked on the door, this time much harder, and again he spoke her name.

This time when she still didn't respond, a warning flashed through his consciousness. What if she had heard and had been so hurt by the knowledge that she had fled?

If she was out there alone in the dark, where would she go?

Determined to find out, Red Feather slowly turned the doorknob.

When he opened the door, the soft glow from a candle revealed that Angela Dawn wasn't there, nor had her bed been slept in.

He wasn't sure what to think. Perhaps she had simply gone to the library to get a book to read.

But when he saw that her large travel bag was open and her belongings lay strewn about on the floor, and he saw the open window, he rushed to it and gazed out.

He gasped when he saw Angela Dawn ride from the stable, a small travel bag hanging at the side of her horse.

"She did hear," Red Feather whispered to himself.

Panic-stricken, Red Feather ran from the room.

He half collided with Larry, then shoved him aside and took the stairs two at a time as Larry stood on the second-floor landing, demanding to know what was wrong.

Even when his mother and father rushed out of the library, Red Feather ignored them and ran outside to the stable.

He led his black steed quickly from its stall,

leaped on it, bareback, and rode from the stable. He had to catch up with Angela Dawn. She would soon get lost in the dark.

Her solitary ride would be frightening and could even be dangerous, for there were evil men who roamed this land at night, men who would like nothing more than to find a defenseless woman they could take advantage of.

He rode hard in the direction that he had seen Angela Dawn traveling and soon caught up with her.

He rode on ahead of her, then wheeled his horse around and stopped directly in front of her to block her way. She had no choice but to draw rein and bring the white steed to a quick halt.

"Let me pass," Angela Dawn said, lifting her chin defiantly.

In the moonlight, she could see again just how handsome this man was.

Yet she could not forget what she had heard him and Larry discussing.

They had played her for a fool. They had used her worse than any whore.

And although she had had a role in her humiliation by accepting a stranger's money to travel to Jamestown, she still could not get over the realization that she had been used as a pawn in a game of poker . . . a poker chip, no less!

"No, I do not think so," Red Feather said, edging his horse closer to hers. "Where do you think you are going at this time of night? And . . . why?"

Of course, he knew without a doubt why she was fleeing, but he wanted to hear her say it. Then he would find a way to make things right with her.

Apologies would not be enough. He would have to take some action.

After listening to her, he would decide what that might be.

For now, he was just glad that he had discovered her flight when he had, or else she might possibly be lost to him forever. Now that he had met her, he did not ever want to lose her.

"I came to Louisiana thinking that I might find a new start in life here, and then I discovered that I had been won in a game of poker as though I were some inanimate object . . . a poker chip," she said.

She fought the urge to cry, for now she was feeling more hurt than angry over what had happened.

"I am a person . . . a person with feelings," she said, her voice breaking. Tears splashed from her eyes as her defenses began crumbling. "I . . . I . . . hate anything that has to do with gambling."

"Why is that?" Red Feather asked. "What has happened in your life that makes you feel so strongly about gambling?"

"My father died because of it, that's why," she

choked out. She wiped tears from her face and lifted her chin again. "Now will you please let me pass? Or do I have to ride around you?"

Feeling so much for the woman, and touched by her vulnerability, loneliness, and loveliness, Red Feather inched his horse closer to hers.

"If you will not flee . . . if you will stay, I will make you feel like anything but a person who was won in a game of cards," he said thickly. "I will see to it that you have a good life. You came to Louisiana thinking that you were to be married. Well, that can still happen. *I* will marry you."

He was stunned that he should have such powerful feelings for a woman he had only just met. He wanted to change his life to include her, despite the other things troubling his mind.

But there was no denying that he cared deeply about this woman. If it took marriage to make things right for her, then that was the way it would be. He knew that if he let her pass by him tonight and something happened to her, he would forever hold himself responsible.

"I appreciate what you are offering, but . . . I . . . I . . . have to refuse you," Angela Dawn said, amazed by the man's generosity. He would marry her when it was Larry's scheme that had brought her to Jamestown, not his.

She swallowed hard.

She lowered her eyes, then raised them again so that she could look directly into his. "Surely you know how cheap and dirty I feel," she said, her voice soft and lilting.

"It's regrettable that you feel that way," Red Feather said. "I apologize, for I am partly responsible. But I just can't let you leave. Where would you go? In a world of men, you would not get far."

She could not stop the tears from flowing as she responded. "I didn't come to Louisiana *only* to have someone care for me, or marry me," she said softly. "The true reason I came here is very different."

"What are you talking about?" he asked. "What else made you offer yourself as a mail-order bride?"

"It was a way to . . . to . . . I had hoped to find my father's murderer," she blurted out. "He was a gambling man, and . . ."

She told him about her father's death and her daring need to find his killer.

"Please tell no one else what I have told you," she said in a rush. "I would not want the man I am searching for to know that I am here, or why."

She swallowed hard. "Yes, I know that the chances of finding this man are slim, but surely someone in the area will be able to give me a description of him."

"I won't tell a soul what you told me tonight," Red Feather said. He urged his horse closer to hers. "I give you my word on that. And I will go farther than that. I offer my help to find the murderer. Return tonight to my house. Tomorrow, when you are rested, we can begin making plans. We can work together on this project."

"You would do this for me?" Angela Dawn asked, searching his face, trying to understand a man who would offer so much to her, a stranger.

She started to accept his offer, then stiffened when something else occurred to her.

Was he hoping to get her into his bed with his soft words of encouragement?

Did he plan to sleep with her before any marriage vows were spoken, then discard her?

She stiffened her spine. "You are probably no better than your brother," she said.

She forced sarcasm into her voice, but she did not feel at all sarcastic about this man. She wanted him; truly wanted him.

"You and your brother are both gamblers," she murmured. "And because my father was a gambler, I have been put in a position that until only weeks ago would have been abhorrent to me."

She sighed heavily. "I know from having lived with a gambling father that once a gambler, always a gambler," she murmured. "Are you not gambling in a way, as you offer things to me that tomorrow you will regret?"

She yanked on her reins and turned her horse away from his. "No thank you," she said flatly.

"No thank you to all of your offers tonight. I plan to leave on the next stagecoach back to Saint Louis."

And to herself she thought, to hell with her plan of finding the killer. She should have known better than to think she ever could.

It was all just a pipe dream.

She hung her head, and tears rushed from her eyes again. "I am such a fool," she sobbed out. "A fool blinded by the need for vengeance."

She lifted her eyes and gazed into his as she wiped her face. "I am probably no better than you or your brother," she said softly. "I used Larry and his money to get me to the place where I'd hoped to find my father's killer. I had hoped to find the killer before actually exchanging vows with anyone. I did not want to go through with the marriage if I didn't have to."

Red Feather rode up next to her. He reached a hand to her cheek, relieved when she did not slap it away. "I am nothing like my brother," he said gently. "You can trust me. Stay. You don't have to worry about marrying me if you do not choose to. You can stay in the family mansion in your own room. We can work together to find the man responsible for your father's death. I am knowledgeable about the gamblers in this area. I will listen to conversations to see if I hear someone bragging about killing a man from Saint Louis. You can go into Jamestown with me to search, yourself. Do you have a description of the man?"

As he dropped his hand away from her face, she lowered her eyes. "No," she murmured. She gazed at him again. "Only that he is a rich man from Jamestown."

"Do you want to return to my house and work with me on this project?" Red Feather asked. "I promise that you can trust me."

Angela Dawn was touched deeply by his kindness, by his sincerity.

And his eyes and his voice mesmerized her.

Yes, maybe what he suggested could work.

But then she thought about his brother. It was obvious that Larry still thought she belonged to him, not Red Feather.

"What about your brother's claim on me?" she asked warily.

"Do not worry," Red Feather said, smiling. "I will take care of any problems my brother might cause."

Thankful that one brother of the two had proved to be decent and forthright, Angela Dawn agreed to everything that Red Feather had offered.

Side by side, they rode back toward the mansion.

For the first time since her father's death, Angela Dawn felt true hope in her heart.

She gazed over at Red Feather.

Surely it was destiny that had brought them together. How else could she have found such a man as he, who was willing to fight for her?

Chapter Eleven

Take all my love, my love, yea, take them all;
What hast thou then more than though hads't
   before?
No love, my love, that though may'st true
   love call.

                              —William Shakespeare

Jewel was standing at her bedroom window, looking in the direction of her people's village. Now
that she knew the outcome of Red Feather's visit
to the Chitimacha, she was almost beside herself
with disappointment.

   She could not stand by and allow Straight Arrow to deny that Red Feather was his firstborn.

She had no choice but to go to him, to plead Red Feather's case.

It might be her last chance to set things right with her first husband. He might be dying.

She turned and gazed at Jon Paul, who was sound asleep in their bed. She knew that he would not awaken until morning. He took a sleep drug each night to combat insomnia.

"I must go," Jewel whispered to herself.

Yes, she must, and now, not later. She knew it would be possible, for Jon Paul no longer had her watched.

She tiptoed from the room.

Warding off all fears of being a woman alone in the dark, Jewel went to a closet at the far end of the corridor and stepped inside. Even in the dark she could find the buckskin dress that she had placed there in a box high on a shelf. She had taken it from its hiding place often to hold it and to dream when her husband was away on a business jaunt.

Tonight the dream was going to come true.

She was going to return to her first love, and to her true people, the Chitimacha.

Ah, the wait had been so long.

She hurried into the buckskin dress and moccasins, then left the house and ran to the river, where a cypress canoe was always beached. She had taught her sons how to paddle it, and they both loved that mode of travel on days when they needed solace from the world.

After shoving the canoe into the river, Jewel climbed into it and began paddling toward what had been her home twenty-five years ago.

Until tonight, she had never allowed herself to get in the canoe and travel in that direction, fearing that she might never return to the white world.

She had always feared that if she disobeyed her white husband, both she and her son would suffer the consequences.

But now Red Feather was man enough to protect himself from Jon Paul. And she did not fear the consequences now, for she had lived her life.

When she arrived at the Chitimacha village, she beached the canoe.

She was overwhelmed by memories of those days long ago when she had worked with the women of her village, when she had strolled hand in hand with her chieftain husband, anxious to tell him that she was with child, only to have that opportunity taken from her when she was abducted and forced into marriage with a white man.

Although she had been stolen away twenty-five years ago, the memories were as fresh as if it had happened just the day before. She could not help standing and weeping over her loss for a while before continuing into the village and facing her chieftain husband for the first time since their last embrace.

She now knew just how much she had missed him, and her people, her life!

The bitter resentment that she had felt for Jon Paul during her first months of captivity was as raw at this moment as it had been when her captivity was new.

It was hard to understand how she had grown to care for Jon Paul in any way when she should have continued hating, loathing, and despising him.

The weakness that had eventually caused her to share in his lovemaking filled her with shame.

A son had even been born as a result of those nights of lovemaking. . . .

She walked onward toward the village with a humbleness she had never felt before.

When she got closer to the village, she stopped, her eyes widening as she saw how different it was now from the way it had been when she had lived there.

Back then, the only dwellings had been tall, stately tepees. But now there were mostly cabins. It seemed most of her people had chosen the white man's dwelling over their own.

What else would she find that was different from when she had last been there?

She lowered her face into her hands and wept

again, for all that she had not been a part of, and for what could never be. If she could only turn back the hands of time . . . !

But she couldn't.

She had Red Feather's future to see to.

She wiped the tears from her eyes with the backs of her hands, held her chin high, and moved onward.

She would not allow herself to feel guilty for anything in her past.

She knew that everything she had done since learning of her first pregnancy had been done for one person—Red Feather!

It still was her goal to see that everything was right for him.

That was why she was risking so much tonight, even her own life, to come and speak with her first husband, her first love, her Straight Arrow . . . her son's true father.

She jumped when two warriors stepped suddenly out of the shadows. Her heart skipped a beat as each man grabbed an arm and stopped her.

"Who are you and why have you come at this late hour like a ghost in the night?" one of the warriors asked, his dark eyes closely scrutinizing her.

"I feel like a ghost as I face my past for the first time in twenty-five years," Jewel said.

She gazed from one warrior to the other.

She was not afraid, for they were Chitimacha and no Chitimacha warrior would harm a woman, not even one who appeared at night in the middle of their village.

"What do you mean?" the other warrior asked. "Who are you? What do you want here?"

"Please do not force me to reveal my identity to you just yet," she pleaded. "Please allow me to speak directly to your chief."

"You ask to have council with our chief?" the other warrior said, arching an eyebrow. "Woman, do you not know the hour of night that you ask this of us? Our chief is asleep."

"I know that, but it is important that we talk," she said. She was glad when the men released their holds on her. "Your chief will want to talk with me if he knows I am here."

The warriors hesitated. They gave each other questioning looks.

Then suddenly someone else stepped from the shadows.

As this warrior moved into the light of the moon, Jewel gasped. He looked so much like Straight Arrow when he was young and a new husband to her, she knew without a doubt that she had just come face to face with his second-born son—Gray Fox.

This young warrior looked so much like Red Feather, it was as though Red Feather stood there. How could anyone doubt her story that these two young men were brothers?

There was only one noticeable difference between them. Beneath the light of the moon she could see a streak of gray that lay amid Gray Fox's raven-black hair.

"Who are you, and why are you asking to have private council with my father?" Gray Fox asked guardedly.

"Just please allow me time with your father," she said softly. "Both you and your father will understand once I reveal truths to him that have been kept secret for too long." She gazed guardedly at the two warriors, then pleaded with Gray Fox. "Please let me speak to *you* in private?"

Gray Fox stood quietly for a moment while his eyes studied the woman's face and he pondered her words.

Then he nodded to the two warriors, who quickly left.

After the warriors were out of hearing range, Jewel poured out her heart and soul to the young man who so closely resembled her own son.

"Please believe what I say is true," she said, once her tale was told. "Your father deserves to hear me. He would want to know that I am alive and well. Please take me to him?"

Gray Fox had listened closely to what she'd said, yet he still had trouble believing all she had revealed.

Still, his father had talked of his first wife often.

He had said that she had been the beauty of the tribe in her youth, and Gray Fox saw that this woman was lovely even now, for a woman of her age.

His father had even left the lodge that he had shared with his first wife as it had been on her last day there. He had made it into a shrine of sorts, even though his second wife had never understood or approved.

"Come with me," Gray Fox suddenly said as he gently took Jewel by an elbow. "I have something to show you."

Jewel's pulse raced as she walked farther into the village. Except for the cabins, so much was the same. It was as though she had never left.

And when she saw the tepee that she was being taken to, her heart skipped a wild beat. It could not be any other lodge than the one she had shared with her husband.

Its buckskin covering was even still painted the way it had been when she had shared it with Straight Arrow, depicting figures commemorative of a dream experience she'd had, oh, so long ago.

Her gaze shifted and she saw the larger lodge situated nearby and guessed it was the chief's lodge today.

Her thoughts were interrupted when she was led into the old tepee, and a new ache filled her heart.

Gray Fox lit a candle that filled the lodge with a soft glow. He held it up so that Jewel could see everything around her.

She knew that he was watching her reaction, and realized now that he had brought her to this tepee for a purpose. It was a test of sorts.

Tears filled her eyes, and moments spent there with her husband came back in a wondrous rush of happy memories.

She was deeply touched to see that it was exactly the way it had been when she'd lived there with Straight Arrow.

He had left everything as though she had just been there moments ago.

Her sewing basket, the reeds that she had brought to the lodge for her basketry, her cooking utensils—all were as she had left them. Her blankets and clothes still lay folded neatly beside the cold ashes of the central fire pit.

He had left their home untouched, as though her spirit dwelled within.

Overtaken by emotion, she wept openly.

Gray Fox now knew without a doubt that this was his father's first wife.

"Come with me," he said.

He again took her gently by the elbow and led her from the tepee, then walked her over to the larger one which she knew was her husband's.

Together they entered the tepee. When she saw Straight Arrow asleep on his thick bed of pelts beside a slowly burning lodge fire, everything she had once felt for him rushed over her with a sweetness that made her sigh. She knew without doubt that what she had done tonight was right.

She folded her hands together as she watched Gray Fox kneel down beside his father and gently awaken him.

Straight Arrow blinked his eyes, then opened them. He gazed up at his son with curiosity. "Why have you come?" he asked. "Why have you awakened me?"

"Someone has come to speak with you," Gray Fox said. He moved out of the way so that his father could see Jewel standing there in the soft glimmer of light from the fire.

"Am I dreaming ... or ... are ... you ... Soft Flower?" Straight Arrow asked incredulously.

He leaned on an elbow, blinked, and rubbed his eyes. At last he was sure that she was real ... that it *was* his Soft Feather who had come back to him. And to him, she was as beautiful as ever.

She had not aged much since he'd last seen her. There were only a few wrinkles on her lovely face, only a few silver threads in her hair.

"Soft ... Flower ... ?" Straight Arrow whispered. "It ... is ... you."

Unable to hold herself back any longer, Jewel went to her husband and knelt down before him.

When he drew her into his embrace, she was

eighteen winters old again, young and in love, and so thrilled to know she was pregnant with this man's child.

"Yes, it is I," she said, sobbing and clinging. "I am sorry that it took me so long to return to you. And you? I have heard that you are not well."

"I am ill, but I will survive this ailment, it seems," Straight Arrow said, his voice drawn. He glanced over at Gray Fox. "Son, I would like some time alone with Soft Flower. Do you understand?"

"Yes, and I will give you those moments," Gray Fox said. He smiled at Jewel. "You are as my father always said—beautiful, soft-spoken, and sweet. And thank you for coming. You have put sunshine back into my father's eyes."

Tears sprang to Jewel's eyes. She was so moved by Gray Fox's words, all she could do was nod at him.

She watched him leave, then turned back to Straight Arrow. "He is a fine young man," she murmured. "You are lucky, Straight Arrow. You have *two* fine sons."

She sighed. "I have so much to tell you," she murmured.

"I will listen," Straight Arrow said, his eyes fixed on her.

His hands were on her face, slowly, softly exploring, as she began the tale of her past, of how she had disappeared from his life so suddenly, and why she had not been allowed to escape her captivity.

Then she talked of Red Feather and how Straight Arrow had rejected his true son when he had sent him away.

"Red Feather?" Straight Arrow repeated. He gently pulled his hands from her face. "The young warrior who came to me was truly my son Red Feather?"

"Yes, your son," Jewel said. She stifled a sob behind a hand. "And you know that my grandfather's name was Red Feather. When our son told you his name and how he had acquired it, you should have realized he was who he professed to be."

"Did he explain that to me?" Straight Arrow asked, his brow furrowing. He kneaded his chin and seemed lost in thought. "I do not recall, yet I do not remember everything anymore. You see, my mind has blank spots. My illness has weakened my memory. Some days it is worse than others."

"But you remembered me," Jewel said, smiling sweetly at him. "And I am so glad that you did. Had you not, my heart would have been broken, as it was that day when I was stolen away from you and my people."

"How could I ever forget you?" Straight Arrow said. He took one of her hands. "You were the first love of my life, and my only true love. I did love my second wife, but not as deeply as I did you. It is said that in one's lifetime there is only one true love. That, my love, was, and still is, *you*."

"As I have loved no one but you," Jewel murmured. "And now that you know why I could not come back to you, do you understand that it was not because I did not want to? I was a prisoner. In a sense, so was our son."

She touched his smooth, copper face. "You should be very proud of this son you have never known," she murmured. "He came almost the instant he learned about you, only to be turned away. I have taken a chance on my own life tonight by coming to speak on behalf of our son. I have no idea what will await me when I return to the mansion."

"Stay with me," Straight Arrow said. His eyes begged her. "Do not return to this other life that has been forced on you. Turn your back forever on that man who sinned against humanity the day he abducted you."

"No, I cannot do that, not just yet anyhow, for Red Feather is the one who might pay for my absence," Jewel said. She swallowed hard. "Although Jon Paul loves him, I am not certain how he will react when he knows that the truth is out about our son's true heritage. For now, he doesn't know that I have revealed any of it to Red Feather. I sneaked away to come to you. I must sneak back in before Jon Paul discovers that I have gone. But believe me when I say that, with all of my heart, I would stay with you if I could. But nothing will keep me away long, now that I have finally found the courage to return to you."

"Send our son back to me," Straight Arrow said thickly. "He will be welcomed with open arms and heart."

"That makes me so happy," Jewel said. She leaned toward him and wrapped her arms about his neck. "It is as though I have been in your arms forever, for at this moment it is easy to believe that I was never gone from you."

"I want you back," Straight Arrow said, returning her embrace. "Somehow we must make that happen."

"For now, let us just feel blessed that we have been reunited," Jewel said, leaning away from him. "And I feel so blessed that you are not as ill as I thought you might be. I do believe that we will still have some time together before we get too old to enjoy one another's company."

"You must find a way to come and stay with me and our people," Straight Arrow said. He reached a hand out for her as she stood to leave. "I have been denied both you and my firstborn for too long. Find a way, Soft Flower. Find a way."

She nodded, then stepped out into the moonlight. She was glad that Gray Fox was there to escort her back to the canoe.

As she paddled away on the river, she waved at him, feeling a bond with him even though he was not a son born of her and Straight Arrow's love.

She hated to envision Straight Arrow in another woman's arms, making a child, yet she had known through the years that he had another wife.

But now?

Yes, she must find a way to rectify the mistakes of the past.

She did want to be a part of Straight Arrow's life again. Somehow she would find a way.

When she reached the mansion, she hurried inside and changed clothes again.

When she reached her bedroom, she was relieved to find that Jon Paul was still asleep. He did not seem to have moved a muscle while she had been gone.

"Red Feather," she whispered to herself, feeling that she had time to go and speak with him before Jon Paul awakened. She could hardly wait to tell Red Feather all that had happened tonight.

His father had asked to see him!

He had actually accepted that Red Feather was his son!

When she reached Red Feather's room, she softly knocked and spoke his name.

When there was no response, she gently opened his door.

But when she saw his bed still made, she was puzzled. It was obvious that he had not been in it tonight.

She had seen him leave the house in a rush earlier. Had he stayed away? If so, where had he gone?

Puzzled about his absence, yet knowing that she must return to her room before Jon Paul discovered her gone, she walked away from Red Feather's room.

When she found Angela Dawn's door ajar, she tiptoed to it and opened it carefully.

She gazed into the room and discovered that the girl was missing, too, surely Red Feather's absence had something to do with Angela Dawn being gone.

They must be together. But why? And where would they have gone?

Concerned, yet knowing that she must get back to her room, Jewel hurried back to her bedroom and eased into the bed beside her husband. But her eyes would not close.

Nor would her heart cease pounding.

So much had happened tonight, but she could not help worrying about Red Feather.

She lay there scarcely breathing as she listened for his return.

She hoped the woman would not interfere in what had just begun for Red Feather—a new life with his people, perhaps even a future as a powerful Chitimacha chief!

Chapter Twelve

These hours, that with gentle work did frame,
The lovely gaze where every eye doth dwell.
—William Shakespeare

The sun swam gently through the dining room windows, casting soft light on everyone at the table.

Jewel paused in the midst of eating her egg to look from Red Feather to Angela Dawn, then at Larry. There was tension in the air. She hated seeing the angry looks being exchanged between her two sons and knew the reason for it without even asking.

The woman!

Jewel would never forget Red Feather's and Larry's loud voices yesterday, and then how Red Feather had rushed out of the house.

She guessed that Red Feather and Angela Dawn had been together late at night. She hated to think that her son might care for her. She could tell that Angela Dawn had feelings for him. It was evident in the way she gazed at him this morning. There was stardust in her eyes, as though she was recalling an embrace? A kiss?

She slid her gaze back to Red Feather and stiffened when she caught him gazing at Angela Dawn with the same sort of mesmerized look as she was giving him.

Yes, Jewel now knew that there was something going on between her son and the woman, and there could be no worse time for Red Feather to have an infatuation with a woman . . . *any* woman.

Jewel wanted him to concentrate on joining his Chitimachi people and becoming close to his true father.

A woman would only complicate matters.

Jewel jerked with alarm and almost dropped her fork when Larry suddenly scooted his chair back and rose so quickly that the chair toppled over backwards, landing with a loud smack against the wooden floor.

She winced when Larry doubled his hands into tight fists at his sides and leaned his face down into Red Feather's.

119

"You haven't won, Troy," he said stiffly. "Not by a long shot."

Stunned, everyone watched Larry stomp angrily from the room.

And then they gazed at each other with questioning looks.

"Alright, Troy, what was that all about?" Jon Paul asked, his voice tight with controlled anger.

Red Feather didn't respond. He looked away from Jon Paul.

Jon Paul slid his eyes over to Angela Dawn. "Alright, young lady, let me ask you if you know anything about Larry's behavior," he said stiffly.

Angela Dawn felt trapped.

She most certainly had no idea how to respond to this man's question.

She felt it was not her place to tell this father anything about either of his sons. She had come to Ratcliffe Manor for all the wrong reasons. And if it wasn't for Troy, she would flee again.

As it was, though, she and Troy did have feelings for one another. He was going to help her find her father's murderer. No one would intimidate her into leaving now.

Although it seemed incredible, she was in love for the first time in her life.

It had happened so magically, she felt as though she were floating. She could hardly believe that this man who sat opposite her at the table could care enough for her to actually offer to marry her.

"Young lady, don't you think you should go after your fiancé to see what is wrong?" Jon Paul said, his voice growing louder and more demanding with each heated word.

Angela Dawn exchanged a quick glance with Troy. Neither Troy's mother nor father knew that she was not Larry's fiancée . . . that she actually belonged to their other son!

Now with Troy's parents' eyes on her, Angela Dawn slid her chair back from the table; then, sobbing, fled the dining room for the privacy of her bedroom.

"Son, your mother and I are both aware that you know what's going on here. We insist that you tell us," Jon Paul said. "It is obvious that there is something between you and the woman. Who could not catch those glances you gave one another?"

Knowing he would have to reveal the truth to them eventually, and deciding that it was better to get it behind him, Red Feather laid his fork on his plate of uneaten eggs, folded his napkin, then looked uneasily from his mother to Jon Paul.

"Yes, it is only right that you know everything," he said. Then he explained how he had won the card game that made Angela Dawn his, not his brother's. He told his mother and Jon

Paul how Larry had called him a cheat.

"And after seeing her, Larry decided he was not going to give her up after all," Red Feather finished. "That's why he tried to make you believe that she was his fiancée, not mine."

"Your . . . fiancée . . . ?" Jewel gasped, her face paling. "No, Troy. It can't be. You have other things . . ."

She stopped herself from revealing too much.

"It is I who will be seeing to Angela Dawn's welfare, not Larry," Red Feather said.

He pushed his chair back and stood up.

His eyes met his mother's. He saw the confusion in their depths and understood why.

She had mapped out his future from the time of his birth. She now saw that all she had planned was threatened by a woman.

He glanced over at Jon Paul, who was looking at him with disbelief, and knew that this was not the time to explain anything else to either of them. He had to give them both time to adapt to the change that this beautiful, sweet, lonely woman was bringing into all of their lives.

"I'm sorry, I don't think it is best for me to say anything else this morning," he said, then left the room.

He breathed much more easily when he reached the foyer. He gazed up the staircase. He hoped that Larry wasn't waiting for him; he needed to go to Angela Dawn.

When she had started crying in the dining room, it took all the willpower he could muster not to rush to her side to comfort her.

But now he would. And if anyone stood in his way, God help them.

Suddenly he was aware of an angry voice wafting down the staircase.

"Larry," he murmured angrily. "That bastard!"

He rushed up the stairs, taking them two at a time.

When he got to the second-floor landing he found Angela Dawn cowering, her back against the wall, while Larry towered over her, his voice filled with venom, his fists at his sides.

"You are nothing but a tramp, a *whore*," Larry growled as he leaned down into Angela Dawn's pale face. "You should go back where you came from. Haven't you caused enough trouble in this family?"

Feeling so angry it was hard to control himself, Red Feather rushed to Angela Dawn. He slid a protective arm around her waist and drew her close to his side.

"Never speak to Angela Dawn in such a way again," he said tightly. "And, little brother, she isn't going anywhere. She's going to be my bride."

Red Feather gazed down at Angela Dawn. With his free hand he brushed her tears away. "If she will have me," he added, smiling gently at her.

Angela Dawn gazed up at him with wonder in her eyes. This man was her hero!

She had never imagined she would actually meet a man she would love in Louisiana, a man who would actually love her back.

Angela Dawn started to respond, but stopped and swallowed hard when Troy's mother stepped into view.

She had arrived at the top of the steps just in time to hear Red Feather announce to his brother that he was going to marry Angela Dawn.

"No!" Jewel gasped. "Oh, please, please, Troy, don't do this."

Jewel had always dreamed of her son finding and marrying a Chitimacha woman. That dream was now dearer to her heart than ever, for she had made a decision that would change not only her life, but that of everyone in this household.

Unable to sleep after her reunion with her chieftain husband, she had decided to return permanently to her true people, to her first husband.

Seeing Straight Arrow again had made her realize just how much she had missed him; she wanted a relationship with Straight Arrow while there was still time left for them.

Yes, she was going to return to her true roots . . . to her true love . . . and she wanted her son Red Feather to go with her.

She was no longer afraid of her white husband, or of what he might do to her or Red Feather once he heard that she had revealed the truth. She no longer believed that this man with whom she had lived for so long would harm her or the son he had learned to adore.

As if her thoughts had conjured him up, she heard Jon Paul call her name.

Chapter Thirteen

I cannot love thee as I ought,
For love reflects the thing beloved;
My words are only words and moved
Upon the topmost froth of thought.
—Alfred, Lord Tennyson

Everyone turned and gazed at Jon Paul as he came up the stairs carrying a leather business satchel in one hand, a packed travel bag in the other. He was wearing his best suit. His dark hair was combed to perfection, and he wore his usual diamond in the ascot at his throat.

"As you all know, I must leave today on a business trip that is necessary to my cotton trade,"

Jon Paul said as he stopped at the second-floor landing. He frowned as he looked from son to son, and then gave his wife a wary look. "But before I go, I need to know if things are going to be alright here." His dark eyes went to Angela Dawn; then his back stiffened as he gazed at Red Feather.

"Troy, can I depend on your getting this mess cleared up?" he asked, frowning. "My business venture is important. I'll be gone a full week."

"I assure you that we will be just fine," Red Feather said. He felt a twinge of betrayal as he stood before this man whom he no longer considered his father.

As he gazed at him now, he tried to envision how it must have been on the day of his mother's abduction. Could this man really have done such a terrible thing?

It was true, he knew, but the part of him that had always idolized Jon Paul Ratcliffe found it hard to fathom.

"And what about your mother?" Jon Paul asked, turning his gaze to his wife.

Red Feather looked at his mother. He saw that she was fighting to keep her emotions under control, and he knew why. It was not only because she was unhappy about his proposing marriage to a woman who yesterday was a stranger to them all, but also because she had plans for Red

Feather that did not include any woman except herself.

It was hard to know what to expect of his mother now. But he knew one thing. He did have to reassure Jon Paul that she was going to be alright in his absence. Otherwise he might not go, and Red Feather wanted the freedom to come and go as he pleased while his father was gone.

He also wanted private time with his mother to convince her that he was making the right decision about Angela Dawn.

"I regret that Mother has been upset this morning," Red Feather said quickly. "Moments ago, she happened upon Larry and me arguing. That is why she is upset. But things will be alright. Just go on. See to your business. I know of its importance to you."

"You should be going with me," Jon Paul said. Then he gazed at Larry. "So should you. It's important that both my sons know how to carry on the business once I am gone. These meetings are the best way for you to learn."

He looked sternly at Red Feather. "Forget this nonsense about the woman and go pack your bags," he said. He clasped a hand on his shoulder. "Your brother shouldn't have sent for such a woman in the first place."

He dropped his hand and went to Larry. "Send her back," he said flatly. "Do you hear, Lawrence? I am not going to insist on either you or your brother joining me today, because you have gotten yourselves into quite a mess here. It's a mess that I expect to be cleaned up by the time I return home."

Both Larry and Red Feather went quiet.

They exchanged bitter glances. Then they both turned and gazed at Angela Dawn.

Angela Dawn felt trapped in the middle of a family dispute and was sorry that she was the cause of it. If she was smart, she would go and pack her things and leave immediately. She could still find someone to purchase her dueling pistols and so acquire enough money for passage back to Saint Louis.

But at this moment she was so in love, she could not see herself turning her back on the first happiness she'd known since her father's death.

No. She was not about to let an angry old man take away from her what she knew was the best thing that had ever happened to her in her lifetime. She had found a man who truly cared for her, and he was offering her the world.

She was going to step into that world with him and never look back.

She tightened her lips and lifted her chin as she challenged Jon Paul with a stubborn stare.

She smiled to herself when she saw how uneasy her gaze made him. He looked quickly away from her.

"Jon Paul, go on," Jewel encouraged as she

went to him and placed a gentle hand on his arm. "Things will be fine here. I shall see to it."

She turned from him and glared at Red Feather. "But your father is right," she said stiffly. "He is right to demand that this woman go back where she came from. It is up to *you* now, Troy, to do it, not Larry, since you lay claim to her."

Jewel went to him and gazed intently up into his eyes. "Son, send . . . her . . . back," she said tightly.

Having always done as his mother asked of him, Red Feather wasn't sure just what to say.

But he did know that what she demanded was absolutely impossible. Although it did seem incredible that he could fall in love with a woman as quickly as he had fallen for Angela Dawn, the truth was . . . he *was* in love, and he wanted to protect her. She was fragile in so many ways, and she had been absolutely alone in the world until he took her under his wing.

Still, he could hardly bear the hurt that he was causing his mother. She had so many plans for him that were now threatened.

But his concern for his mother now came second to his need to love and protect Angela Dawn.

He glanced at Jon Paul, who had slid a gold pocket watch from his inner coat pocket and was checking the time. His father looked impatiently from his wife to Red Feather.

"Mother, I promise to talk to you later about

this," Red Feather said. "Father must leave now or miss the stagecoach to New Orleans. And it is imperative that he leave with a clear mind so that he can do his best at the meetings."

Not giving his mother a chance to disagree, Red Feather went to his father and placed a reassuring hand on his shoulder. "I assure you that you have nothing to worry about here," he said. "And I'm sorry that I can't accompany you this time. Perhaps the next?"

"Is that a promise, son?" Jon Paul asked, his eyes searching Red Feather's. "You do know how important it is that you know every aspect of the sugarcane business. It is vastly more important than the tobacco industry. I see a time when the tobacco trade may fall off. But never sugar."

Red Feather heard the quick intake of his mother's breath and knew what she was thinking without her even saying it. She did not want him to get any more involved in the sugarcane business than he already was. His future with the Chitimacha would not include sugar.

"Yes, I shall plan to go with you the next time," he replied, regretting what might turn out to be a lie. He dropped his hand away from Jon Paul's shoulder and turned to Larry. "And so will Larry, won't you?"

Larry's only response was to give Red Feather an annoyed, forced nod.

Jon Paul turned to Jewel. "Can I truly leave without worrying about you?" he asked. He went to her and placed a hand gently on her cheek. "Or . . . should I cancel my business trip?"

Panic seized Jewel. She knew the importance of Jon Paul's being away these next several days. His absence would give her time to carry out her plans.

"You know I am capable of handling things while you are gone," Jewel said. "I always have, haven't I?"

"Before, there was never any woman involved with our sons," Jon Paul said. He gave both sons a bitter look, then gazed again into his wife's eyes. "But if you are certain, I truly must be on my way."

"Yes, I am certain," Jewel said softly. "Please concentrate only on business, not on me or your sons. Things have a way of working themselves out."

Jon Paul smiled, nodded, then drew her into a gentle embrace. "I shall miss you," he whispered in her ear.

She didn't respond, only smiled at him after he stepped away from her and hurried down the stairs.

The thud of the front door was proof enough that he had left and would soon be well on his way to New Orleans.

Larry gave Red Feather and Angela Dawn a hard glare, then also left.

Jewel ignored Angela Dawn, addressing herself to Red Feather. "Son, we must have a talk," she said, her voice drawn. "A serious talk."

She gave Angela Dawn a cold stare, then turned to Red Feather again. "We must have that talk *now*, Troy, not later, and it must be in total privacy, away from the woman."

"Mother, she has a name. It is Angela Dawn," Red Feather said, annoyed at his mother's rudeness. "She deserves respect, for she has done nothing to deserve ill treatment."

He sighed heavily when his mother, who had always been so sweet and gentle, refused to give Angela Dawn even a smile or a kind word.

He went to Angela Dawn and took her gently by the hand. They gazed into each other's eyes; then Red Feather spoke.

"Will you be alright while I have this talk with my mother?" he asked. "As you can see, it must be done."

"Yes, I'll be fine," Angela Dawn said, feeling sympathy for Troy. It was so obvious that his mother disliked her. To a mother, it must be painful to see a son care so much for a woman who, only a short time before, had been a total stranger.

She turned to Jewel, gave her a weak smile, then hurried to her bedroom and closed the door

133

between herself and the mother who seemed so adamant about keeping her son from her.

She stood with her back to the door, her heart pounding as she worried that Troy's mother might change his mind about her.

Her eyes filled with tears. She had brought trouble into this household, and the more she thought about it now, the more she felt guilty for her role in it.

Although she knew that Troy's feelings for her were genuine, and that she loved him with a passion she had never known before, she wondered if she was wrong to stay where so many did not want her.

If she was gone, Troy could resume his life as he had always known it.

"I *must* leave," she whispered, although every fiber of her being cried out against doing such a thing. It would break her heart into a million pieces.

But she just could not see how she could marry Troy when the whole family was against their loving one another. Worst of all, their love had pitted brother against brother.

"Yes, it is best for Troy that I leave," she whispered, blinded by tears as she went to her smaller travel bag and packed it again. "And this time, no one will find me and stop me."

She must find someone to purchase the dueling

pistols so that she could book passage with the money and flee Jamestown.

She had been foolish to think that she could change her own destiny by coming to Louisiana with vengeance on her mind.

That was where her life had begun to go wrong in the first place . . . planning to find and kill a man.

"I'm sorry, Father, but it just wasn't meant to be," she whispered, securing everything in her bag.

Yes, she must leave, even though by doing so she would be leaving behind her heart forever.

Tonight. She would flee into the darkness, but this time she would make certain no one followed her.

Chapter Fourteen

Look in thy glass, and tell the face thou
  viewest,
Now is the time that face should form another.
                                   —William Shakespeare

In the privacy of her bedroom, Jewel sat opposite
Red Feather in a plush, overstuffed chair before
the fireplace. There was much tension in the air
as mother and son gazed into each other's eyes.

Red Feather was trying to remain focused on
why he was there with his mother, yet his mind
and heart were elsewhere. He was afraid that Angela Dawn might decide to leave.

"Red Feather, I went and met with your Chitimacha father," Jewel began. "I left last night while your . . . while Jon Paul was asleep."

She took one of his hands in hers. "Son, your true father now knows that you are his son, and that you are called Red Feather, and why," she murmured. "He will now not only address you as Red Feather, but also as son."

"You went to him?" Red Feather gasped out, realizing the dangers that would have faced her if Jon Paul had awakened and found her gone.

"I had to go, Red Feather," Jewel said, her voice full of deep emotion. "Not only to set things right in your life, but also in my own. For so long I have craved a reunion with my only true love. His rejection of you gave me all the reason I needed to go and speak with him."

"And what happened when he realized who you were?" Red Feather asked, his eyes searching his mother's face. "Was he glad? Or too confused to feel anything?"

"He was, oh, so very glad that I was well, alive, and that I had finally returned to him," Jewel said. She lowered her eyes, then lifted them again. "I explained why I had not come earlier."

"Then he knows about the threat that kept you away, as well as me?" Red Feather asked.

"Yes, and he has urged me to return to him for good," Jewel said. She lifted her hand from his. She rose, took a poker from its stand, and began absently toying with the glowing coals of the fire. "And I have decided that my true place is with him."

Red Feather stood quickly and went to her. He placed a gentle hand on her shoulder and turned her toward him. "You are leaving? You are taking your place among your people as their princess again? As the wife of their chief?" he asked warily. "Mother, is that so?"

"Yes, just as I want you to take your place, among our people," Jewel said. She replaced the poker in its stand, then framed his face between her hands. "I am no longer afraid of Jon Paul, and neither should you be."

"But the threat is as real today as it has been every day since you were stolen from your people," Red Feather said, sighing heavily. "Mother, please do nothing that might bring harm to you." He sighed again. "I am not concerned for myself. But you? Yes, I do believe Father . . . Jon Paul . . . will retaliate if you humiliate him. Your leaving him to go live with your Indian husband will be the worst of humiliations."

"No, I do not fear the threat he used through the years to keep me at his side," Jewel said. She turned from him and went to the library window and gazed out. "No. He will not do anything to either of us."

She turned and gazed at Red Feather again. "He loves us both too much to harm us," she murmured. "And he also loves his respect and standing in the white community too much to raise a fuss. I believe he will quietly accept what we have done, and realize that he no longer has any say in the matter."

"But he has spent a lifetime loving us both," Red Feather said. "He always treated me so grandly. I never wanted for a thing."

He frowned and inhaled a deep breath, then slowly exhaled again. "Yet he had no choice but to treat me grandly, did he?" he said tightly. "Perhaps it was his guilt that made him shower me with personal possessions—horses, the best of firearms and clothes . . ."

"Son, let's not talk any longer about him, when we have so much else to discuss," Jewel said. She took his hand and urged him back to the chairs, where they again sat opposite one another. "It is imperative that you go back to the Chitimacha village and meet with your true father. He is waiting for you."

She paused, then said, "But, Red Feather, you should forget about the white woman. You have your father to consider now. Is he not more important than the woman? Your father is not as ill as I first thought. He has a different sort of ailment. It is not one that kills, but instead robs a person of his memory. I urge you to go to him before he forgets everything. Let him know you now, while he can, for soon I believe that he will not remember anything."

"His memory is failing him?" Red Feather asked.

"Yes, and it will worsen as time goes on," Jewel murmured. "Son, how do you feel about everything? Can you leave the comforts of this mansion and way of life and live the way you were meant to live? Can you exchange your expensive suits for buckskin? Would you be willing to marry into the tribe? The son of a chief can only marry into nobility."

"Marry . . . into . . . nobility?" Red Feather gasped. "And . . . it would be required of me to marry into the tribe?" His eyes narrowed as he gazed more intently at his mother. "Mother, you did not teach me that when you were teaching me all of the customs of the Chitimacha people."

"I did not think it necessary at the time, because there was no white woman in your life," Jewel said. "I thought that once you left this life and went to live with your people, you would meet a woman and fall in love."

"Mother, in truth you had no idea how any of these plans you had for me would work out in the end," Red Feather said tightly. "Nor did I."

He rose, leaned an arm against the fireplace mantel, and gazed into the fire. "I had never dreamed of meeting someone like Angela Dawn, who would steal my heart the moment our eyes met," he said softly. "It never made any difference to me whether the woman I fell in love with was white or not."

He wheeled around and gazed down at Jewel. "But as it turns out, Mother, the woman I am love with *does* have white skin," he said. "And please hear me when I say that I will do what my heart leads me to do. I will go to the Chitimacha village and spend more time with my people before making any decisions. But no matter where I am, or where I plan to live, Angela Dawn is a part of that life. Except for me, she is alone in the world. From now on, where I go, she goes. I *will* be loyal . . . to the woman I love."

"Son, I am going to try to forget the sharpness with which you just spoke to me," Jewel said. She found it hard to realize that this son she had tutored to be Chitimacha was now uncertain which life he should pursue.

She blamed the woman.

Had this Angela Dawn person not arrived in his life at this time, surely he would have no doubts about what his future should be.

"I did not mean to speak sharply to you, but you are so adamant about whom I should love, and where I should live, when it must be my own decision," he said, his voice calmer and softer.

"Son, I cannot believe you might be considering staying with Jon Paul after learning what he did to keep us both from our true people. As I told you, I have decided to go and live with our

141

true people; so should you," Jewel declared. "I am leaving the comforts of this life behind me; so must you. So must you choose your people over the white woman. What do you even know about this woman? Surely she has a dark side . . . like your white father, who held a terrible threat over both our heads all these years. Surely all whites have a dark side."

Knowing that no matter what he said about Angela Dawn, his mother was not yet ready to accept the truth.

Afraid that he might hurt his mother's feelings even more than he already had, he walked to the door and opened it. He turned and gave her a soft look of apology, then left without another word.

He felt the need to be totally alone. He needed time to think all of this through, even though he knew that he had already made his decision about Angela Dawn.

He would never desert her.

But what should he do about his other loyalties?

Although Jon Paul had practically enslaved his Indian wife, holding a terrible threat over her head for years, nothing would take away the fact that Jon Paul had been good, otherwise, to his wife and the son that he knew he had not fathered.

Yes, Red Feather had to think seriously about

his situation. And he knew the perfect place. He had gone there often to think things through.

He even prayed often as he sat there on the bluff, where he felt as though he could reach up and touch the sky.

He saddled his midnight-black steed, then rode at a hard gallop from the plantation grounds and did not stop until he reached a high bluff that overlooked his father's land on one side, the Indian village far away in the distance, on the other.

After dismounting and securing his horse's reins, Red Feather gazed toward the Chitimacha village and saw smoke spiraling from the smoke holes of the tepees and the chimneys of the cabins, and a larger swath of smoke that he knew came from the outdoor central fire that was kept burning day and night.

So much of his heart belonged there, yet he had had another life, the only one he had known except for those moments when his mother had taught him the Chitimacha history and customs.

Yes, he had begun long ago to feel a tugging at his heart to be among his true people, and to get to know them.

But there was no doubting that part of his heart that had never been unhappy while he lived his life at the plantation.

But now that he knew *why* he was a part of Jon Paul's life, and how this man had stolen a princess from her people, it made all the difference in the world.

He knelt down and gazed heavenward. He reached his hands skyward and prayed.

He prayed to know who he was, and why he had been put on this earth.

He prayed to know what his role should be. The life of a white man? Or red?

He felt the soft caress of a breeze and felt suddenly at peace with himself and the world.

He knew that somehow his prayers had been answered. He felt a sudden urge to go to the Chitimacha. He felt a strong need to wear his buckskin attire, not the expensive wool suits that hung in his closet.

He was destined to leave the life of a white man behind him, as well as the name that belonged to that life.

He would go and live with his true people, not with the man who had forced his mother and him to live a lie.

Yes, he would claim his birthright!

He hoped that his people would accept the white woman, for she was a part of his life, now and forever.

But what if Angela Dawn did not want to follow him to the Chitimacha village and be a part of his life there? What if she saw the Chitimacha as uncivilized?

He prayed he would not be put in the position of choosing between his Chitimacha people and Angela Dawn.

Chapter Fifteen

Dost thou truly long for me?
And am I thus sweet to thee?
                    —William Blake

Having seen Troy hurry from the house as though he was distraught about something, Angela Dawn concluded that his talk with his mother had not gone well.

Now that she had seen the man she loved so distraught, she could not help wanting to go to him. He had offered her so much comfort the night before. How could she not want to go to him now and see if she could help him in some way?

Just that quickly she had decided not to leave after all. She could not give up on their future. She knew that something extraordinary had brought her and Troy together. It was surely destiny! She would not let an angry, selfish mother stand in their way.

Angela Dawn was now on a horse, herself. She was searching for Troy, and when she saw him on a bluff on his knees, she knew that he had sought solace there . . . through prayer.

That made him even dearer to her. He was not only a noble, caring man. He was spiritual as well.

Having been denied the chance to practice any religion because her father was a gambler, a profession frowned upon by all religions, Angela Dawn had not learned much about religion herself.

But she did pray.

One did not have to practice a specific religion to pray. It could be done in the privacy of one's own room.

Prayer had sustained her after her parents' deaths.

Now she prayed silently to herself that what she was about to do was right. If she interfered in this man's life, and he eventually despised and resented her for it, she would not be disconsolate.

Even before she started to climb the bluff, he saw her.

When he smiled down at her and waved, her

heart did a somersault of joy, for she could tell that she was welcome. He *did* want her there.

When he motioned with a hand that she should stay, not climb to the bluff, then turned away from her and mounted his steed to descend the steep slope himself, she dismounted and waited.

Angela Dawn's breath caught in her throat as he leaped off his horse, wrapped his arms around her, and brought his lips down on hers in a kiss so sweet, her insides tingled from the joy of it.

She twined her arms around his neck and returned the kiss, knowing now for certain that she belonged with him, and he with her.

When he softly drew away from her and framed her face between his hands, their eyes met and her insides melted at the sincere love she saw there.

"I was afraid that I would be interfering by coming to seek you out," Angela Dawn murmured. "When I saw you leave the house in such a rush, I worried that the talk with your mother had been disturbing to you."

She lowered her eyes, swallowed hard, then gazed up at him again. "Am . . . I . . . the cause?" she asked, her voice breaking. "If so, perhaps I should go back to Saint Louis—"

"No, do not think that," he said, interrupting her before she said any more about leaving him. "Can't you see that you mean the world to me?"

He smiled and smoothed a fallen lock of her auburn hair back from her brow. "I do not know how it happened that I fell in love so quickly, but the truth is . . . I have. And I never want to let you go."

"Nor do I want to leave," she gulped out. When he leaned down and brushed a soft kiss across her lips, her knees trembled from the rush of passion that sped through her.

"Then do not ever speak of leaving again," Red Feather said. He smiled again into her eyes. "Come and let's sit by the stream over there and talk all this out."

"Yes, I'd love to, especially if it will help you feel better," Angela Dawn murmured.

Hand in hand they walked to the stream that meandered beneath an umbrella of old live oaks. They sat down on a thick bed of grass; then he put his arm around her waist and drew her close to him.

"It seems so right . . . so natural, to be with you like this," he said. "It is as though I have always known you."

"Perhaps we met in another time?" Angela Dawn suggested, shivering deliciously when he lifted one of her hands to his lips and kissed its palm.

"No matter how we have come to care so much for one another, our love is something to protect . . . to cherish," he said.

Then he gazed intently into the clear body of water, where minnows whipped like flashes of sunlight just beneath the surface. "But I have much to explain to you," he said. "I am not altogether what I seem to be. I am someone even I did not know until recently."

"What do you mean?" Angela Dawn asked, aware of pain in his voice. "What did you not know?"

He poured his heart and soul out to her, explaining how his mother had begun teaching him his Indian heritage, how only a few days ago he had discovered who his true father was, and that his mother had been abducted by the man he had always called Father.

He told her about having gone to meet his Indian father, and being rejected by him.

He told her that his mother had gone to his father then and explained who he was, and that his Indian father now understood, and believed her.

"Now I am going to go to him myself and make peace with him and my Chitimacha people," Red Feather said. He turned to her and took both her hands. "I will no longer be called Troy. I was given an Indian name at birth and feel that I am right to use it. Red Feather is my true name. There is no part of me that is white. I am totally Chitimacha."

"Then your brother is not your full-blood

brother," Angela Dawn said, amazed by what he had just told her. "Does he know?"

"No, but he will soon enough," Red Feather said, his eyes narrowing. "Everyone will know, for I am accepting my Indian heritage and turning my back on the world I have known. In my heart, I believe that it is the right decision for me."

He squeezed her hands. "Does knowing all of this change your feelings about me...about wanting to spend your future as my wife?" he asked. "You came to Louisiana because you thought you were marrying a rich man. When I turn my back on Jon Paul and the riches that are his, I turn my back, as well, on all that would have been mine had I stayed."

He leaned closer to her. "Would you have a problem calling me Red Feather and...and...living with me in a tepee or cabin instead of a mansion?" he asked hesitantly. "I need to know now, for it is my desire to take you to my father with me. He should know that when I come to stay with him and my people, you will also come."

His mother's words, about how he should marry into nobility since he was the son of a powerful chief, came to him in a flash, and then were gone again as quickly. This woman was everything noble anyone would want in a wife. And no one could be more generously sweet.

"Red Feather?" Angela Dawn said, searching his face. She eased a hand from his and reached it to his hair. She ran her fingers through the black thickness, adoring it, and then she placed a hand on his smooth copper cheek. "Chitimacha?"

"Yes, I am Red Feather of the Chitimacha tribe," he said, pride in his eyes and voice. "Will you come with me and be a part of my happiness there?"

"Yes, I would be proud to do that," Angela Dawn said, then flung herself into his arms. "I would be proud to live with you in a tepee and cook your meals over the open flames of a fire. I will be proud to wear buckskin along with you. I will even learn how to make moccasins."

Then she eased herself from his arms. "I am anxious to do those things, but . . . what . . . if your people deny me the chance?" she said, her voice breaking. "What if they do not approve of your bringing a white woman amid them, especially after they hear that you are going to marry me?"

She shook her head slowly back and forth. "No, maybe it wouldn't be the best thing for you to take me with you," she blurted out. "I have already seen your mother's resentment of me. I am not sure if I can bear having your father dislike me, as well."

Red Feather understood her hesitation; even

he was wondering about his father's reaction to her.

"Let us work these things out together," he said softly. "We are as one in heart and soul now. We shall show our oneness to the world. If my father wants me to be part of his life, he will have no choice but to accept you, as well."

"You truly want me to do this, don't you?" Angela Dawn murmured.

"Yes, with all my heart," Red Feather said. He drew her into his arms again. "When we kiss, does not the world seem to be only ours?"

"Yes," she said softly, then melted into his arms as he kissed her, this time passionately.

When they leaned away from one another and gazed in wonder into each other's eyes, they both knew that nothing would ever be able to stop this love that was so strong between them.

Red Feather stood and offered her a hand. "Let us go now," he said thickly. "I am anxious to embrace my father and brother."

"You have a Chitimacha brother?" Angela Dawn said, taking his hand and rising to her feet.

"Yes. We have different mothers, but that does not make us any the less brothers to one another," Red Feather said. "It is just that we have much time to make up since we have not been together during our growing years. It will be good to learn from each other."

They mounted their steeds, and when they

rode into the village, people stopped and stared.

But they traveled onward until Gray Fox stepped from a cabin and came toward them.

"Red Feather, I have been waiting for you to return to us," Gray Fox said, lifting a hand of welcome to his brother. "Welcome." His eyes slid over to Angela Dawn. "And who is the lady?"

"Her name is Angela Dawn and she will soon be my wife," Red Feather said, aware that his brother's hand stiffened within his and slowly lifted away. "She has only recently become a part of my world. I will explain later, brother, how this came to be, and how our love for one another blossomed so quickly."

"I shall listen well, and, Angela Dawn, I welcome you to my village," Gray Fox said, smiling up at her.

"Our father?" Red Feather said. He looked past Gray Fox at the large tepee which he knew was his father's. "How is he faring today?"

"He is strong enough physically, but his mind weakens each day," Gray Fox said as Red Feather slid from his saddle and Angela Dawn dismounted.

She watched as a young brave came and took the two horses' reins and led the steeds away.

Her heart beat rapidly as she was led toward the large tepee with Red Feather.

She was overjoyed that Gray Fox had accepted her so quickly, but how would the chief react?

They all went to the larger lodge.

Gray Fox held back the buckskin entrance flap as Red Feather went inside, with Angela Dawn close behind him.

Soon they were standing before Straight Arrow.

Angela Dawn held herself stiffly until the older man wrapped his arms around Red Feather and spoke of his happiness about his firstborn coming home. He was quick to add an apology about his earlier behavior when he had not believed Red Feather.

After a long embrace, Straight Arrow stepped away from Red Feather and first looked at Angela Dawn questioningly, then took a closer look at Red Feather, his smile having faded.

"You are dressed today in white man's attire, not buckskin," he said. "And you have a white woman with you. Why?"

"Clothes do not make me any less Chitimacha, nor does my choice of women," Red Feather replied. "The Chitimacha side of me is in my blood. My mother awakened it in me long ago."

Suddenly there was a familiar voice outside the tepee.

Red Feather turned with a start when he realized that his mother was there.

His eyes widened with surprise when she stepped into the tepee dressed in buckskin, even down to the moccasins on her feet. And her hair now hung in long braids down her back.

It was hard for him to imagine her looking otherwise, for now she seemed to be her true self . . . Chitimacha!

Chapter Sixteen

Mankind is composed of two sorts of men—
Those who love and create it—
And those who hate and destroy.

—José Marti

Larry was pacing the floor in his bedroom. From his second-story bedroom window he had seen everyone leave. He had seen Troy ride away at a hard gallop, then shortly after that, he had seen Angela Dawn follow him on horseback.

But what puzzled him most of all was his mother.

He raked his fingers through his thick black hair as he recalled how she had looked as she hurried to the river and stepped into the canoe that was always beached there.

He had never seen her travel in the canoe, *ever*. She had always quietly refused whenever he had asked if she might want to join him or Troy on one of their outings.

But today she had paddled off in the canoe wearing a fringed buckskin dress and moccasins.

Did her unusual garb mean she was seeking out her Indian roots?

Yes, that had to be the answer, for she was in a canoe headed downriver toward the Chitimacha village.

"Why would she do that?" he whispered to himself as he hurried to the window and gazed again toward the river.

Had he imagined seeing his mother boarding the canoe?

Had he imagined her wearing Indian attire?

No. What he'd seen had been real enough, and the absence of the canoe was proof positive.

He turned from the window and slouched down in a heavily cushioned chair. His shoulders slumped as he placed his fingertips together, his dark eyes narrowing in thought.

Never had he been as confused as now.

He had always thought that his mother had willingly left her Indian life long ago because she had fallen in love with a white man and married him.

If so, what was drawing her back to her Indian roots now?

His father had showered her with everything a woman could ever want: beautiful clothes. A mansion. Diamonds. Servants!

And an enduring love that was obvious every time he looked at her, even though they had been married now for many, many years.

"Mother, what is in your mind?" Larry said aloud, his gaze moving again to the river.

Surely she had reached the village by now.

Would they accept her arrival there? Or would they send her away since she had chosen a white husband over one of their own skin color?

There was more to this situation than met the eye.

He felt that she had kept secrets not from only her husband, but also from him.

His mother's actions today made him feel left out of her life even more than those other times when she and Troy had their secret talks.

He knew what the two of them discussed. He had found out one day recently when he had gotten the courage to place an ear to the door. He had heard her talking of her Chitimacha heritage to Troy, but because she talked so softly, he had not been able to hear any details.

Could those secret talks have something to do with what was happening now?

Yet Troy had not accompanied her to the Indian village. He was surely with Angela Dawn somewhere.

Did the mail-order bride have anything to do with his mother leaving? he wondered, his eyes widening at the thought.

He stomped toward the door and opened it so quickly and furiously, it banged back against the wall as he stepped into the corridor and half ran toward the steps.

He had no choice but to try to stop his father from leaving Jamestown. Once gone, Jon Paul would be in New Orleans in business meetings for a full week.

A lot could happen here at home in a week in his absence, and Larry was afraid those things would alter not only his father's life, but also his sons' lives.

"Mother, how could you?" he whispered. "Don't I know you at all? Has your life here all been a lie?" He swallowed hard. "Don't you love me at all?"

He rushed outside, down the steps, and to the stable.

Without telling the stable boy why he was taking his white stallion from the stall in such a rush that he did not even take the time to saddle it, he secured the bridle and reins.

He rode away from the plantation bareback, desperate to get to his father as quickly as possible.

He leaned low over his horse, his teeth clenched.

It seemed an eternity before he saw the outskirts of Jamestown come into view.

"Thank God," he whispered.

He sank his heels into the flanks of his steed. "Come on, White Snow, surely you can go faster than that," he shouted.

Again he pounded his heels on his prized stallion's flanks, unaware of the sweat that pearled the animal's neck, or its labored breathing.

All that was important now was to alert his father to the strange behavior of his wife, and then the rest would be up to Jon Paul Ratcliffe.

He thundered into the city of Jamestown and down the main street.

He ignored the stares of the well-dressed women who stopped before the fancy shops of the city to see who was stirring up such dust as the horse's hooves pounded into the dirt roadway.

He did not see the looks of disgust as the dust settled onto the faces and delicate hats and clothes of some of the women; he didn't even hear their squeals of anger.

All his attention was focused on the stagecoach office, where the coach had just pulled up and was unloading its passengers.

He looked past it and saw his father standing patiently with his travel bag and work satchel, smiling and nodding to the women and men who brushed past him.

And then the stagecoach was empty.

He knew that his father was moments from boarding it.

"Father!" Larry shouted as he approached the stagecoach. "Wait!"

He saw that his father had finally noticed him. Jon Paul gave Larry a confused look, then stepped out into the road as he waited for his son to reach him.

Just the sight of his father made Larry feel calmer.

Yes, his father would know how to stop whatever madness was driving his wife to go among Indians, dressed as one of them.

Larry had not even realized that she owned Indian attire. He had only seen her wearing the beautiful dresses that all the other white wives wore. She stood out from them like a rose among thorns; she was always so much more beautiful than other women. And he had always loved the way diamonds sparkled even more elegantly against her copper throat, contrasting so beautifully with the lovely color of her skin.

"Larry!" his father shouted, waving. "Why are you here?"

Larry finally pulled his stallion to a shuddering stop beside his father. Larry, too, was breathing hard, his nostrils flaring.

"Father, you must hurry home," he gasped out.

When he told his father why, the color rushed from Jon Paul's face.

"You were right to come for me," Jon Paul said. He glanced over his shoulder at the suitcase and satchel that he had left beside the stagecoach, then gazed at the livery stable where he had left his horse and carriage.

"Father, you must *hurry*," Larry insisted.

He dismounted, secured the reins on a hitching post, then went with his father to gather up his travel bag and satchel. In the livery stable it was the work of moments to hitch the horse again to the carriage, then throw the satchel and travel bag in the back as his father climbed in.

"I'll follow you," Larry shouted as he ran back toward his horse. His father slapped the reins and started off in a cloud of dust.

When they returned to Ratcliffe Manor, Jon Paul rushed breathlessly up the steps and into the house.

His heart pounding with anxiety, Larry dismounted and followed him in, only to find his father standing in the foyer, his head lowered in despair.

"She's still gone?" Larry asked.

"Yes, she's gone," Jon Paul said, slowly raising his eyes.

Larry was startled by the anger in the depths of his father's eyes. There was more anger than confusion . . . and that truly bewildered Larry.

Then his father pulled something from behind him that he had been holding. It was the dress that his mother had worn at the breakfast table.

"Why are you holding that?" Larry asked, raising an eyebrow.

"I found it along with her other things, along with her shoes, where she had discarded them hurriedly," Jon Paul growled out.

"Father, I'm sorry," Larry gulped out.

Jon Paul threw the dress to the floor and angrily ground a heel into it, then placed a hand on his son's shoulder. "You were right to come to me and tell me what you saw," he said. "You will be rewarded for your loyalty."

"I don't need payment, Father, for helping you," Larry said, then sighed. "Father, aren't you going after her? I will go with you, if you wish."

"No, I'm not going anywhere," Jon Paul said, easing his hand from Larry's shoulder. "The business trip is ruined, as . . . is . . . my life, it seems." He gave his son a look that Larry could not identify. "And, son, it seems that yours will be changed, as well, because of your mother's decision to . . ."

"To *what*?" Larry asked when his father seemed unable to finish what he was saying.

"Son, I'm going to my room," Jon Paul said, turning slowly. "I shall remain there until your mother's return. Go on about your business. I'm sure you have something to do to occupy your mind and time until things here are sorted out."

"I've a need to go riding," Larry said, disturbed by his father's response. "Father, will you be alright? Are you certain you do not want me to stay here with you?"

Without turning to look at Larry, Jon Paul started slowly up the stairs. "There's not much anyone can do now, Larry," he said sorrowfully. "Not much at all . . ."

His father's behavior caused Larry to wonder about what in the world would happen when his mother did return.

As his father stepped onto the second-floor landing and headed toward his bedroom, Larry went outside and shouted for the stable boy to come and tend to the horse and carriage. Larry took the travel bag and satchel inside the house and left them in the foyer, then went back out and mounted his steed.

He already had his destination in mind.

The Chitimacha village.

He would try to discover what had drawn his mother back there!

Being part Chitimacha himself, and curious about that side of his heritage, Larry had gone several times and stood on a bluff that overlooked the Chitimacha village. He had watched the people from afar.

Much that he had seen had intrigued him, but he had fought that side of him that hungered to know more about his people. He longed to be happy in the world he knew, so he had given up some time ago his trips to the bluff to watch, to study.

But today? He had a different reason for being there.

Once he arrived at the bluff, he tied his horse back in the trees, then stretched out on his belly so that only his head would be visible should anyone look in that direction.

He gazed down at the activity of the village.

It was the usual scene . . . some women were coming and going from the river, while others worked on their beading beneath the shade of old live oaks.

The elderly men were sitting together, smoking their long pipes and talking, and children ran around everywhere, playing, laughing, and chatting.

But Larry's eyes were focused on the large tepee which surely belonged to the chief. Surely his mother would have gone to him and explained that she had been one of his people long ago, and perhaps had come to reacquaint herself with them.

He glanced toward the river.

Yes, he did see his family's canoe beached there, a little away from the others. His mother was somewhere in this village.

After waiting and watching for what seemed a

lifetime, he finally saw his mother come from the large tepee.

He gasped when he also saw his brother step from the tepee, as well as Angela Dawn!

He was too stunned to think clearly now. What could have brought not only his mother there, but also his brother and Angela Dawn?

The mystery mounting, he watched Troy and Angela Dawn escort his mother to the canoe, where she boarded and paddled off in the direction of her home.

But his brother and Angela Dawn stayed at the village. They were even going back inside the large tepee, as though it was a natural thing for them to do . . . as though they belonged there!

"Why?" he whispered.

He felt betrayed, and left out of his mother's and brother's lives.

A part of him wanted to go down and march right into the village and demand answers.

But the part of him that did not want anything to do with his Indian heritage kept him away.

Then he thought of his mother. The color drained from his face when he realized that she would soon arrive home and walk right into a lion's den.

He knew his father would not treat what she had done lightly.

And although Jon Paul had always adored and loved her dearly, he might not excuse this betrayal. And it was a betrayal; she had gone to the Chitimacha while she had thought her husband was away on a business trip and would never be the wiser!

He felt he should warn his mother about what awaited her, yet he was ruled by the part of him that resented both his mother and Troy for having left him out of whatever it was they were about. His mother had made her bed; now she must lie in it.

Instead of returning to the mansion himself, he headed for Jamestown to lose himself in drink.

His brow furrowed. He felt betrayed, not only by his mother, but also by Troy.

They had both purposely left him out of things.

"Big brother, I cannot help loathing you," he snarled. "One day I'll teach you to ignore that I exist."

A shudder ran through him when he suddenly saw something in his mind's eye that was not new to him. Those times when he had felt so angry and left out, he had often imagined his brother dead!

A slow, menacing smile curled his lips as he thought that maybe this was the time to make that vision a reality.

Then there would be just him for his father and his mother to dote on!

Chapter Seventeen

Heaven sends down the love of her as a
Flame falls in the hay.
   —Love Songs of the New Kingdom

Almost as soon as Red Feather entered his father's tepee with Angela Dawn, he saw the weariness in Straight Arrow's eyes and knew that it would not be wise to stay long.

But Red Feather stayed there long enough to feel a real connection to his heritage and his father and brother.

Being told about them was one thing. Being there in person was another.

168

He was glad, as well, that Angela Dawn seemed so interested in everything.

But it was obvious to Red Feather that his father was still against Angela Dawn, though luckily not to the point of being hostile to her.

In time, though, Red Feather believed that his father's attitude would change. How could anyone disapprove of Angela Dawn after getting to know her? No one could be as sweet, as caring, or as kind as the woman he loved.

Yes, he must find a way to help change his father's feelings for Angela Dawn. Red Feather must have her with him wherever he chose to live, and he wished to live among the Chitimacha people. He had been denied them for too long already.

And he had seen how much his mother cared for Straight Arrow. He knew she loved him so much, she was willing to give up everything she had in her white world to be with him again.

Red Feather, too, was ready to give up that world, a world where he had never truly belonged. He was ready to begin anew in the world that was his.

And he must make this change soon, for his father's memory lapses might get worse.

As his father's eyes drifted closed and his head slowly bowed, Red Feather decided it was time to leave.

Gray Fox had also seen his father fall asleep. He gave Red Feather a silent nod, then motioned toward the entranceway with a hand.

Red Feather and Angela Dawn left the tepee with Gray Fox. "I thank you, brother, for the time you spent with me and my woman," Red Feather said. He noticed how Gray Fox stiffened at the words "my woman" and gave Angela Dawn a slight frown.

Red Feather ignored it.

"And thank you for making me welcome," he added.

"Our father accepts you now as his son, and I accept you as my brother," Gray Fox said. He placed a hand on Red Feather's shoulder. "Come again. We shall sit and talk longer with our father, and we shall also share food."

Red Feather noticed that Gray Fox had left Angela Dawn out of that invitation.

He wanted to say something in her defense, yet knew this was not the time.

He had only just been accepted himself. In time, his woman would be welcomed, too.

Gray Fox walked Red Feather and Angela Dawn to their horses.

Farewells were said, and the brothers exchanged a brief hug; then Red Feather and Angela Dawn left. They rode for a while until they came to a secluded place beside the river where many trees gave them the privacy that Red Feather sought.

He wanted to talk things over before they went back to the house.

He was not sure what to expect from Larry when they returned. He only hoped that his mother had arrived home at a time when Larry would not see her in her Indian attire.

He knew that his mother wanted to disclose her decision to return to her people in her own time and in her own way.

If Larry forced her hand, it might be dangerous for his mother, and even for Red Feather.

Who was to say what his father would do when he realized that he would be losing a wife and a son?

Red Feather helped Angela Dawn from her steed, secured both their reins to a tree limb, then took Angela Dawn gently by the elbow and led her down onto the soft cushion of grass at the riverbank.

"I truly enjoyed going with you and meeting your father and brother," Angela Dawn murmured. She grew warm all over when Red Feather took one of her hands and held it. "Do you think things went alright? Do you think your father truly accepts you as who you are? He did seem resentful of what you wore, you know."

"It was foolish of me not to think of that before I went to the village," Red Feather said. "But he

171

seemed to get over that resentment."

"There was something else that he resented more than your clothes," Angela Dawn said, her voice breaking. "*Me*, Troy. He resented me."

"As most Indians resent white people, both women *and* men," Red Feather said. "Whites have taken so much from my people. How could they not resent them?"

"Do you think he will never accept me, then?" Angela Dawn asked softly. "And if not, what shall we do? I am eager to spend the rest of my life with you. I love you, Troy."

"Red Feather," he said thickly. "Please call me by my Indian name. Now that I know the truth of my heritage . . . of my true parentage, it does not seem right to be called by anything but my Chitimacha name."

"Red Feather . . ." Angela Dawn said, as though testing the name on her lips.

"My mother named me Red Feather on the day I was born, yet only she and I knew that secret," Red Feather said. "But now? Soon everyone will know."

"Even Jon Paul Ratcliffe?" Angela Dawn asked warily.

"Even Jon Paul Ratcliffe," Red Feather said, then smiled. "*Especially* Jon Paul Ratcliffe, for it was he who robbed me and my mother of our heritage on that day he abducted my mother. Had he not interfered in our lives, we would have always been a part of the Chitimacha. I would have always been my true father's son."

"It's sad how lives can be manipulated like that," Angela Dawn said.

Red Feather placed a finger beneath her chin and urged her face around so that their eyes could meet and hold. "I'm sorry about my father's attitude toward you. But that doesn't change things, Angela Dawn, as far as I'm concerned. Now that you have seen how the Chitimacha live, some in buckskin lodges, others in cabins, does it change anything for you? Can you be comfortable living the life of an Indian wife? When you traveled to Jamestown, it was not to live in a tepee or crude cabin."

"No, but that doesn't matter," Angela Dawn said. She smiled sweetly at him. "What's important is our being together . . . our becoming husband and wife. Don't you know that I would live anywhere if it meant that I would be with you?"

She sighed, then said, "I will welcome any home that I can call my own. I have never had roots. While my father and mother were alive, we always lived in hotel rooms. Red Feather, you will be giving me roots, a home, and oh, so much more. Thank you. Oh, darling, thank you, thank you."

"You do not need to thank me for anything," Red Feather said.

He twined his arms around her waist and drew her close to him.

He lowered his lips to her mouth.

Their kiss was soft and sweet, and then became hot and passionate.

It did not take long for them to undress each other. Then they stretched out on the thick, soft grass. Angela Dawn's soft, white body was blanketed by Red Feather's muscled, copper-colored one.

He lifted his lips away and reverently breathed her name. "Angela Dawn," he whispered huskily. "Angela Dawn, I need you so badly."

He brushed a soft kiss across her lips, then asked, "Do you need me as much?"

"Yes, I need you. My body aches for you, but ... but ... Red Feather, I have never made love before," Angela Dawn said, her voice breaking. "What if I disappoint you? Will you still love me?"

"Nothing you could do would ever disappoint me, especially not while making love," Red Feather said, then kissed her again on her passion-moist lips with a kiss all-consuming.

He moved a hand between them and cupped one of her breasts, causing Angela Dawn's world to begin melting away with an ecstasy never known by her before.

But there had never been a man like Red Feather in her life.

She had never even wanted to kiss a man, much less lie naked in his arms, ready, even hungry, for lovemaking.

Feeling the heat growing in his loins, his need for Angela Dawn almost a sharp pain inside him, Red Feather lowered his hand away from her breast and slowly ran it down and across her belly.

He then sought her womanhood nestled beneath auburn fronds of hair at the juncture of her thighs.

He twined his fingers through the feathering of hair, then swirled them around her womanhood, causing her to gasp with pleasure.

Then he parted her legs with his knee.

He felt the heat of his manhood against the warmth of her thigh.

Being cautious, being gentle, he placed the throbbing tip of his manhood against her wet, moist opening.

Slowly he pressed into her. Knowing that he was the first man to be inside her, he was careful, oh, so careful, not to rush things. He did not want to cause pain or frighten her out of wanting to join with him.

Aware of that heat probing where no man had ever been before, and somewhat afraid of having a man inside her for the first time, Angela Dawn stiffened.

He felt her stiffen. He understood.

He leaned a little away from her lips so that their eyes could meet. "I shall be gentle," he said, his voice husky.

"I know you will be," Angela Dawn murmured, her cheeks hot with a blush. "But I am ready. Truly I am. Just please kiss me as . . . as . . . you do it?"

"You are truly ready?" Red Feather asked, searching her eyes. "If you are too afraid to do it now, we can wait until later. Even if you wish to wait until we have spoken vows before we make love, I will understand."

He placed a gentle hand on her cheek. "Beautiful woman, you are worth waiting for," he said.

"Would I disappoint you if I said we should wait?" she asked guardedly. "I want you so badly, yet I . . ."

"I understand," Red Feather said. He gave her a soft, sweet kiss, then rolled away from her and stretched out on his back.

So touched by his understanding, and feeling somewhat guilty for having asked him to wait, Angela Dawn was uncertain what to do.

She ached to be made love to. Yet there was the fear of disappointing him.

He was a handsome, virile man. Surely he had bedded many women . . . women skilled in every way of making love.

Knowing that she must get past her fear of not knowing how to please him, she turned to him

176

•

and began slowly running her fingers over his bare, muscled chest.

She leaned up on an elbow and swallowed hard when she saw his manhood and how her caresses were making it grow larger all over again, so large the smooth skin looked much too tight.

"Are you hurting?" she asked innocently. "If so, is it because . . . ?"

He laughed because he had seen how she stared at his manhood, and understood what had caused her to question him in such a way.

"Yes, I am hurting, but not in the way you think," he said, smiling.

He reached for her hand and placed it on his manhood. "Forget being shy," he urged. "Move your hand on me. Then you will see just how much pleasure you give me."

Having never seen a man nude before, much less touched his sex, she blushed, then began moving her hand on him.

She saw his eyes close with ecstasy and heard him groan. She knew the sound was not caused by pain, but instead by pleasure.

When he reached over and began caressing her between her legs again, she closed her own eyes with rapture and sighed. Then he was suddenly atop her.

He thrust himself into her.

The pain was brief, and then all she felt was ecstasy.

She clung to him. She was lost in his kiss, his embrace.

She yielded to him, her whole body suddenly aflame with pleasure. As his own body suddenly quivered and shook, she knew that they both had just experienced their first moments of ecstasy together.

Stunned by the beauty of having given herself to the man she would always love, Angela Dawn lay quiet in his arms.

He gazed down at her with a soft smile.

He kissed her lashes closed, then the tip of her nose, then bent low and flicked his tongue across first one nipple, then the other.

Every new thing he did to her, each new pleasure he gave her, made Angela Dawn hunger for more.

She knew now that he was not only going to be teaching her a new way of life among the Chitimacha, but also how to be a woman in all respects.

"You will marry me, won't you?" Red Feather asked huskily as he brushed fallen locks of her hair back from her brow.

"I wish for nothing more than to be your wife," she said softly.

"Perhaps we had best be on our way, for the sooner we get things settled at my house, the sooner we can concentrate on making a home for ourselves at my people's village," he said thickly.

He rose away from her, then held a hand out. "My wife. I truly like the sound of that. Soon, Angela Dawn. You will be my wife very, very soon."

She eased into his arms.

She pressed her nakedness into his, then giggled as she moved quickly away, for she knew that if she did not stay away from him, they would never go anywhere.

She hurried into her clothes, as did he.

Then they rode away from the river toward home.

When Angela Dawn looked at Red Feather, she saw he was no longer smiling. She realized that he dreaded what lay ahead of him.

He had to turn away from one father in order to go to another.

She only wished that she had a father she could still claim was hers!

She frowned when she thought of why she had originally come to Jamestown. She should never forget. She still must find a way to find her father's murderer!

She could not . . . she would not . . . abandon the plan that had driven her to offer herself as a mail-order bride.

Thank heaven destiny was going to make her something more than that. She was going to be a true bride to the man she loved!

Chapter Eighteen

"Speak, I love thee best!"
He exclaimed:
"Let thy love my own foretell."
—Robert Browning

Filled with emotions—renewed feelings of love
for her Indian husband, happiness that Red
Feather and his father had come together in such
a wonderful way, disappointment that Red
Feather had taken Angela Dawn to the Chitimacha village with him—Jewel beached the canoe, then ran toward the house.

She felt like a young girl again who has received a first kiss from her young lover.

She felt as though she were floating on clouds when she thought of the way her eyes and Straight Arrow's had met so often in an exchange of devoted love.

She could hardly wait now to leave the life she had known these past twenty-five years, and return to where she had always belonged.

And she would try her hardest to talk sense into Red Feather about the white woman. Angela Dawn was the only obstacle to her son's illustrious future among the Chitimacha people.

Although there had been another son born to Straight Arrow, it was only right that Red Feather be chief. He was the elder.

The day was beautiful, the sun warm, the air clear and sweet as she ran up the steep incline past the sugarcane fields. In those fields, the slaves were hard at work.

She caught several stopping to give her curious looks and she only now remembered how she was dressed. Oh, Lord, she had forgotten that she had on her Indian dress.

She had not been concerned about it earlier because her husband was away on a business trip. But she had forgotten that other people might see her in it.

When she had left, no one had been in the fields.

But now? Her secret was out!

She ignored the slaves and hurried to the

house. But no sooner had she entered than she saw something that made her heart almost stop dead.

The dress that she had been wearing at breakfast was all wadded up and lying on the floor in the foyer!

But how?

And who would have placed it there?

And . . . why . . . ?

Then her gaze shifted and she saw Jon Paul's business satchel and travel bag sitting against the far wall of the foyer.

She turned pale. Something had brought him back home. Had he found out . . . ?

Feeling a presence, she looked up the steep staircase and sucked in a wild breath of shock when she saw Jon Paul standing there, his fists on his hips.

"Jon . . . Paul . . ." she said in a shaky whisper, her knees suddenly gone weak with the fear that swept through her.

She could see quiet rage in his eyes. His face was beet red with anger.

She was afraid now, even more afraid than she had been on the day of her abduction.

She had no idea what to expect from him.

If he hated her as much as he seemed to at this moment, then she was truly afraid for her life.

She took slow, shaky steps backward as he came heavily down the stairs.

Her back against the wall now, Jewel waited for him to reach her.

And when he did, she gazed up at him, her eyes searching his face. She had never felt so trapped . . . so afraid . . . as now.

"It has always been the worst of my fears that you would one day return to your Indian husband and take your son Troy to the Chitimacha village," he said, his eyes slowly raking over her, taking in the attire she wore. In his mind's eye he recalled her wearing a dress like this on the day he had abducted her. He had to wonder where she had gotten this dress, and when, for he had burned the dress she had worn long ago.

He leaned down into her face. "Jewel, did you?" he asked, his voice filled with venom. "Did you take Troy to the village? Is . . . he . . . there even now?"

"You are calling me by the wrong name," she found herself saying.

She couldn't even believe that it was she speaking, that she was actually standing up to this man who now looked as though he loathed her with every fiber of his being.

She lifted her chin proudly.

"My name is Soft Flower," she said. "When you address me, call . . . me . . . Soft Flower."

She stood still as Jon Paul took a stiff step away from her, his eyes wide, his lips agape.

"And, yes, Troy, whose true name is Red

Feather, is even now with his true father," she boldly said. "He never should have been denied his true people and father for so long."

"Red Feather?" Jon Paul gasped. "You have even given him an Indian name?"

"He has had that name from the day he took his first breath," Soft Flower said quietly. From this moment on she would never think of herself as Jewel again. "Of course, I was not free to call him that except when we—Red Feather and I—were alone."

"How long has he known that name?" Jon Paul asked, his voice drawn. "How long has he known that I was not his true father?"

"He has known for many years that he had an Indian name, but he only recently discovered that you were not his true father," Soft Flower murmured. "I was afraid to tell him too soon, for fear that he might go to Straight Arrow before he was man enough to protect himself against you."

She again held her chin high. "He is man enough now, but I see now that nothing can protect me," she said stiffly. "What are you going to do, Jon Paul, now that you know what I have done, and where I have been, and where my son is even now?"

"What . . . am . . . I going to do?" he growled out.

He raised a hand and slapped her hard across the face, so hard she spun around, then stumbled and fell down onto the floor, on her knees.

"You savage," he screamed as he stood over her, his fists doubled at his sides. "I thought I got the savage out of you long ago, but now I know that I was wrong, and that I never will."

He bent to a knee beside her. He grabbed a thick lock of her hair and yanked her face close to his. "So, *squaw*, if you want to behave like a savage slave and betray your master husband, then so be it," he growled. "You must be treated like one. I will teach you a well-deserved lesson, and then I will release you so that you can go to your redskin husband. I want nothing more to do with you."

He yanked her up from the floor.

Soft Flower sobbed as Jon Paul half dragged her through the house to the back door, then shoved her down the steps, so that she fell onto the ground.

Again he yanked her to her feet by her hair.

Humiliated, and hating this man now with a passion, Soft Flower forced herself not to cry, or to react in any way to what he was doing to her.

He took her to one of the slave's cabins that sat away from the others. There, Jon Paul shoved her through thick cobwebs and then threw her against the back wall.

She crumpled to the floor, then gasped when she saw chains hanging from the wall, and realized what his plans were for her.

Quickly, he shackled her to the wall. Her wrists ached as the iron bonds there pressed into her tender flesh.

"Please, I do not ask for mercy for myself, but for my son," she begged, no longer able to stop herself from crying. "Please do not harm Troy. Please remember the closeness you have shared through the years. He is innocent. He can't help that you are not his true father."

"Now that you beg for mercy for this young man I treated as my very own son, you call him the name I gave to him?" Jon Paul said, his fists on his hips. He laughed sardonically. "Where has the name Red Feather suddenly gone?"

"Please, just think about what you will do to Troy, because you know that he doesn't deserve to be mistreated," she cried. "Think of how proud you have always been of him. Has he ever given you cause to hate him? Has he?"

"What he has done by going to the Chitimacha village and acknowledging another man as his father is all I need to despise the very ground he walks on," Jon Paul said, then slapped her again across the face. "You whore. How could you have done this? You have robbed me of everything today. My dignity. My life. My son . . . and . . . my wife whom I adored."

He leaned into her face. "Apologize, woman," he growled out between clenched teeth. "At least apologize for tearing my world apart."

"Like you apologized to me those years ago when you tore mine apart?" Soft Flower sobbed out. "No. I think not, Jon Paul. I . . . think . . . not."

"Then you deserve what happens to both you and your son 'Red Feather,' " he said mockingly. He turned on a heel and left the cabin, slamming the door behind him.

Jewel hung her head. She now knew more than ever before that she had been wrong to live a lie with this man for so long. She was ashamed that she had never had the courage to do what she should have done when her son was small.

When she heard a movement, she opened her eyes and gasped in horror when she found a rat sniffing at her feet.

Chapter Nineteen

So, one day more I deified,
Who knows but the world may end tonight?
—Robert Browning

Hating what he had done, Jon Paul went slowly up the back steps. He had ignored the stares from the workers in the fields, not even caring that they had seen what he had done with his Indian wife.

They all knew about the chains in that cabin.

If any slave stepped out of line, he punished him by shackling him to the wall. He had always felt that was a better punishment than whipping his slaves as he had seen many slave owners do.

No. Whipping was not something he could ever do.

But shackling them made them understand that he was the boss. And it had always worked.

Nothing would help what Jewel had done. He would not punish her, then forgive her.

He could not see himself ever touching her again. Surely she had gone to her Indian husband's tepee and embraced him there.

He shivered at the thought, then hurried into the house.

Feeling defeated and betrayed, he went to his study and poured himself a drink, then slouched down into a chair before a roaring fire.

He emptied one glass of whiskey after another, hoping to get drunk enough to stop all the thoughts that kept swirling inside his head.

"How could she have so little faith in me and my feelings for Troy?" he said, his words slurred.

Yes, she had begged for mercy for Troy.

Did she truly think that he could actually harm the son he had loved so much even though he was not of his own blood?

Troy, who was now called Red Feather, had betrayed him as much as his wife, yet it was a different sort of betrayal. Troy had just learned that he had been raised by someone who was not his own blood kin. What normal person wouldn't want to seek out the man he knew was his true father?

No, he just could not hold Troy accountable for the actions that were caused by Jewel's betrayal.

And Jon Paul hoped that Troy would have enough respect for him to come and talk things over with him.

Of course there would be some confusion and anger over Jon Paul having abducted Jewel and holding a threat over her head to keep her with him.

But how could he have assured her compliance otherwise?

He had loved her instantly. He could not live without her.

"Yet now I must," he mumbled. "She is now the same as dead to me."

He glanced toward the window. He was not sure just how long he would keep her shackled in the cabin. He would leave her there long enough to teach her a lesson.

Then he would release her.

He would even place her in the cypress canoe himself and send her to her people, for as far as he was concerned, she was now a true savage, not at all the woman he had adored through the years.

"Father?"

Larry's voice drew Jon Paul's eyes toward the door just in time to see Larry stagger into the library, his eyes bloodshot, his suit and white shirt soiled. It looked as though he had vomited after having consumed far too much alcohol.

Even though Jon Paul was drunk himself, he still could not help feeling deep disgust over this son who continued to disappoint him by drinking and gambling to excess in the saloons of Jamestown.

He had warned Larry time and again about the family's reputation, and how drinking in public only tarnished the good name that Jon Paul had always protected, almost with his life.

"How could you?" Jon Paul growled out. He threw his empty whiskey glass at Larry, seeing that Larry was too drunk even to step aside so that it would not hit him.

Larry winced as the glass bounced off his chest, then smiled awkwardly at his father.

"Again you darken the name . . . the reputation . . . of the Ratcliffes?" Jon Paul shouted. "I've suffered enough setbacks today without you adding to the list."

"What . . . do . . . you mean, Father?" Larry mumbled. He staggered into the room and fell awkwardly into a chair opposite the one where his father had seated himself.

Larry was sober enough to recall what he had seen at the Indian village. He wondered whether his father had discovered the truth, too.

Larry wasn't about to be the one to reveal it to him.

191

If his father did know, then both Troy and his mother had hell to pay. Larry wanted to be far away when that happened.

"What do I mean?" Jon Paul said. He went silent as he stared at Larry again. He could not help comparing his two sons.

Ah, Troy. He had always been the thoughtful one, steady, studious, and dependable, whereas Larry was lazy, shiftless, a womanizer, a drunk who got in barroom brawls, and then there was the gambling. Larry was addicted to it.

Although his son Troy also enjoyed a game of cards, he did not do it often enough to draw attention to himself.

Troy had never disappointed Jon Paul the way Larry did.

Filled with blind rage at this son who had not turned out to be what he had expected, Jon Paul picked a book up from the table next to him and threw it at Larry.

It grazed the side of Larry's head, causing him to cry out with pain. He turned to his father with a bewildered, hurt look.

"You are nothing but a disappointment to me," Jon Paul shouted. He rose from the chair and stood over Larry, causing his son to cower. "You are a drunk who doesn't even know what he does half the time, who in a drunken stupor stupidly sent for a mail-order bride."

Jon Paul stopped and leaned his face down until their breath mingled, each smelling of whiskey. "You are such a disappointment to me, I cannot possibly will my wealth to you," he said, his voice filled with loathing. "Look at you. You are a drunken slob. How could I ever expect you to handle my money properly once I am gone? You'd spend it all on whiskey and women, or you'd squander it away, gambling and entertaining."

Jon Paul straightened his back, flailed a hand in the air, then glared at Larry again. "I don't give a damn that Troy has an Indian father," he declared. "Yes, his father is a Chitimacha Indian chief. But that doesn't matter. Troy will still inherit everything."

Jon Paul got a twisted look on his face. "Yes, that's how it will be," he said, nodding. "Surely if Troy knows that he alone will inherit my wealth, he will think better of going to his savage father instead of remaining with the one who has always provided for him and made him the man that he is."

So stunned that he became instantly sober at his father's words, Larry pushed himself from the chair and stared in disbelief at Jon Paul. "How could you do this?" he asked. "Do you forget so easily that it was I who came and warned you about your wife? Did you not say then that I would be rewarded for my loyalty? Is this how you repay me?"

Then he recalled what Jon Paul had said about Troy not being his son, but instead an Indian chief's. "And what do you mean about Troy having an Indian father?" he asked, then went cold inside when he recalled Troy stepping from Chief Straight Arrow's lodge.

He felt the color drain from his face when he thought further about that, and the implications of his father's revelation.

If Troy was Straight Arrow's son, then Jewel must have slept with the chief. Had he been her lover all those long years ago?

"Father, please tell me what all of this means," Larry begged. "Why should I not know it all? And if Troy isn't your true son, how could you give him what is rightfully mine?"

"Why?" Jon Paul asked darkly. Again he leaned his face into Larry's. "Because you disgust me, that's why."

Jon Paul straightened his back and pointed to the door. "Get out!" he screamed. "Get out of my sight!"

Devastated by his father's rejection, and totally confused about everything else, Larry rose from the chair and stumbled from the room.

As he took the stairs to the second floor slowly and carefully, he tried to think matters through. He would go to his mother and get answers from her.

Surely she was home now and in her room.

Probably she was hiding from a husband who was so drunk he was capable of anything!

He rushed to his mother's room and knocked on the door. When she didn't respond, he knocked again.

Still there was no response, and a sudden fear gripped his heart. Perhaps his father had already done something to her. Had Larry's father punished her somehow?

He pushed open the door.

"Oh, Mother, what have I done?" he sobbed.

He went to her dresser, opened a drawer, and took a lacy handkerchief from it.

He cried as he held her scent close to his nose.

He regretted everything now, especially having told his father about his mother's strange behavior. That had surely led to his current predicament.

He suddenly remembered what his father had said about the inheritance, that it would all go to Troy. How could his father love Troy, even though he knew that he was not his true son?

Larry felt keen resentment building in his heart. He had known for a long time that his father favored Troy over him. But now he realized that his father had felt that way even though he'd known that Troy was not his biological son, and that Larry was.

He went to the window and gazed toward the Indian village.

He vowed there and then that he wouldn't let Troy get the best of him any longer.

He would make certain that his brother couldn't inherit the family riches that by rights should be Larry's. He had walked in his brother's shadow for much too long.

It . . . must . . . stop!

In an angry rage, Larry threw the handkerchief to the floor, then hurried to his room, where he paced back and forth.

Then, still unable to control his hurt and anger, he began throwing things from his room out into the corridor.

"What the hell are you doing?" Jon Paul shouted as he rushed into the room. "Stop that this minute, do you hear? And clean up that damn mess in the corridor."

Then Jon Paul was gone as quickly as he had arrived, leaving Larry alone again with his hurt pride, his disgust at life in general, and a hatred for his father that was consuming him.

But most overwhelming of all was his resentment of Troy.

Crying, Larry ignored his father's command to clean up the hallway. Instead he stumbled back into his bedroom and threw himself onto his bed.

He pummeled the mattress with his fist, the hatred he was feeling growing with each minute, with each memory of what his father had said about the inheritance.

He was filled with too much hate and jealousy now to think of anything but vengeance . . . vengeance that would lead him to his brother.

Yes, at all costs, Troy must be stopped.

Chapter Twenty

My whole heart rises up to bless
Your name in pride and thankfulness.
          —Robert Browning

Red Feather dismounted from his steed, then turned to help Angela Dawn. "I've got to go and talk with Mother," he said, walking his horse into the stable, while Angela Dawn followed with hers. "I've got to make her understand how things are between us . . . that we *will* be man and wife."

"But I can understand why she would be against your caring so much for me," Angela Dawn said. She nodded a silent thank you to the stable boy as he took her horse's reins and led it toward its stall.

"First, you have known me for only a short time. Second, she has planned all of your life how things would be for you once she explained about your true father. She thought that once you were introduced into the Chitimacha way of life, you would stay with your people, and that you would marry a woman from the village."

"I understand that as well, yet no mother can make definite plans for a son and truly believe that is the way it will be," he said, putting his horse into its stall and closing the door. He turned to Angela Dawn. He gently framed her face between his hands. "I am my own man, and I have my own definition of happiness. Yes, I do want to be a part of my true father's life, as well as his people's, but I also want to follow my heart. I must choose my own woman, and I *have*. Nothing will stand in the way of our marriage."

Suddenly Angela Dawn noticed that he was staring past her. He dropped his hands from her face; there was a look of alarm in his jet-black eyes. "What do you see?" she asked, slowly turning to follow the path of his eyes.

"My father's horse is in its stall," Red Feather said warily. He took a slow step backward when he also saw that his father's carriage was in its place in the stable.

A warning rushed through him.

"That could only mean that he's home . . . that something changed his mind about leaving on his business trip," he blurted out. "And as adamant as he was about going, nothing except a tragedy would have brought him back home."

He stepped quickly from the stable and looked down toward the river. Yes, the family canoe was beached there, which meant that his mother had made it home alright.

But if Jon Paul had arrived back home before Red Feather's mother had returned from her visit with the Chitimacha, Jon Paul might have caught her wearing the Indian dress.

"What is it?" Angela Dawn asked as she stepped to his side. She followed the path of his eyes again and this time saw that he was staring up at a bedroom window.

"I'm afraid for Mother," he said anxiously. "If Father was home when she arrived, and she did not have the chance to change her clothes . . ."

"Oh, Lord," Angela Dawn said, understanding why Red Feather was so alarmed. "Do you think . . . ?"

"I've got to find out, and *quick*," Red Feather said, breaking into a hard run.

Lifting the skirt of her dress, Angela Dawn ran after him.

When they entered the house, they both saw the discarded dress.

"He does know," Red Feather said, his heart

pounding. He turned to Angela Dawn. "I don't want you to get in the middle of this. Please go to your room, close the door, even *lock* it, if that will make you feel more comfortable. I will come to you and explain everything when I can."

"Alright," Angela Dawn said, then hurriedly rose on tiptoe and gave him a quick kiss.

She stepped away from him just as they both heard a noise in the study.

"He must be in there," Red Feather said, his spine stiffening. "Perhaps things are alright. Mother is surely in her room, knitting or reading. Maybe something unforeseen happened that caused Jon Paul to return home and it had nothing to do with Mother."

"But the dress . . ." Angela Dawn said, gazing down at the garment, which lay strangely twisted on the floor.

"Yes, the dress," he said, his voice drawn. "Finding it here is surely a bad sign."

"Do you want me to go check on your mother?" Angela Dawn asked.

"No, I still believe that it is best if you go to your room and wait there for me," Red Feather said. "I hope nothing has happened to Mother. She only did what she should have done long ago."

"Please be careful," Angela Dawn said, placing a quick hand on his arm. "If your father is upset about things, might not he take his anger out on you?"

"I don't believe he would," Red Feather said. "I don't see how he could love me for so long, then turn on me so quickly."

"Then maybe he feels the same about your mother," Angela Dawn said.

She turned and started up the stairs. She paused and faced him again as he moved toward the study. "Please, oh, please be careful," she said, her voice tight with fear.

Red Feather gave her a reassuring nod, then walked away from her as Angela Dawn went on up the stairs. It was now dark enough for the corridor to be filled with dark shadows, making it hard for her to see her way to her bedroom.

She went onward, though, and then tripped on something, making her fall clumsily against the corridor wall.

She looked down, but it was too dark to see what had tripped her.

She went to her bedroom, lit a candle, then returned to the corridor.

Her eyes widened when she saw an assortment of things just outside of Larry's door.

She gazed at the closed door, and then at his belongings again, wondering why he had thrown them there.

She stooped to get a closer look at the things on the floor. There were clothes, books, and . . .

Her heart seemed to go dead still when she spied something else lying farther away in the dark shadows.

Scarcely breathing, she stood and held the candle nearer in an effort to see the object.

"Oh, Father, it *is* yours, I *know* that it is yours," Angela Dawn whispered. Everything within her went cold, and tears fell from her eyes as she stared down at her father's pearl-handled walking cane.

She recognized the two places in the handle where it had been chipped, and she recalled how it had happened. They had been riding along a street in Saint Louis and the cane had bounced from the buggy onto the cobblestone street.

When her father had retrieved it, he had discovered that two pieces had been chipped out of the pearl handle.

But loving the cane so much, and having already carved the name of his wife and daughter in the wood at the bottom of the cane, he continued to use it.

He had had it with him on the day of his murder, but it had never been returned with his other possessions.

Angela Dawn had forgotten about it, with so much else on her mind. Until now.

Seeing it brought a rush of memories. She missed her father now almost as much as the day she had heard that he had been shot.

Oh, how she missed him!

Trembling, she bent and picked the cane up and held it closer to the candle's glow while slowly turning it so that she could see the bottom.

If there were carved names on the bottom of the cane, it most certainly was her father's.

She felt as if the air had been sucked out of her lungs when she spotted them ... her name and her mother's. They were so faint with age that no one but those who knew they were there would have noticed.

She knew that she had, without a doubt, just found her father's killer.

The man who'd shot her father had not taken his dueling pistols that day, but he *had* taken his walking cane. The killer would have imagined that no one could identify it as her father's, for there were many such canes owned by other men.

But there *were* differences, differences that only a daughter would recognize!

She glared at Larry's bedroom door. She felt a surge of hatred for him that frightened her.

But she knew without a doubt that she had found her father's killer! Ironically enough, she had not had to look farther than this house to find the murderer.

She breathed hard as she battled the feelings within her. She glanced toward her bedroom door, then looked at Larry's again. It would be so simple to go and get one of her father's dueling pistols and end his life. But then she would die for the act, even if she was ridding the world of a murderer.

She did not want to hang for killing a worthless coward. She would find a different, better way to get her vengeance.

Except for the resentment of Red Feather's parents, everything was going her way for the first time in her life. She had a man who loved her, who would care for her until her dying day. And she loved this man with all her heart.

Clutching the cane to her heart, she went back to her room and closed the door.

She set the candle on a table, then went to the bed and lifted a corner of the mattress. Smiling, she slid the cane beneath it, hiding it from Larry should he discover it missing and begin searching the house for it.

"Let him come," Angela Dawn said, turning toward the door, her arms folded across her chest. "You damn, stinking coward, if not for my love for your brother, I would kill you *now*, without blinking an eye."

But as it was, she *did* have someone to live for now and would not allow anyone to ruin it all for her. Larry had already ruined her family by shooting that one fatal bullet into her father's back.

He had all but killed her mother that day when

he took her father's life. Even Angela Dawn had felt dead . . . until Red Feather gazed that first time into her eyes.

A smile replaced the frown on her face; then she remembered what he might be going through himself at this moment. She wanted to go to him and stand at his side, to offer what comfort she could.

But she knew that he had his own battles to fight, which did not include her, just as she had her vengeance to take care of, which did not include him.

In time, surely all of this would be behind them, and they could live in peace. A family. Would it not be wonderful to have a family that included both a daughter and a son?

She went to the window and gazed into the dark heavens, where the moon had replaced the sun in the sky and stars twinkled like small lamps against the backdrop of black. "Please, God, please let this happiness come to Red Feather and me?" she prayed. "Please, oh, please . . ."

Chapter Twenty-one

See golden days,
fruitful of golden deeds,
With joy and love triumphing.
          —John Milton

As Red Feather stepped into the library, he smelled the strong stench of alcohol. That alone was enough to alarm him. His father loved a drink of whiskey as much as the next man, but he had never made it a practice to drink much at home except for an occasional glass of port. He mainly drank with friends during card games at one of the more secluded saloons in Jamestown.

The fact that he had drunk so much that the

room reeked of it made Red Feather certain that something had gone terribly awry.

He looked slowly around the room.

The glow of the fire from the massive stone fireplace at one end and the faint light of a lone kerosene lamp revealed to him a man who sat slumped in a high-backed overstuffed chair before the fire, his eyes glassy as he gazed into the slow-burning flames.

Red Feather noticed that his father was so lost in thought that he had not heard him enter the room.

And as Red Feather stepped farther into the room and walked slowly toward his father, Jon Paul still did not notice him.

But when Red Feather was close enough to see the shine of tears in his father's eyes, he was taken aback, and stopped. His father had always been a strong man who would think a man's tears a terrible weakness.

At that moment Jon Paul turned his head quickly toward him, having finally realized that he was no longer alone.

When his eyes met Red Feather's, and Red Feather saw the pain and anger in their depths, he had no doubt that his father knew everything. Red Feather prayed that his mother was alright.

"Father, I'm surprised to see you here," Red Feather said, working at controlling the tone of his voice. It was hard now to call him 'Father,' when he had so recently called another man by that name. "Did something happen to cause you to return home?"

"Troy, just leave," Jon Paul said, his voice breaking. He hung his head in his hands, then gave Red Feather another weary gaze.

"But, Father, why did you return home?" Red Feather asked, not wanting to be dismissed when there were so many truths to iron out.

"Things came to light that were so disturbing, I could not go on a lengthy business venture," Jon Paul said thickly. "Leave, son. For now, let me be. I have much to think about . . . to work out. Come later. Then . . . we will talk."

"No, Father, I will not be dismissed so easily," Red Feather said. He went and sat opposite Jon Paul. "I have much to say. I need to say it now, not later."

"I do . . . not . . . want to hear it," Jon Paul growled out. He clenched his hands into tight fists on his lap. "Son, it is best not to get into this now. You might—"

"It must be said now, for I have places to go," Red Feather said. He stiffened when he saw rage fill his father's eyes.

"You should not say anything to me right now about anything," Jon Paul said. He stumbled to his feet. He leaned an arm against the fireplace mantel as he stared into the flames of the fire. "Troy, please just let it rest for now."

"I cannot do that," Red Feather said, slowly rising. He went and stood beside his father. "I must tell you everything now. Please listen with an open heart?"

Jon Paul refused to look at him as Red Feather began pouring his heart out to him.

He blurted out everything.

He told Jon Paul that he wanted to live with his true father . . . his true people, and that he was going to, because he should have been among them all his life.

When it was all said, Red Feather scarcely breathed as he waited for his father to say something.

Instead, Jon Paul remained standing with his arm resting on the mantel, his eyes still watching the flames of the fire. Then suddenly Jon Paul dropped his arms to his sides and turned to Red Feather.

His eyes wavered as he spoke. "You cannot leave here," he said tightly. "You cannot do this, Troy. You are *my* son, not some . . . savage's. Son, it is my decision that you will inherit all of the family wealth, not your drunken sot of a brother. If you leave, Troy, you will be leaving so much behind—money, this mansion, the vast fields filled with sugarcane and tobacco. How could you want to leave? I have raised you to follow in my footsteps. Larry is not capable of handling my affairs. Troy, I am ordering you to stay."

Red Feather gave his father a sad stare, because he knew why his father was being so adamant about his inheriting everything. It was only to save face.

If Red Feather went to live with the Chitimacha, everyone would realize that Red Feather was not his son. And that his wife was not truly his wife, after all. People might guess that his Indian wife had an Indian husband. Eventually it would come out that she had been abducted and forced to live with Jon Paul Ratcliffe as his wife.

Jon Paul was begging Red Feather to stay for all the wrong reasons, for selfish reasons.

"You call my people savages," Red Feather said sadly. "Then that is how you truly see me, for I am Chitimacha through and through. There is no part of me that is white. So ... then ... this 'savage' bids you adieu, Jon Paul Ratcliffe."

He leaned closer to his father. "And, by the way, my name is not Troy," he said proudly. "I am called by the name Red Feather, the name of my Chitimacha grandfather. When you address me from here on out, I would appreciate being addressed by my true name, not one that you forced my mother to give me so that it would appear as though I were your true son."

"All that I did for you ..." Jon Paul said,

reaching a hand out to Red Feather. "How can you forget?"

"I do appreciate so much, yet it was all done for the wrong reasons," Red Feather said. "I did love you . . ."

He spun around and hurried from the room before he said something he might regret later.

His mother was his priority now. He had to go see if she was alright.

Oh, surely she was!

Had not Jon Paul treated *him* respectfully?

He rushed up the steps and hurried to his mother's room. He saw immediately that she was not there.

A warning shot through him as he recalled just how despondent Jon Paul had been. Was it because he had done something to his Indian wife?

That look in Jon Paul's eyes when Red Feather surprised him in the study, the coldness in their depths, caused a jolt of fear to go through Red Feather's heart.

If this man did have a dark side, would he have carried out his threat against Jewel?

"Mother, oh, Mother, where are you?" he whispered harshly as he raced from the room and rushed down the steps.

Red Feather searched each and every room on the first floor except the study. When he didn't find any signs of his mother anywhere, he was overwhelmed by a feeling of foreboding.

"Mother, Mother . . ." he whispered.

Chapter Twenty-two

I, too, at love's brim
Touched the sweet:
I would die if death bequeathed
Sweet to him.
                    —Robert Browning

Knowing that his father would not tell him where she was, Red Feather began asking questions . . . he asked the cooks, servants, and maids if they had seen his mother.

Everyone shied away from him, their wavering eyes telling him they knew something was wrong.

But did they know where she was? If so, none would say.

He stopped just outside the study and glared at the closed door. He doubled his hands into tight fists at his sides as he tried to gain the courage to go and demand answers from Jon Paul.

He did not hesitate because he was afraid to face Jon Paul. He hesitated because he was afraid that Jon Paul would ignore the questions even though he knew where his wife was.

His heart pounded as he reached his hand out for the doorknob. If Jon Paul continued to refuse him, Red Feather was afraid of what he might do. He was beginning to wonder if he had ever really known the man he'd always called Father.

If anyone was guilty of deceit, it was Jon Paul. And if he kept his silence today, Red Feather did not want to even consider what he might do to this rich landowner to get the answers from him.

Red Feather had never agreed with Jon Paul's ownership of slaves, yet had not outwardly questioned it because Red Feather had grown up knowing that slaves were a part of his life, just as his brother was.

Knowing that time was passing quickly and that his mother's life might be in danger, Red Feather again reached his hand out for the doorknob but drew it back quickly when Hannah, the pretty little daughter of his mother's maid, came tiptoeing toward him. She held a finger to her lips in a way to keep Red Feather from saying anything.

Understanding, and thinking this child had come with answers about his mother, Red Feather nodded, then followed Hannah into the parlor, where a solitary lamp diffused a soft glow throughout the room.

Red Feather slid the double parlor doors closed, then bent low before Hannah. Her dark eyes revealed her fright, yet also quiet determination.

She stood on tiptoe and leaned close to his face. "Yo' motha' was taken away by yo' fatha'," she whispered, her tiny, black, round face shining beneath the light of the lamp. Her hair hung in long pigtails down her slim back. Her plain cotton dress made from a gunny sack hung around her ankles. Her feet were bare.

His heart pounding with fear, Red Feather placed gentle hands on the girl's frail shoulders. "Where did my . . . father . . . take my mother?" he asked, finding it hard now to refer to Jon Paul Ratcliffe as his father.

"To the slave qua'tahs," Hannah said, her eyes searching his face. "Masta' Troy, why would Masta' Ratcliffe do such a thing to the missus? There was such feah in her eyes. I went later and looked in the door at yo' mama but didn't dare go inside for feah of gettin' whipped by Masta' Ratcliffe."

"He . . . took . . . her to the slave quarters?"

Red Feather gasped out, dropping his hands to his sides.

For a moment he was too stunned to say anything more.

His mind was whirling with questions as to how Jon Paul Ratcliffe could do such a thing to the woman he had always adored, and to a woman who was good through and through, who had been his wife in every respect even though her heart was left behind at the Chitimacha village so long ago.

"He shackled her, Masta' Troy, to the wall," Hannah blurted out. "I cried when I saw her."

"Shackled?" Red Feather gasped, his face draining of color.

He bent low before Hannah so that he could peer directly into her eyes. "Which cabin, Hannah?" he asked thickly. "I can't ask you to take me there because I wouldn't want to chance Jon Paul seeing you doing it. Just tell me, Hannah . . . which cabin?"

"The one that is abandoned and only used for disciplining slaves," Hannah said, then stepped quickly away from Red Feather as he rushed from the room.

Afraid of being caught in the parlor, where she was only allowed when she helped her mother dust the furniture, she left at a run.

Red Feather ran as quickly as his legs would

carry him. He knew the cabin well and hated it. He had never played a role in disciplining the slaves, but knew that his brother Larry had.

Larry had even laughed about it. He had bragged about using a whip a time or two on the male slaves, a practice that Red Feather abhorred.

Breathing hard, Red Feather finally reached the back of the estate where the slaves' cabins stood in a long row beneath the low-hanging branches of live oak trees.

Most cabins had candles lit in them; kerosene lamps were forbidden as being "too costly for the help," as his father said.

But there was one cabin where no light showed through the windows.

In that cabin his mother was enslaved in a way that sickened Red Feather. He envisioned her with those horrible iron bands around her wrists, and possibly even her ankles.

He almost wrenched the door off its creaky hinges as he entered the cabin.

Then he stood still as the moon slid from beneath clouds, revealing to him a sight that he would never be able to erase from his mind.

His mother was asleep on the floor, her wrists bound by iron bands. Her dress was hiked up past her ankles and revealed a bloody bite on her flesh which made Red Feather flinch with horror.

"Mother," he said as he knelt down beside her.

As he gently drew her into his arms, she slowly

217

awakened and gazed up at him through tear-drenched lashes.

"Son, you shouldn't be here," Soft Flower said, thinking more of his safety than hers. She knew that if Jon Paul found him there, he might chain her son in the same ghastly way.

"Mother, I'm going to get you out of this place," Red Feather said, holding her close in his arms. He hated to let her go, but knew that he needed to hurry or he might be discovered, and he knew that Jon Paul Ratcliffe would not hesitate to chain him beside his mother.

He left her momentarily as he went to where his father kept the key hidden beneath a floorboard. He loosened the floorboard, then reached down and got the key.

He hurried back to his mother and unlocked the bonds at her wrists, then again gazed at her bloody, swollen ankle.

"A rat," Soft Flower sobbed. "A rat bit me."

"A rat?" Red Feather said, shivering at the thought of what she had endured.

He reached his hands beneath his mother and lifted her into his arms.

"Jon Paul won't get a chance ever to touch you again or chain you," Red Feather said thickly. "Mother, I'm taking you home . . . to your . . . our . . . true home."

She twined an arm around his neck and laid her cheek against his chest.

She sobbed as he carried her from the cabin and headed toward the river.

"Mother, I am going to take you to the canoe and leave you there for only as long as it takes for me to fetch Angela Dawn," he said, keeping hidden beneath the low-hanging limbs of the live oak trees so that his father could not see him from the house.

"Angela Dawn?" Soft Flower repeated softly. "Must . . . you . . . ?"

"Mother, would you want to leave her in the house with such a man as Jon Paul Ratcliffe and chance her being mistreated like you?" Red Feather asked. "You know that Jon Paul is very unhappy about Angela Dawn. If we don't take her with us, who is to say what he will do to her?"

"He will just send her away," Soft Flower murmured. "Please allow it, Red Feather."

"Mother, I love her," Red Feather said, stopping next to the canoe.

He gently placed his mother inside.

He knelt beside the canoe. "Please understand my feelings for her and understand that I am going to marry her," he said softly. "She is alone in the world, Mother. So alone. Without me, or my love, what do you think would eventually happen to her?"

"You are right," Soft Flower said. She reached a gentle hand to his cheek. "I have been so selfish. Do go and get her, Red Feather. I shall say no more about your feelings for her. Just hurry. I . . . so . . . fear Jon Paul, for *all* of us. He is a madman, Red Feather. A man without a heart."

"He is more than that now," Red Feather growled. "He is a man without a family."

"He has Larry," Soft Flower murmured.

"Yes, he has Larry," Red Feather said. He chuckled sarcastically. "They deserve one another."

"I do love Larry," Soft Flower said, tears filling her eyes again. "He is my son. But . . . he is, oh, so much like his father."

"Mother, I must go," Red Feather said. He reached inside his jacket and removed a knife from its leather sheath. He handed it to his mother.

"Use this if anyone threatens you," he said. He saw her look disbelievingly at the knife, the moon's reflection caught in its sharp blade. "Mother, if necessary, defend yourself. Do you hear?"

"Yes . . . I . . . hear," Soft Flower choked out. She gazed up at him with wavering eyes. "What if Jon Paul sees me waiting for you?"

"I doubt that he can see much of anything right now," Red Feather said dryly. "When I left him, he was drunk. I'm almost certain he emptied another bottle after our talk."

"Be careful, son," Soft Flower said, then

winced when renewed pain shot through her rat-bitten ankle.

"Mother, you will soon be at our village where the shaman will care for you," Red Feather assured her.

It seemed strange to him to refer to the shaman as though he had never known any other way of doctoring the ill, whereas Doc Rose had always been the Ratcliffe family doctor.

But it felt good to speak of the customs of his people. He was becoming more and more Chitimacha with each breath he took.

"I will be alright," Soft Flower said. "Hurry, son. Hurry."

He bent low and brushed a kiss across her brow, then broke into a mad run toward the house.

When he reached it, he went to the back, where it was less likely that Jon Paul would hear him enter the house or climb the stairs.

It was necessary that neither Larry nor Jon Paul hear him and Angela Dawn as they made their escape.

Once they were gone, once they were safe at the Chitimacha village, let Jon Paul and Larry discover the truth.

Breathless from rushing up the steps two at a time, Red Feather finally came to the second-floor landing at the rear of the house. He moved softly along the corridor, the carpeting muffling his footsteps.

When he came to the corridor where Larry's room was situated, Red Feather gazed curiously at the things strewn across the floor. He stared at Larry's closed door, then shrugged and went on past, to Angela Dawn's room.

He tried the knob. He couldn't enter. That meant she had wisely locked herself in.

"Angela Dawn," he said only loud enough for her to hear.

When she opened the door, he slipped into the room and took her in his arms.

"We must leave," he whispered into her ear. "Now, Angela Dawn. I'll explain later. But it is necessary to get out of here while we can."

"You are so pale," Angela Dawn murmured. "You look as though you've seen a ghost."

"I would have rather seen a ghost than what I did see," he said thickly.

"What happened?" Angela Dawn asked.

"What happened?" Red Feather said, his voice breaking.

He gazed at the door, then slowly and quietly closed it.

"My mother . . ." he began, and Angela Dawn's eyes widened more with each and every revelation.

Chapter Twenty-three

That was all I meant,
—to be just, and the passion
I had raised,
To content.
          —Robert Browning

After hearing everything, Angela Dawn was suddenly truly afraid of Jon Paul Ratcliffe. At this moment he might be too drunk to act any further on his anger, but once he was sober? Might he then take everything out on Red Feather?

If he could do what he'd done to the woman he loved, surely he was capable of doing anything.

Yes, she was afraid—so afraid that her knees trembled.

She hurriedly shoved her most precious belongings into the smaller travel bag along with the dueling pistols, then turned to Red Feather. "I'm ready," she said, her voice quivering. "Let's get out of this place. Who is to say when Jon Paul might decide to punish you? He might come hunting for you. I feel you are lucky that you got out of the study without him harming you."

"He seems too adamant about my staying and inheriting everything from him to harm me," Red Feather said.

He raised an eyebrow when he saw Angela Dawn make a sudden turn, reach down, and grab a pearl-handled walking cane from beneath the mattress on the bed. She tucked it beneath her left arm.

"Where did you get that?" he asked, staring at the cane. "Whose is it?"

"It's a long story, not one that I should take time now to tell," Angela Dawn said. "But I must make room for it when I leave here today. It is special to me in many ways."

"Then you should take it," Red Feather said, reaching out and taking her bag. "Come on. We must get back to my mother. I am anxious to get her to my people's village so her bite can be seen to. I cringe to think of how much pain she is in.

It is so hard to believe that my . . . that Jon Paul . . . left her in that place where rats are known to be, but he did, and who can say what else he might do?"

They crept as quietly as they could out into the corridor. The servants had not lit the candles in the wall sconces. It was as though all of the servants were being wary tonight of whatever they did in the house, for surely they all knew by now what their master had done to his wife.

No one could feel safe under those circumstances, and most were keeping to their rooms. If they were smart, they had locked themselves safely inside.

Just as Red Feather and Angela Dawn fled down the back stairs, Larry stepped sleepily from his room.

He rubbed his eyes with his fists and swayed drunkenly from side to side as he looked one way down the corridor and then the other.

He had heard a noise, but there was no one in sight. Strangely enough, no one had lit the candles along the wall.

Not seeing anything or anyone, Larry turned to go back inside his room, then stumbled over the debris that lay just outside his door.

He grumbled to himself as he stared at everything he had thrown out during his fit of rage.

Now he recalled his father demanding that he get his things back inside his room.

Thus far his father apparently had not noticed that he had not followed his orders, but Larry did not dare leave the mess there any longer.

Who was to say when his father would come to see if the corridor was clear? If it wasn't, Larry knew he would have hell to pay.

He began taking things one at a time back to his room.

Once his belongings were all there, lying in a pile along one wall, his eyes went slowly over it all to see if anything had been broken. Beneath the pale light of a candle, he went from item to item. Suddenly his breath caught when he realized that one thing was most definitely missing.

"The cane," he whispered.

He scratched his brow as he tried to figure out who would want the cane enough to steal it. Should he go and demand answers from the servants? Could one of them have taken it, thinking he would not care since he had thrown it into the hall?

Perhaps the thief would take it to a pawn shop and make money from it.

"Oh, well," he whispered, shrugging. "It's worthless anyhow. They can't get much for it."

He threw himself onto the bed, on his belly. Soon he found himself drifting back to sleep, but not before he went over the way he had acquired that pearl-handled cane. He had grabbed it from beside a dead man he had shot in the back.

Yes, it was worthless, just like the man he had shot.

Strange that he had never asked the man his name. To Larry, he had been just another face holding another hand of cards. They had played poker into the wee hours of the morning until harsh words became harsher accusations.

A duel was the man's suggestion as a way to settle the differences between the two men.

Larry had acquiesced, knowing that he would not allow that man to get a shot at him. It had been his plan all along to kill the man before the duel even began.

He had regretted, more than once, that he hadn't taken the man's dueling pistols. But there had been a good reason to leave them behind. Larry had feared they could be easily identified. They would provide a link between him and the dead man.

But still, they would have been a much better prize than that banged-up cane.

"To hell with it," he mumbled in a drunken slur. "Sleep. I . . . need . . . more sleep."

His eyes closed again, and in his sleep he relived the duel, as he had so many times since that day he had taken another man's life.

Sweat beaded on his brow as the dream changed, and it was he who was the victim of a bullet in his back. His eyes flew open wide as the fear of what he had dreamed shook him.

It was so real!

The bullet entering his back had been so real.

He climbed from the bed, went to his dresser, and pulled out a drawer.

He took a half-emptied bottle of whiskey from it and hurriedly removed the top.

He held the bottle to his lips and guzzled the whiskey down until it was all gone.

His head spinning, he dropped the empty bottle and made his way back to the bed, then again fell into a stupor-like sleep.

Again he dreamed that he had been shot.

He cried out for help in his sleep.

But no one came.

Chapter Twenty-four

Come, on wings of joy we'll fly.
To where my Bower hangs on high.
                    —William Blake

Not wanting to leave his horse behind, Red
Feather had asked Angela Dawn to ride his stallion to the Chitimacha village while he paddled
his mother there in the canoe.

Angela Dawn was glad to ride the beautiful,
sleek black stallion. She felt proud to be able to
do something to help Red Feather since he was
doing so much for her. Without him, she would
be so alone.

Now she had a future, one that included the

love of a man, and not just any man . . . someone very, very special.

She arrived at the outskirts of the village ahead of Red Feather. She was nervous waiting for him in the dark by the river.

She gazed over her shoulder at the village, which was shrouded in beautiful moonlight. There were no sounds; everyone was asleep.

She shivered as she only now realized the chill of the autumn night. She had not taken the time to grab a wrap.

She hugged herself as she again gazed down the long avenue of the river.

She smiled and whispered a silent thank you to heaven above when she finally saw the canoe slicing through the water.

She dismounted and met Red Feather as he beached the canoe, then gently lifted his mother into his arms.

"What should I do with the horse?" Angela Dawn asked, glancing over her shoulder at the village. She spied a large corral of horses beyond the lodges, then smiled at Red Feather. "I see the corrals. I shall take the horse there."

"Meet me at my mother's tepee," Red Feather said, already walking toward the village. "I shall return later for your bag."

Angela Dawn looked into the canoe. The pearl handle of the cane picked up the shine of the moon and seemed to look back at her, as though warning her to hide it as quickly as possible.

"After I secure the horse, I shall return for my bag myself," Angela Dawn said, already walking the horse ahead of Red Feather toward the corral. "You just concentrate on getting help for your mother."

He gave her a nod and hurried onward with his mother as Angela Dawn led the horse into the corral.

Soon they had all reassembled in Soft Flower's tepee.

Within minutes Red Feather kindled a fire in its firepit.

Angela Dawn stood back with Red Feather and his father, who had summoned a *katcmi'c*. The shaman knelt low over Soft Flower and ministered to her ankle after cleansing it thoroughly.

She lay on a comfortable thick pallet of furs beside the warm fire as the shaman rubbed a fine powder on the wound. In a small bag he had brought his medicine, which tonight was the gizzard of a bird called *ku-nsnu*. It had been mashed fine, and was now being rubbed upon the wound by the elderly man's bony fingers.

Angela Dawn was in awe of the shaman, whose name she now knew to be Raven Wing. He seemed too old even to be able to walk, much less tend to those who were ill.

His hair was thin and gray, and when he stood, his hair reached the floor. He wore a long, full buckskin robe, upon which were beads sewn in the design of many ravens. His face was gaunt and lined with deep wrinkles. His eyes were pale, yet alert.

Angela Dawn was aware of a strange medicinal smell about him, and she assumed it was because he handled herbs all day long, either preparing them to be used or inventing new cures.

Angela Dawn inched closer to Red Feather, who was avidly watching the shaman. All of this was new to him, as well, even though he was as much Chitimacha as the man who ministered to his mother.

Angela Dawn could tell that he was fascinated by it all, and seemed at peace with the decision he had made to join this world.

"How does a man become a shaman?" she whispered to Red Feather. "Did your mother teach you that?"

"Yes, and it is interesting," Red Feather whispered back, making sure his voice did not reach the shaman and disturb him. "Mother told me about Raven Wing many times. She knew him when she lived among her people. She said that in his vision one day a raven came to him and took him far away, where he saw a spirit effecting a cure, and then he knew that it was his calling to become a shaman."

"That's a beautiful story," Angela Dawn said

softly. At that moment, Raven Wing's voice stilled everyone else's.

"I am finished," he said after having applied all of the fine powder that he had brought in his buckskin bag.

He rose slowly, turned, then smiled at Straight Arrow.

Angela Dawn noticed that he continued to purposely avoid looking at her, as though he felt that not to see her made her not truly there.

She knew that not only did she have a lot of adjusting to do in order to live this new life, but so did all of Red Feather's people.

"My chief, Princess Soft Flower will be well soon," the elderly shaman said in a low, soothing voice. He turned and smiled at Straight Arrow. "It is good that she has come home to us," he said softly. "I mourned her disappearance those long years ago, thinking she was gone from us forever. She, who is my cousin, was, and will always be, special to me."

Again he turned, then smiled down at Soft Flower, who returned the smile. "Soft Flower, I will go now but I will come again tomorrow and check on your wound," he said. "I shall again minister to it and will do so until all signs of the wound are gone."

"Thank you, Raven Wing," Soft Flower murmured. "And it is so very good to be here again, to be with you and all of my people." Tears filled her eyes. "It is so good to be called princess again after that title was denied me from the day I was abducted."

"I will come tomorrow, but until then, rest, my princess," Raven Wing said, then quietly left the lodge.

Soft Flower smiled up at Red Feather. "Straight Arrow, are you not pleased that our son has returned to be with his people?" she murmured. "He was denied his heritage for far too long."

Straight Arrow turned to Red Feather. "My son, all will welcome you with open arms," he said. "They will know you as your mother has known you."

Then he turned back to his wife and knelt beside her. "We will leave you now so you can rest," he said softly. "Tomorrow you will be all but well."

"I would like to stay with her," Angela Dawn blurted out, since she knew that Red Feather needed time with his father to speak on her behalf. She had seen his father give her occasional frowns and knew that she still was not welcome. She hoped Red Feather would find the right words to change that.

She went and knelt at Soft Flower's other side. "May I stay with you?" she murmured. "Red Feather needs time alone with his father."

Soft Flower gave Angela Dawn a long look,

finally understanding her son's deep feelings for this woman, and realizing that she had no choice but to accept her. Now that she had seen the good in this woman, she smiled and took one of Angela Dawn's hands.

"Yes, please do stay with me," she murmured. "I shall welcome the company."

"You can sleep when you want to sleep," Angela Dawn said softly. "I just want to be here if you need anything."

"Your kindness is appreciated," Soft Flower said, then turned to Red Feather. "My son, go with your father. Talk, then take the time to rest. Angela Dawn can sleep here. There are enough pelts for her comfort."

Angela Dawn's stomach clenched when she saw Straight Arrow frown as he gazed over at her. She knew that she had much to do to convince this elderly chief that she was worthy of his son's love, and of living among his people.

For now she decided not to say anything else. Perhaps Red Feather would be able to convince him.

"Father, let us go to your lodge," Red Feather said, holding a hand out for him. "Mother can sleep. Angela Dawn will see to her needs if she awakens."

Straight Arrow gave his wife a questioning gaze.

When she nodded in quiet encouragement for

him to go on, he leaned over and brushed a soft kiss across her brow, then rose and left the lodge with Red Feather.

When they reached his tepee and fresh wood was added to the fire, Red Feather and Straight Arrow sat down opposite each other on spread blankets.

"There is so much to tell you," Red Feather began. "I have not yet had the time to tell you how Mother was injured. I shall tell you now, but do not become so enraged that you will do something you might regret later."

"Tell me, and I will listen with an open heart," Straight Arrow said. "I am a man of peace, but sometimes I wonder if that is the right road to take. Tell me now, my son, what seems so hard for you to say."

Red Feather's jaw tightened as he began telling his father how he had found his mother.

He saw his father fighting deep emotions as he heard about his wife having been shackled in a cabin all alone, and why. He saw Straight Arrow wince when he told about the rat.

"But, Father," Red Feather continued, "all is well now. Mother is here to stay. So is this son who has been denied too much already of his heritage. We should look ahead now, not behind. Jon Paul Ratcliffe would not dare attempt to come here for either me or mother. If he does, I shall be the one who will escort him away again.

I will put the fear of God into his heart, Father, so do not bother yourself with thoughts of vengeance."

"It is hard not to go directly to that white man and sink a knife into his heart," Straight Arrow replied. "But it is enough that my wife is home and will be well, as it is good that I have my firstborn with me now, forever. Our people will cherish your presence."

"That is so good to know," Red Feather said. He sighed. "But there is something more that we must talk about . . . some*one*."

"The white woman," Straight Arrow said, his eyes narrowing with an anger he could not hide from his son. "It is not good that she has come with you. It would be best if you sent her away."

"Father, that is not possible," Red Feather said tightly. "She is going to be my wife. She is a part of my life now, and I cannot turn my back on her."

That word "wife" seemed to have turned his father's heart cold. Red Feather said nothing more, but waited.

"I have missed so many years with you, how can I deny you the woman if she will make your stay here happier?" Straight Arrow said. "Yes, my son, I am so anxious to have you with me, a son that I never knew existed until now, I will do whatever I can to make you happy."

"Thank you, Father," Red Feather said,

stunned by his father's quick decision, a decision that made Red Feather's heart pound with gladness.

"But," Straight Arrow suddenly added. "My son, because of her, you can never expect to reach the status of chief."

"Yes, Mother explained to me that a Chitimacha chief must marry a woman of his own status," Red Feather said. "This woman is white, and in your eyes she is a commoner."

"She *is* a commoner," Straight Arrow said dryly. "There is no way that she can be allowed to be the wife of a powerful Chitimacha chief. Therefore, my son, at the time of my death, your younger brother will become chief."

"I would not expect anything but that," Red Feather said softly. "My brother deserves to be chief. He has always been here among his people. He knows all of the customs, so many that I do not know yet. He is loved by all of our people."

Red Feather paused, then said, "My mother has taught me much, but there is much that I still do not know, that I must learn by actually doing. It would not have been fair to our people to have a chief who was only partially aware of their customs."

"You speak wisely, my son," Straight Arrow said, smiling. "It is good that you understand how it must be."

"It is just so good to be here, to know you and

my people, to be a part of my heritage," Red Feather said proudly. "And I cannot thank you enough that you will allow Angela Dawn to be a part of it."

"So often a man is what he becomes because of a woman," Straight Arrow said with emotion. "We shall see, my son, just how right I am to accept her into our lives."

"Mother was good for you, was she not?" Red Feather asked, his eyes smiling into his father's.

"So very much, and when she was gone, there was such a void left inside my heart," Straight Arrow said, nodding. He smiled broadly. "But she is with me again. Everything within me feels warm and good."

"And you seem to be feeling better altogether," Red Feather said, searching his father's eyes, then his face. "Are you?"

"I feel young again, if that is what you mean," Straight Arrow said, chuckling. Then he frowned. "As far as what ails me? We shall see, my son. We shall see."

He sighed, then rose and spread blankets and pelts for Red Feather's bed. He gestured with a hand toward it. "My son, we must sleep. Tomorrow we shall begin the rest of our lives as a true family," he said.

Red Feather went to embrace him, then stretched out on his bed of blankets and pelts as his father stretched out upon his own closer to the fire.

They nodded a quiet good night to each other, and Red Feather watched his father's eyes close. When he began softly snoring, Red Feather knew he was asleep.

But sleep would not come quickly to Red Feather. He was thinking about what his father had said about his being denied the title of chief because of Angela Dawn.

There was one person who wouldn't be happy about that decision. Red Feather's mother.

It had always been her secret dream to one day see Red Feather as chief.

She surely felt that she had taught him all that he should know to be a Chitimacha leader.

But he knew his mother well enough to know that she would accept this decision and be silent in her feelings about things. Fortunately, she was beginning to accept Angela Dawn in their lives.

He hoped that soon she would be happy that her son had a woman he loved with all his heart. This woman, ah, yes, this woman . . . *his* woman.

Chapter Twenty-five

That was't that all to me, love,
For which my soul did pine.
          —Edgar Allan Poe

Concerned that Jewel had not had anything to eat since he had shackled her in the cabin, and having slept off his drunken stupor as he sat slumped in his chair before the fireplace, Jon Paul eased himself from the chair and went to the kitchen, where he found untouched food that had been prepared by the cook.

The kitchen was dark with shadows created by candles that had burned down almost to their wicks in a chandelier over the preparation table.

The room still smelled of baked chicken and potatoes and milk gravy.

He went to the preparation table and broke off a piece of chicken and put it in his mouth, then raked a finger through the cold, stiff mashed potatoes and sucked a dollop from his finger.

He cringed when he saw how the gravy had formed a strange sort of gel across the top.

But as hungry as he was, and Jewel must be, none of that mattered. He went to a cabinet and took a dish, then piled food onto it.

He left the kitchen and went outside where the moon was high and spreading its white light across the tops of his vast fields of sugarcane and tobacco.

Everything was quiet except for an occasional hoot from an owl somewhere in the live oaks.

He saw candlelight at the slaves' cabin windows and hoped that none of the blacks would see him taking food into the farthest cabin.

He knew that many had seen him leave his wife there, but they knew not to interfere with the decisions of their master.

A part of Jon Paul dreaded seeing Jewel after having left her there for so long.

Yet that part of him that still ached from her betrayal caused a wicked smile to quiver across his thin line of lips. She had not only betrayed him, but also turned his son against him.

He wondered whether, if she had it all to do

over again, she would choose not to tell Troy the truth about his heritage.

Or had she been determined to do this from the very beginning of her marriage to him? Had she only been biding her time until Troy was old enough to be told?

"You wench," he growled to himself.

Yes, he was glad that he had chosen to make her pay for her crime against him. She had also sinned against the son who would have had everything any young man could want once Jon Paul died.

Everything grand would have been Troy's.

He would have carried on the tradition of the Ratcliffes and made everyone bow down to that name, or regret not having done so.

Jon Paul held much power in his hands. Troy could have had the same.

Now his son Larry would have it all, and Jon Paul knew without a doubt that he would squander it away until the name Ratcliffe had no meaning. His family might even become a laughingstock in Jamestown.

Sighing heavily, his whole world having been turned upside down by Jewel's decision to tell Troy the truth, Jon Paul went up to the cabin.

He immediately noticed that the door was ajar.

When he had left the cabin he had made sure the door was closed, though not locked. He knew that none of the slaves would dare enter.

Then . . . who . . . would have entered? he wondered.

His pulse racing, he set the plate of food on the ground, then drew a pearl-handled pistol from his front coat pocket.

He moved stealthily into the cabin.

The moon shone through the window and door, giving enough light for Jon Paul to see everything within. And what he saw made his heart almost stop still within his chest.

Jewel was gone!

And there was dried blood on the floor where she had sat shackled to the wall!

"Lord almighty," Jon Paul gasped out. "How did she get loose? And where did the blood come from?"

He stared for a moment longer where he had last seen his wife, then hurried outside.

He placed his hands on his hips as he looked from cabin to cabin. Everything seemed quiet.

Surely none of the slaves had been brave enough to help Jewel. Then that left only one person who would do this.

Troy!

Somehow he had discovered that his mother was chained there. He had come for her! He had rescued her.

How had Troy learned the truth?

Who among the slaves had told him? And why was blood involved in her escape?

A rat suddenly scurried across Jon Paul's foot and stopped where the plate of food sat on the ground close to the cabin door.

It did not even take the time to sniff. It began consuming the food as though it had been placed there for it.

"A rat . . ." Jon Paul said, paling.

He had known that rats dwelt among the slaves' cabins. Surely a rat had gone into the cabin and bitten Jewel! That was where the blood had come from.

"You sonofabitch!" Jon Paul shouted as he aimed the pistol and fired. The rat flew into the air as the bullet made contact, then fell down onto what was left of the food on the plate, dead.

He was aware of scurrying feet.

He turned and saw numerous slaves—men, women, and children. The gunshot had obviously alarmed them. They were standing behind Jon Paul, their eyes wide and wondering.

Instant rage engulfed Jon Paul. He raised his pistol into the air and fired. The slaves lurched with fear, and grasped one another as they gazed at him with wide, dark eyes.

"I need answers!" he shouted. "Who among you knew about my wife being shackled in this cabin?"

When no one responded, but instead all looked even more afraid, Jon Paul's eyes narrowed as he gazed from one to another.

"I know that several of you saw me take Jewel into the cabin," Jon Paul growled. "Did any of you decide to go and check on her? Did any of you dare to let her go? Or . . . did you see who did?"

Little Hannah stepped forward from the others. "Masta' Troy was here," she innocently admitted. "I seed him take Miss Jewel away in a canoe. The lady with him as well, on Masta' Troy's beautiful black horse."

"Troy," Jon Paul said, his teeth clenched.

Then he grew even angrier. "Troy would not have known about his mother being here unless one of you told him," he said. He took quick steps toward Hannah. He grabbed her arm. "Did you tell him, Hannah?"

Hannah's eyes were wide with fright. "No, suh, Hannah nevah tol' Masta' Troy anythin'," she said, lying. "Please let Hannah go?"

Believing the child since she had been truthful enough to reveal what she had seen, Jon Paul yanked his hand back from her. "Sorry, Hannah," he mumbled.

He glared at everyone again, then waved a hand in the air. "Get back to your cabins," he cried. "Don't let me see the whites of your eyes until morning. Do you hear?"

They all nodded, then ran together back to their cabins, their doors closing with loud bangs.

Jon Paul sighed heavily.

He gazed down at the dead rat, then looked at the cabin again. Dejectedly, he walked back toward the house.

He did not have to think hard to know where Troy had taken his mother, and Jon Paul knew for certain that after Troy had seen how his mother had been treated, Jon Paul would never see either of them again.

And he was not about to go to the Chitimacha village and demand that they return home, for in truth they *were* home. They were now among their true people.

He did not want to arouse the wrath of the Chitimacha any more than it was already. Now they must realize who had abducted their princess those long years ago.

No, he didn't want any more trouble.

He just wanted to be left alone to live his life as it would be without the woman he had loved with all his heart, and the son he had cared for so much.

Yes, he had just lost a wife and a son in one blow. It would be hard to accept.

"Red Feather?" he said, shivering as he thought of what his son was now being called, and why.

Tears streamed from his eyes when he saw Jewel in his mind's eye, then whispered her true name—Princess Soft Flower.

The thought of her Chitimacha name awoke a hatred for her that moments ago did not seem possible. "You double-crossing wench," he growled.

Chapter Twenty-six

What is love? It is the morning
and the evening star.
                    —Sinclair Lewis

Deep in thought, and enjoying the morning, Angela Dawn sat with one of Red Feather's wid-
owed cousins, Pretty Moon, with whom she was
staying until her marriage to Red Feather.

Red Feather would be living in his mother's
tepee until she recovered entirely from the terrible rat bite; then he had been invited to stay
with his brother for a while, so that they could
get to know one another. Then he would spend
his final days before the marriage with his father.

Angela Dawn was excited about so many things—her upcoming marriage and how she had been accepted by everyone as Red Feather's future bride. Today, she was excited about learning the customs of the Chitimacha women.

Pretty Moon, a radiantly beautiful woman of fifty years, was her teacher. She had no wrinkles, and her thick black hair was not yet threaded with gray. Today it lay in heavy braids down her back, and she wore a doeskin dress that was beautifully decorated with variously colored beads.

Angela Dawn wore doeskin today, too, a gift from Pretty Moon on the very day that Angela Dawn had met her and had been invited to stay in her lodge. Pretty Moon was without a husband now, and she had never been blessed with children.

Yet Angela Dawn marveled at how happy the woman was, how what she had in life was more than enough; she shared all she had with those who seemed less fortunate than she.

Pretty Moon was teaching Angela Dawn the art of basketry today. As Red Feather was meeting with his family in his father's lodge, Angela Dawn had gone with Pretty Moon and some of the other women to the bayou to gather cane for the baskets.

She had helped them cut the green canes, strip them, and then bring them to their homes, where each woman went into her own lodge to work on her basketry. She had assisted in the preparation of the reeds for the baskets. Seated on a bench just outside Pretty Moon's tepee, Angela Dawn held a four-foot length of reed in her bare hands, and with a quick twist of her wrists, split it open.

She had learned that the ripe cane was very hard, and found it difficult to work with.

She had been aghast when Pretty Moon had not hesitated to use her teeth to divide the cane into narrower strips. When all of them were the right width, she had taken a sharp knife and split them into flat lengths, making them very thin and workable.

Angela Dawn had then learned that the cane splints must lie out in the sun and dew for eight days and nights, after which they would be ready to be dyed.

Besides the natural greenish tan of the dry cane, there were three colors—dark brown, red, and yellow—all of which blended into the most harmonious combinations.

Today Angela Dawn and Pretty Moon were working with aged cane that had already been dyed and made ready for basketry.

But she had been taught by Pretty Moon that to produce the brown color, one must boil the cane splints with black walnut hulls. For red and yellow, Pretty Moon had said that one must dig the root of the *po-wah-ahsh*, a species of plant commonly called *dock*, which grew in abundance along the bayou.

When yellow was desired, the cane was boiled with the root alone. But red required more labor. The splints must be soaked in lime water for eight days, then dyed with *po-wah-ahsh*, when a rich red was obtained.

Lime was made from gathered shells that were burned and crushed.

"You are doing fine work," Pretty Moon said as she looked at what Angela Dawn was making. "You have listened well to my teachings about how to make a double-walled basket."

"I have discovered that this is not all that easy," Angela Dawn said, smiling up at Pretty Moon. Then she concentrated on the chore at hand as her fingers continued to work with the reeds. "But I know that with a very fine splint, I must begin at the bottom inside, and work up to the top, then turn back down and weave the outside, finishing at the bottom."

"Yes, and then the leftover ends of the splints are broken off, leaving a smooth finish," Pretty Moon said. "Angela Dawn, when the basket is completed, it will be impossible to detect a beginning or an ending, so perfect is the workmanship that I have taught you. Even the lid of the basket will be doubled.

"The most remarkable feature of Chitimacha basketry is this double-weaving process that I have taught you, which produces two baskets, woven one inside the other, sharing a single rim, and showing no visible stopping or starting point," Pretty Moon said, resuming work on her own basket. "Like the one you are making, I, too, am making a double-woven basket. Upon reaching the rim, I am bending the cane over and weaving it down the sides and across the bottom. The inner basket will be constructed of undyed strips, while the exterior will display glorious colored designs."

"And you said that these baskets are heavy, strong, and durable, so tight they can even hold water?" Angela Dawn asked as her fingers continued to weave and bend and straighten.

"Yes, and remember this," Pretty Moon said, pausing in her own basketry. "The durability of the double weave is the joy of a basket owner, and its beauty and complexity are the envy of basket weavers."

"I love the designs you have taught me for my basket," Angela Dawn said. "For example, I love how it looks like there are startled minnows swimming through diagonal ripples of red and black water. I also admire yours, how it looks as if somber cow eyes are marching in pairs around the midsection of the basket."

"My favorite, which I will weave into my next basket, is a popular design of many Chitimacha women. It features alligators undulating horizontally across the basket, while mouse tracks pitter-patter up, down, and around the rim and lid," Pretty Moon said. "The art of basket making has been passed down from generation to generation. Over the years, our women have developed many beautiful designs."

Angela Dawn paused in her sewing, then looked behind her, where many lovely baskets were displayed. Pretty Moon had explained that she had made this large collection with every known pattern of the Chitimacha. The work had kept her mind occupied since the death of her husband.

"You will learn it all, Angela Dawn," Pretty Moon said, drawing Angela Dawn's eyes back to her. "I have already taught you how to gather and split the cane, but I will also teach you how to cure the cane, how to gather roots and actually make the dyes, how to dye the cane, and make the many designs and shapes of our baskets."

"Why are you being so kind?" Angela Dawn asked as she watched Pretty Moon slide a piece of wood into her lodge fire.

"Why?" Pretty Moon said, settling back down and folding her arms across her chest. "Because you have been chosen by our chief's son to be his wife, and because you are someone I feel close to although we have only just met. Even though you are white, I feel you have the heart of a Chitimacha."

"Perhaps that is because I have fallen in love with one," Angela Dawn said, also laying her basketry aside. She moved closer to the fire and held her palms up to absorb the warmth.

"No, it is more than that," Pretty Moon said, studying Angela Dawn's friendly smile. "You have a good heart, a sweet, soft voice, and you hold no prejudice toward us Chitimacha, as so many white women do. You sit here with me as though you have known me forever. You talk with me as though we are blood kin. Yes, Angela Dawn, you will bring sunshine into the hearts of my people."

"I hope that Red Feather's father will learn to accept me," Angela Dawn murmured. "At first, his mother resented me also. But now that she knows just how much Red Feather loves me, she has accepted me. But his father?" She lowered her eyes. "I doubt he will ever accept me. He . . . has . . . even said that I am beneath him, as though I am not worthy of his son's love."

"Yes, you are called a 'commoner' among my people because you do not have any birth status," Pretty Moon said, sighing. "But soon all will know you as Red Feather and I know you. You will be accepted. You will be loved."

"But I can never become a princess in their eyes," Angela Dawn said softly. "And I understand why. I am white. Your princesses are Chitimacha."

"In my eyes and Red Feather's, you *are* a princess," Pretty Moon said, reaching over to gently touch Angela Dawn's face.

"You are so kind," Angela Dawn said, taking Pretty Moon's hand from her face and squeezing it affectionately.

Then she released her hand. "You live alone," she murmured. "You have no parents?"

"My parents were swept away one day when the winds and water overcame our people's village," Pretty Moon said solemnly. "They were here one minute, gone the next. There was a search for them, but no one could find them, or my husband. He died on that same day, in the same way."

"You lost so many so quickly," Angela Dawn said, reminded of her own circumstance. She lowered her eyes. "So did I. My father died, and shortly after, my mother. I had never felt so alone . . . until . . ."

She raised her eyes and smiled warmly at Pretty Moon. "I was so very alone until I met Red Feather," she murmured. "Now I have never felt so loved, so needed."

"How did your parents die?" Pretty Moon asked, resuming her basketry. Her eyes were on her work, not Angela Dawn, or she would have seen the instant hurt in her eyes.

"How?" Angela Dawn said, her voice drawn. "My father was murdered, and then my mother died . . . I truly believe . . . of a broken heart."

Pretty Moon looked quickly up at Angela Dawn. "Your father was murdered?" she gasped. "Who murdered him? Did the murderer pay for his crime?"

"I only recently discovered who the murderer is, and no, he has not paid for the crime . . . *yet*," Angela Dawn said, then looked quickly at the entrance flap as it was held aside. Red Feather was there, smiling at her.

"Come with me," he said, motioning toward her with a hand. "There is news that I wish you to hear." He smiled at Pretty Moon. "Come, as well, Pretty Moon. You will enjoy hearing the news, too."

"News?" Angela Dawn said, sliding her basketry materials from her lap. She rose to her feet just as Pretty Moon stood up and walked toward Red Feather. "What sort, Red Feather?"

"You shall see," he said. He reached a hand out for her. "Come with me to my father's lodge. My mother and brother are there. We have had a long visit. Mother is feeling much better, and things are going well between me and my father, and my brother, as well. It is as though my mother and I have lived here always. We are truly, truly home."

"I am so happy for you," Angela Dawn said. She was especially pleased that his mother was almost well, and had accepted the fact that Red

Feather could never be chief; she did not even hate Angela Dawn any longer. Soft Flower was so radiantly happy to be with her husband and people again, and to have her son Red Feather there with her, that other things just no longer seemed so important.

As they walked toward his father's tepee, Red Feather put his arm gently around Angela Dawn's waist. Pretty Moon walked quietly beside them.

The village was filled with activity, the people busy with their daily chores. The children romped and played, and the elders sat around an outdoor fire, gossiping and smoking.

The sun was lowering in the sky. The air smelled fresh and clean from the river. Birds sang overhead in the trees.

"Aren't you going to give me a hint of what the news is about?" Angela Dawn asked as she drew even closer to Red Feather's side. "Please? Pretty please?"

"Pretty please?" Red Feather said, chuckling. "No. Not even pretty pleases will get me to tell you what is about to happen. Just be patient. When you do know, you will be as happy as this man who loves you."

"Alright," she said, sighing. "If you want to keep it a secret, so be it."

"A secret for only a few more minutes," Red Feather said, stepping away from her when they reached the large tepee. He held the entrance flap aside. "Go inside. I shall follow."

Pretty Moon and Angela Dawn went into the tepee. They found Red Feather's brother, mother, and father sitting around a fire, their faces all smiles as they looked up at Angela Dawn. Red Feather ushered Angela Dawn and Pretty Moon to a thick pallet of furs beside the fire.

He then sat down beside Angela Dawn and took her hand. "Mother, should I be the one to tell, or do you wish to?" he asked, smiling almost mischievously at Angela Dawn as she glanced up at him curiously.

"You tell it, son," Soft Flower said, reaching over to take one of her husband's hands.

Red Feather nodded, then turned and faced Angela Dawn. "There is to be a wedding soon," he said excitedly. "There is a celebration planned for tomorrow. After that feast, plans will be made for our wedding, and not only ours . . . but also Mother's and Father's. You see, Angela Dawn, they are going to renew their vows, vows that were broken all those years ago when my mother was forced to live with another man."

"There will be a double ceremony?" Angela Dawn gasped, her eyes wide. She was touched that she was accepted by his mother and father to such a degree that they saw nothing wrong with renewing their marriage vows as Red Feather and Angela Dawn spoke their own.

"Yes, we will all speak our vows together," Red Feather said. He looked past Angela Dawn and saw tears running down Pretty Moon's cheeks. He did not know her well yet, but had seen that she had taken to Angela Dawn.

Why was she crying?

"I see you are questioning my tears," Pretty Moon said as she brushed the tears away. "They are not sad or unhappy tears. They are tears of gladness. I am happy for you all."

She rose to her feet and knelt beside Soft Flower. "It will be a wonderful day when you and our chief speak vows of love again before our people, for I wept often for you and your special love when you suddenly disappeared from our people's lives," she said. She flung herself into Soft Flower's arms. "This is so good, oh, so good."

"Thank you," Soft Flower murmured, clinging to Pretty Moon. "I am living a dream, one that I hope never to awaken from."

"And you won't, Mother," Red Feather assured her. "No one will take away your happiness again."

Then Pretty Moon turned to Angela Dawn. "As you can see now, you are even more accepted than you ever hoped to be, since our chief has agreed to stand with you on the same day that you speak vows with Red Feather," she said. "You can stop worrying about how you are received among our people, because our chief and princess have taken you into their hearts."

Angela Dawn reached her arms out for Pretty Moon. They hugged, then Pretty Moon turned and walked toward the entrance flap. "I will leave you all alone now, so that you can be together and rejoice in everything," she murmured. She smiled at Gray Fox. "One day you, too, will find a woman who will make your heart sing. You will see, Gray Fox. You will see. If I were younger . . ."

Giggling, she left the lodge.

Red Feather looked from his mother, to his father and brother, and then to Angela Dawn. "You have all made me happier today than I had ever thought possible," he said. "And, Father, it is so good to see that you are feeling stronger."

"Even in my mind, son," Straight Arrow said. "Even in my mind. I feel that having all of my family with me again has renewed me in all ways."

He gazed at Angela Dawn. "And, yes, I do accept you into my son's life," he said. "But only as his wife, nothing more, you understand."

"Yes, I understand, and he is all that I will ever want," Angela Dawn said, smiling sweetly. She slid a hand into Red Feather's. "He is my reason for breathing."

"Then we are all set for a wedding, I see," Gray Fox said, beaming.

261

"Go and round up our people, Gray Fox, for the announcement," Straight Arrow said, slowly rising to his feet. He held a hand out for Soft Flower. "Wife, join me as we make the announcement."

He looked at Red Feather, and then at Angela Dawn. "We shall stand before our people and tell them together of the plans for a day so wonderful that it is hard for me to believe it will be happening," he said. "I have my Princess Soft Flower back with me."

Red Feather smiled and swept an arm around Angela Dawn's waist. He drew her close as he looked upon the two older people, who were smiling, then kissing, as though they were young again and just about to be married.

Angela Dawn smiled at Red Feather. "How can anyone be as happy as I am at this moment?" she whispered. "How is it possible?"

"Because we have made it so," Red Feather said, brushing a soft kiss across her lips.

"Let us leave now and speak before our people," Straight Arrow said, leading Soft Flower past Red Feather and Angela Dawn.

After his father and mother left the tepee, Red Feather placed a finger beneath Angela Dawn's chin and lifted her lips to his as he bent low and gave her an all-consuming kiss.

"I love you," Angela Dawn breathed against his

lips. "Oh, thank you, my Chitimacha warrior, for making life wonderful for me."

"As you have made it for me," he said, then swept her outside, where all his people stood listening to a chief whose voice seemed stronger and happier than it had been for many moons.

Chapter Twenty-seven

In loving thee, thou know'st
I am forsworn,
But thou are twice forsworn,
To me love swearing.
                    —William Shakespeare

The day was brilliant with sunshine. It seemed made for a celebration ... the celebration of a family's reunion ... of a chief whose health had blossomed after realizing that the woman he loved so long ago was alive, and had returned to him with a son he never knew.

This family sat together now on a platform cushioned with many pelts and blankets. A roaring outdoor fire had been built, around which dancers performed. Later there would be games, stories, and then a feast of feasts.

Angela Dawn had at first felt awkward sitting with Red Feather and his family, for she was the only white person in attendance.

But it had not taken long for her to relax and enjoy the entertainment. For what woman would not have fun with Red Feather at her side?

She sat at the far left of the family. Red Feather was seated beside his mother, and his mother sat next to Straight Arrow.

Gray Fox sat on Straight Arrow's right side, a man of regal bearing even at his young age, a warrior who would one day be chief.

But everyone hoped that would be a long time in the future, for Chief Straight Arrow was a beloved chief, and his wife, Soft Flower, had been a popular princess. Already, it was as though she had never been gone from them.

When Angela Dawn felt eyes on her, she turned to her left and found Pretty Moon smiling at her.

Angela Dawn returned the smile, and with it, a softly whispered "thank you," for Pretty Moon had given Angela Dawn a new, beautifully beaded doeskin dress to wear today. She had also given her moccasins beaded with a matching design.

Angela Dawn wore her hair in long braids down her back.

Were she not white of skin, she would look just like the Chitimacha. She even wore a necklace and bracelet of beads that Pretty Moon had loaned her for the celebration.

There was only one thing that kept coming to her mind to momentarily spoil this perfect day. It was the fact that her father's murderer was still walking around free, when he should have been incarcerated long ago for his crime.

She had to find a way to make him pay. But how? When?

Now that she was with Red Feather, soon to be his wife, would there even be any opportunity for her to avenge her father's death?

She glanced over at Red Feather. He was quite unaware of her discovery and her need to take vengeance.

She ached to share her discovery with him. But Larry was his brother!

Although there had always been some bad blood between them, mainly stemming from Larry's jealousy of Red Feather, Red Feather loved his brother.

How could she spoil Red Feather's world now that he had finally found his true father and his people?

And Red Feather was eagerly anticipating his wedding. How could she place a dark shadow over the wedding?

She was so torn.

But for today, she must put the knowledge behind her as best she could and enjoy these precious moments with her betrothed.

She wanted to feel his joy, his utter peace now that he had been united with his father and brother.

"Are you enjoying yourself?" Red Feather asked softly as he leaned closer to her. "I have noticed that sometimes you breathe harder, then scarcely breathe at all. There is something on your mind. Do you want to leave the celebration and tell me about it? Is the celebration of the Chitimacha making you uncomfortable?"

Alarmed that he had realized she was thinking about something besides these wondrous moments with him, when he was beaming with pride and happiness, Angela Dawn gave him a quick look of surprise.

Then realizing just how astute he was, she forced a smile so that she might assure him that all was well with her.

"Truly, I am alright," she whispered back. "It is just all so new to me. The dancers. The music. The children who seem anxious for something. What are they anxious for? Is something planned for them?"

"Stories," Red Feather said, smiling. "Soon there will be stories." He glanced quickly over at his father, pride filling him.

"It will be my father who will tell the stories

to the children," he said. "Do you see the significance of that? Angela Dawn, he is remembering more than he was even a few days ago. He remembers enough to tell stories of bravery to the children, and myths that he was told when he was a young boy himself."

"That is so wonderful," she said, believing that the chief's returning memory was something of a miracle.

Only a few days ago he could remember only things that had happened to him recently.

Only a few memories of his past would come to him, and only occasionally.

But now? His great happiness seemed to have brought his memory alive again, along with his wonderful smile.

There was going to be a double wedding!

That was something so sweet to think about, Angela Dawn wondered why it was not enough to distract her from ugly thoughts about Larry Ratcliffe.

"Yes, wonderful," Red Feather said.

Even though some of his people had not yet fully accepted this white woman among them, he slid an arm around Angela Dawn's waist and drew her closer to him.

"And after the celebration is over today, I have a surprise for you," he said, causing Angela Dawn's eyes to widen. "No. I will not tell you what it is. You will see with your own eyes. But later, not now."

"Waiting will be hard," Angela Dawn said, then smiled sweetly at him. "Can you just give me a small hint?"

"It is something big, and that is all I shall tell you," Red Feather said in a teasing fashion. "And it will be yours . . . and mine, together."

"Big? Yours and mine?" Angela Dawn said, raising an eyebrow. "I cannot imagine what it might be."

"That is why it is called a surprise," Red Feather said, chuckling. "Now let us get back to enjoying the celebration. It is a time of love and camaraderie for my family and people. It is a time of joy."

"Yes, I see it and feel it," Angela Dawn murmured. "I am enjoying it so much, Red Feather."

"That is good, for it is important that you share the emotions of my people, as well as understanding their customs," Red Feather said.

He nodded toward the musicians, who played as women and men danced rhythmically around the fire.

"The horns being played today are made of cane or reed," Red Feather explained to Angela Dawn. "The drums are made by stretching a deerskin hide over the top of a large clay pot or the end of a hollow log. Music is also being made by scratching an alligator hide with a stick."

"An alligator hide?" Angela Dawn gasped out. "Truly . . . an alligator hide?"

"The skins are prepared by first exposing the slain alligator to ants until all of the softer parts are eaten out," he explained. "And then the skins are dried. As you can hear, the music made by this instrument is interesting."

"Very interesting," Angela Dawn said, smiling.

Then she sat back and observed as the dancing ended and games began.

Several women participated in a chunkey game, and then a woman's game that included pieces of cane, and then the men joined in a game in which a ball had to be thrown through a ring.

After these games were over, the children excitedly formed a wide circle before their chief, their eyes round as they watched and waited for his stories to begin.

"Long ago, young braves built their stamina by running around the outdoor fire, over and over again," Straight Arrow began. "After a certain period passed, certain individuals had practiced running so assiduously that wonderful stories were told of their swiftness. These young braves trained by eating nothing but raw eggs and drinking only a kind of tea that makes people supple. One young brave could run even faster than the horses that were raced against him. So you see, my young braves, even you could become someone of myth if you work hard."

The children, especially the young braves, sat attentively quiet as their chief continued. "There was a man long ago who became angry with everybody, so angry that he set the sea marshes on fire, intending to destroy them," Straight Arrow said, and the children scooted even closer to him.

Red Feather beamed as he saw the pleasure the children's attentiveness was causing his father. He saw the pride in his father's eyes, pride that he was remembering things he had thought gone from his memory forever.

Red Feather reached over and took his mother's hand with his free one. He squeezed it affectionately.

When she turned her eyes to him, he saw tears. He knew they were joyous tears, for she was feeling the happiness that Red Feather was feeling for his father.

When he had moments like this, when he saw just how much he had missed by not living with the Chitimacha, sadness engulfed him.

But now he vowed to erase that sadness forever. He would not think back to what should have been.

He would rejoice with his mother over finally having the life they both wanted, and together.

When Jon Paul entered his thoughts, he blinked his eyes and the man was gone, just as quickly as he had disappeared from both his and his mother's lives.

He looked back at his true father as Straight Arrow continued with his latest tale.

"After the angry man set the marshes on fire, a little bird flew up into a tree and shouted at him, '*Ku-naxmiwican*! *Ku-naxmiwican*! The water and all is going to burn.' The man replied to the bird, saying that if it did not go away, he would kill it. The bird lingered. The man threw a shell at the bird and hit it on the wings, making them bleed."

The children gasped, then grew silent again when Chief Straight Arrow continued his tale.

"Children, the story I have just told you reveals to you how the red-winged blackbird came to have its red wings," he said, smiling from child to child. "But I am not finished yet with the story about the red-winged blackbird. You see, the fire burned on past the marshes that day, onto land of the Chitimacha. Then after it was finally out, the bird said to the man, 'You have done me good, for I can find plenty of good food to eat now that you have burned the grasses away.' The man watched the bird devouring small prey, and before the bird flew away, its belly filled with food, it gave off a call that sounded like laughter to the evil man. The red-winged blackbird comes often even today to the marshes, its pretty red wings flashing in the sun, its song beautiful and sweet."

The stories went on and on, and then the feast began as women brought the food they had prepared earlier from their lodges. They placed the dishes on the ground close to the warmth of the fire.

As everyone filled their wooden plates with delicious-smelling food, Red Feather took Angela Dawn gently by the arm and led her away.

"Where are you taking me?" Angela Dawn asked, looking over her shoulder as the people began sitting in groups, eating and chatting.

"To the surprise that I told you about earlier," Red Feather said, smiling down at her. "Yes, now is the time for me to reveal it to you. Are you ready?"

"Very," she murmured, then hurried with him to the far edge of the village. She gave him a questioning look when he led her toward a large, freshly erected tepee, its deerskin covering having been bleached snow white by the sun.

"Our home," Red Feather said, stopping to gesture with his free hand toward the large lodge.

"Ours?" Angela Dawn gasped out, awed by the beautiful tepee, and its hugeness. Even the chief's was not as large.

"While you were learning basketry with Pretty Moon yesterday, and I was in my father's lodge with my family, many warriors came together and erected this lodge for us," he murmured. "It is a gift from the heart of those who built it for their chief's son."

He gazed down at her. "Do you want to go inside?" he asked. "I have already seen it. I know already of its grandness."

"I do wish to see it," Angela Dawn said. She sighed. "Our home? Yours and mine? It is all so wonderful to behold, Red Feather. And it is all because of you."

"And I want to continue giving you a life that will make you happy," he said, lifting the entrance flap. He led her inside.

She stopped and stared in wonder at everything that had been prepared for her and Red Feather. A fire burned in the firepit, casting light around the interior, showing many rolled-up blankets, pelts, cooking utensils, and even a wooden vase of wildflowers on the mat-covered floor.

"I have always lived in a spacious house, with riches everywhere, yet nothing I have ever had compares to this, my true home with my future wife," Red Feather said. "Will this smaller space be enough for you, as well?"

"As you know, I have never in my life had a true home," Angela Dawn said as she wandered around the tepee. She continued to look about her. "But this? This is truly ours? A true home?"

She turned to him and flung herself into his

arms. "I do love it so," she murmured. "And sharing a home with you? Ah, how can I express my true feelings to you about this?"

"With a kiss?" Red Feather said huskily as he led her down onto the floor on a thick pallet of pelts that he had prepared for them himself.

"Yes, a kiss," she murmured, twining her arms around his neck as he moved his lips to hers and they shared a kiss that spoke of everything sweet and wonderful.

"I know that vows have still not been spoken, but do you think we can . . . ?" he asked as he gazed in a pleading manner into her eyes.

"More than kiss?" she asked, her heart pounding as the passion rose within her at the thought of their being totally together again.

"Yes, more than a kiss," Red Feather said, slowly running one of his hands up under her dress, caressing her legs with feathery touches all the way.

She trembled with ecstasy as he again kissed her, his fingers finding her most sensitive spots.

She became breathless with desire.

"I had better secure the entrance flap ties, don't you think?" he asked, leaning away from her.

She smiled and nodded. "Yes, I think that might be a good idea," she said, then waited with a thumping heart for him to do it.

When he came back to her, he drew her to her feet before him.

Slowly, almost methodically, he began undressing her.

Chapter Twenty-eight

The little Love-god, lying once asleep,
Laid by his side his heart-inflaming brand,
Whils't many nymphs that vowed chaste life to
   keep,
Came tripping by.
                    —William Shakespeare

As Red Feather pulled Angela Dawn's dress over
her head, then tossed it to the floor behind him,
he stared at her body. Although he had already
seen her nude, he could not help marveling over
her again. She was petite; her breasts were well
rounded and firm, her nipples were tight peaks
of pink.

Her belly was flat, the flesh there leading down to a thick feathering of hair which covered that part of her that would soon again be awakened to total bliss.

"Until you, I had never been undressed in the presence of a man," Angela Dawn said, her voice quavering as she stood before him; his gaze seemed to scorch her flesh. "Do . . . you . . . truly find my body beautiful? My father always teased me about being too skinny. Am I? Do you think I'm too skinny?"

Red Feather chuckled as he reached his hands out for her breasts. "I find your body exquisite in every way," he said huskily.

He saw how her eyes closed and she gasped with pleasure when he cupped both of her breasts. Then he bent over and brushed them with quick flicks of his tongue.

"And the taste of your body is just as exquisite," he said. He quickly undressed, tossing his buckskin shirt aside, then dropped his breeches to the floor. That part of him that ached for her immediately sprang into sight.

He saw her face become red with a blush, and saw her look quickly away from that part of his anatomy that she still found somewhat embarrassing.

Smiling, their eyes holding, he took her hands and led her down onto the soft pallet of furs.

"Do you want me to hold you for a while before we make love?" he asked as he spread himself atop her, yet resting on his forearms so that his body just barely touched hers.

"I want you to make love with me," she murmured. She ran her fingers slowly across his lips. "Kiss me. Hold me. Make love with me. I have waited a lifetime for a man I could adore so much that I would be breathless with passion for him, as I am now for you."

He did not have to be coaxed any more, for his whole being was crying out for her.

He swept his arms around her and drew her against him as he fully blanketed her with his body.

"Part your legs," he whispered against her lips. "Let me touch you there, and then I shall again show you what paradise truly is."

Her heart thumping, her eyes wide, she slowly parted her legs, then sucked in a wild breath of rapture when he reached a hand between them and began caressing her womanhood.

"You are not only touching, you are . . ." she started, but stopped when his lips came down upon hers in a maddening, trembling kiss.

Angela Dawn lurched with surprise, then relaxed into a soft, sweet pleasure when Red Feather slowly pushed a finger within her, then began rhythmic movements that almost brought her over the brink of something too beautiful to describe.

Hardly able to hold back for much longer, he slowly pushed his manhood into her. He could hear her erratic breathing as he began his rhythmic strokes, her sighs proving that she felt the same bliss he was experiencing as her every secret became his.

"I love you so," Red Feather groaned against her lips.

He plunged into her, withdrew, and plunged again and again.

He kissed her with a fierce, possessive heat, her repeated moans proof that she was feeling the rapture he so badly wanted her to feel.

His body continued to move rhythmically with hers.

Fighting off the inevitable conclusion of these wondrous moments while he taught his woman the true meaning of love, he drew a ragged breath and held on for a while longer.

As before, Angela Dawn was awed by how wonderful being with a man in this way could be. Sweet currents of warm pleasure swept through her. She was flooded with emotions—all wonderful.

Red Feather paused for a moment.

He cradled Angela Dawn close as his steely arms enfolded her.

He gazed into her eyes. "Can you feel how much I love you?" he asked huskily. He flicked his tongue across her lips, then looked at her again. "Can you see the passion in my eyes? Do you hear it in my voice? Angela Dawn, I do love you so. It was our destiny to meet."

"Yes, a savage destiny," she whispered back, then melted when he covered her lips with his and again his body moved with hers.

She clung to him.

She strained her body against his.

And then the moment came when neither could hold back any longer. They embraced each other as their bodies rocked, quivered, swayed, and their moans and groans of pleasure mingled.

When it was over, Red Feather rolled away from Angela Dawn and stretched out on his back, panting. Their bodies were pearled with sweat.

Angela Dawn didn't move. She breathed hard and closed her eyes, realizing that she was still throbbing with pleasure.

She tingled all over when she felt his fingers on her moist cleft, which was now swollen and rapturously tender.

She sighed with pleasure as he stroked her, and soon she felt that wonderful splash of rapture overtake her again.

When her body subsided once more, she opened her eyes and turned to face him. "What you just did . . ." she murmured. "Your fingers gave me the same sort of pleasure that being locked in your arms gave me. Why is that?"

"There are many mysteries of the body that I

shall awaken you to," Red Feather said, turning on his side to face her. "Once we are man and wife, I shall teach you everything I know about lovemaking."

Her lips curved into a pout. "I hate to even think that you have been with other women, yet at your age, and as virile as you are, I could not expect anything less than that," she murmured. "But now I am here. You need no one else."

She scooted over and pressed her body against his. "Will I be enough?" she asked softly. "Will I be able to please you so much that you will never again want another woman?"

"There was never any woman for me until you, nor will there ever be again," he said. He reached a hand to the braid that lay across her shoulder. He smiled. "I love the braids."

"Pretty Moon advised me to wear them," she said, smiling softly. "I like them, too."

"Pretty Moon will teach you traditions of my people that I cannot teach you," Red Feather said. "In time, we both will know everything about my people."

"I hope that all of your people will eventually accept me as one of them," Angela Dawn said, her voice breaking. "If not, will you still be comfortable with me as your wife?"

"If ever you feel uncomfortable here in my village, please tell me," he said. "I will right all wrongs for you."

"Will you be able to?"

"Am I not their chief's son?"

"Yes, but is that enough?"

"I will make it so."

"I adore you," Angela Dawn said, moving her lips to his. "Darling, hold me. Please hold me."

He embraced her, then laughed softly when both of their stomachs growled at the same time. "We have fed one hunger today; do you think we should feed another?" he asked as he leaned up on an elbow. "Would you like to go and eat some of that delicious-smelling food that awaits us?"

"Do you think your people will be able to tell that we . . . we . . . just . . . you know . . . ?" Angela Dawn said as she rose to her feet, taking her dress as Red Feather handed it to her.

"If so, it should not matter," he said. He pulled on his breeches. "The wedding will be in two days. Pretty Moon came to me and asked for that much time to ready things for the wedding, especially since there will be more than one wedding on that day."

"I wonder what she has planned," Angela Dawn said, smoothing her hands over her braids to make sure they were still in place.

"It will be a day of days," Red Feather said. He reached for Angela Dawn and pulled her against his hard body. "What if my brother Larry had not seen your poster that day? What if we never had the opportunity to meet?"

"But that was not the way it was meant to be," Angela Dawn said, laughing softly. "Remember, darling. Destiny."

"Any way we look at it, I still owe my brother a debt for having made it all possible," Red Feather said, going and unknotting the ties at the entrance flap. He gave her a look over his shoulder and wondered why the mention of Larry had changed her mood. There was something in her eyes vastly different than what had been there moments ago.

He went to her. "What did I say?" he asked, searching her eyes. "It is about Larry, isn't it? Why? What does he have to do with any of this except having brought us together?"

Angela Dawn felt trapped. She did not want to tell Red Feather the truth about Larry just yet.

The truth would ruin everything right now.

After the wedding. Then she would tell Red Feather everything.

"No, it's not Larry," she said, forcing a soft laugh. "It's just that everything has happened so fast. My head sometimes seems to spin from it all."

"Yes, mine, too," he said, then took her hand and walked with her from the tepee.

He gave her a half glance, for he sensed that she was not being entirely truthful with him.

He knew that something was bothering her, and he guessed it was about Larry.

284

In time he would get her to tell him. But for now he would leave it alone. He wanted nothing to spoil this newfound happiness.

Especially not his brother Larry.

Because of jealousy, Larry had tried to interfere too often in Red Feather's life.

But not this time.

Damn it, not this time!

Chapter Twenty-nine

Now must I depart from the brother . . .
As I long for your love,
My heart stands still inside me.
  —Love Songs of the New Kingdom

Red Feather stepped into Gray Fox's cabin, surprised by what he saw. He stepped closer to get a better look.

"That is my violin," Gray Fox said proudly when he saw Red Feather's interest.

Red Feather ran a hand over the smooth exterior. "It is so beautiful," he said, then turned to Gray Fox when his brother picked up the violin, and a bow and began playing it.

As Gray Fox pulled the bow across the strings, magical sounds came from the instrument, soft and soothing, sweet and delicate.

Red Feather watched his brother's fingers march across the strings, each new sound that he made more magical than the last.

And then Gray Fox lowered both his violin and the bow. "None of my people play the violin," he said. "Some had never even heard the music of a violin. But one day I passed the concert hall in Jamestown and heard the sweetness of the music wafting from inside it. I followed the sound, as if it was drawing me to it. It was then that I discovered the loveliness of the violin."

"Did you take lessons to learn how to play the instrument?" Red Feather asked, enjoying this exchange of confidences with his younger brother. There could have been such a battle between them over who would follow their father in the chieftainship.

But being a sensitive man, who was grateful to know this brother, Red Feather had never for one moment thought to challenge Gray Fox over the title of chief.

"I took no lessons," Gray Fox said, gently laying his bow and violin down on a soft bed of pelts. "I traded many pelts for my violin. I taught myself the art of playing."

"I see ten pelts lying here," Red Feather said, smiling.

"Do you play for your people often?" he asked as he began walking around the cabin, looking at his brother's other things.

"Whenever my people request it, yes, I do play for them," Gray Fox said, walking slowly beside Red Feather around the front room of the two-room cabin. "Would you like me to play for your wedding? My father has already hinted at it, since he and Soft Flower are exchanging vows on the same day as you and your woman."

Red Feather turned to his brother. He placed a hand on his shoulder. "It would please me so much, my brother, if you would do this for Angela Dawn and me," he said thickly. "Your playing the violin would make our marriage day even more special."

"Then I shall play special music for you," Gray Fox said, beaming.

Then his brother showed Red Feather other things that he was proud of; his second love, after the violin, was making intricately carved wooden figures of animals and birds.

As he showed him his creations, Red Feather felt as though he were walking in a museum, except that every object had been created by his brother.

Something in his brother's bedroom caught Red Feather's eye. He had heard much about the headdresses of Indian chiefs, and how beautiful they were. And here was one in his brother's cabin. He turned to his brother with a question in his eyes.

Gray Fox had followed the path of Red Feather's gaze and saw that he was interested in the headdress that hung from a peg on the wall. It was beautifully decorated with the various feathers that his father had chosen for the head-dress long ago, when he first became chief.

And he understood why Red Feather would be interested in it. Surely his brother knew that the headdress belonged to his father. It would be handed down to the next chief in line only when the chief to whom it belonged had died, or had decided to step down from chieftainship so that his son might take his place.

Yes, it was only natural that Red Feather would question his possession of the headdress. As of now, only Gray Fox knew of his father's decision, which he had revealed just this morning.

"Father brought the headdress to me this morning," Gray Fox said warily. He was not sure how his older brother truly felt about not being able to be chief; usually it was the eldest son who received the honor.

"I thought the headdress of a chief was only given to his successor when the chief passed on," Red Feather said.

"Father has not yet told anyone but me of his decision to step down," Gray Fox said, reaching a hand to the feathers and lovingly running his hand over them.

"I still don't understand," Red Feather said, turning to his brother. "Now, don't take me wrong. I am not upset over you having this, for I have not ever anticipated being chief. But . . ."

"Father wants to leave the chieftainship now so that he can have time with Soft Flower, time that was stolen from him so long ago," Gray Fox said, placing a gentle hand on Red Feather's shoulder. "And . . . I believe he gave me the headdress before he announced his decision in council because he wanted to reassure me. Perhaps he feared that I still did not know for certain it would be I who would be chief, since you are known now to be his firstborn."

"I see," Red Feather murmured. "He did it in this way so that it would set your mind at ease. But, Gray Fox, I thought you knew that I had accepted how it should be."

"I do not believe that Father was sure of your reaction," Gray Fox said, lowering his hand to his side. "He loves me so much, he wanted to give me peace in my heart that I would be chief, for he has known for many moons that I aspired to it. But never would I have expected that it would come so soon, and especially before he passed on to the other side."

"My mother's return has changed a lot, it seems," Red Feather said, nodding. "And so has my sudden appearance in my father's life."

"And it has all been for the good," Gray Fox said softly. "Our father's mental state is better than it has been in many moons. It is good to see him remembering the myths of our people. It made my heart sing yesterday as I listened to my father telling stories to the children."

"Yes, I felt proud and happy, as well," Red Feather said. Then he reached for one of his brother's hands. He squeezed it affectionately. "Gray Fox, it makes my heart glad to know that I have a brother besides Larry." He chuckled. "What a difference there is in my brothers. One is noble, the other is too often a sneak . . . a coward. I do not take pride in speaking of my other brother in such ugly terms, but I am one who always speaks the truth."

"Will you ever introduce me to this brother?" Gray Fox asked as Red Feather lowered his hand and they walked together back into the front room of the cabin.

"Do you want to meet him?" Red Feather asked, raising an eyebrow as he and Gray Fox went through the door and stepped out into the sunshine.

"If he is of your blood, yes, I do wish to know him," Gray Fox said, nodding. "And soon, if possible."

"I think it would be better to wait a while before returning to Ratcliffe Manor," Red Feather said, walking around to the back of the cabin, where a large horse corral was located. "Jon Paul is surely filled with such jealous hatred, he might not even think before lashing out at me. And my brother? Who is to say how he will react to my choice in life."

"He is a prejudiced man?" Gray Fox asked as he stopped at the wood fence, his eyes on Red Feather's beautiful black mustang, which was in the corral.

"My other brother is half Chitimacha," Red Feather said, drawing Gray Fox's eyes quickly back to him. "He has my mother's skin, hair, and eyes. But he has the heart of a white man. And . . . yes, even though his mother is Chitimacha, he does have prejudice toward Indians that he has come face to face with in Jamestown. You see, he wears expensive clothing such as I wore until I chose to embrace my Indian heritage. He would never wear buckskin attire. But he does wear his hair long as you and I do."

"Why?" Gray Fox asked, raising an eyebrow.

"Because when we were children and my mother encouraged me to wear my hair long, as our Chitimacha warriors wear theirs, my brother became jealous of my hair and began to wear his long, as well."

Red Feather gestured toward Gray Fox's streak of gray hair. "If not for the gray threads in your hair, some would find it hard to tell us apart now that I dress like you," he said, smiling. "I am proud of our resemblance."

"As am I," Gray Fox said, then once again turned toward the horses.

Red Feather leaned both hands onto the wooden fence. "I have noticed you watching my steed more than once," Red Feather said. "I believe you recognize its quality."

"Yes, and I have silently wished to ride your horse," Gray Fox said, then turned eagerly toward Red Feather. "Might I ride him now?"

"It pleases me that you admire my horse so much. Yes, take him for a ride," Red Feather said, already walking toward the gate. "I have never had such a horse as this. It is as though we were destined for one another. I chose it for my own when it was newborn, still wobbly on its long, new legs. Everyone who knows me knows my horse."

"I enjoy riding bareback, so do not concern yourself with readying the steed with a saddle," Gray Fox said as he went inside the corral with his brother. He stood aside as Red Feather bridled the horse, then handed the reins to his brother.

"He is yours for as long as you wish to ride him," Red Feather said, proudly watching his brother mount the steed. "Ride far, brother. Enjoy. And know this. You can ride my steed as often as you wish, whenever you wish. He is an astute horse. He will recognize someone who rides him with pride, as I know you will ride him."

"Would you like to ride my horse? Then we could go riding together," Gray Fox suggested as he smoothed a hand along the sleek lines of the stallion's muscled neck.

"No, I'd best not, at least not this time," Red Feather said, walking from the corral as Gray Fox walked the horse out. "Angela Dawn is waiting for me. We have made plans to gather clams for our supper."

Red Feather smiled broadly at Gray Fox. "Would you like to join us for supper?" he asked. "It is so good to have you as a brother. I want much time with you, as much as we can find to spend with one another. I would enjoy being taught the traditions of our people by you."

"I will enjoy being your teacher," Gray Fox said, returning his smile. "Whatever you want to know, just ask your little brother. And, yes, I will gladly join you and Angela Dawn this evening. Thank you for including me."

"It is something I wish to do often, now that we are together," Red Feather said. "Now go. Enjoy. Ride with the wind, Gray Fox."

"And so I shall!" Gray Fox said, sinking his heels into the flanks of the steed and riding away from the village.

Red Feather watched his brother until he could

no longer see him, then turned to go to Angela Dawn. He had left her with Pretty Moon, who was continuing to teach her basketry.

But this was Red Feather's time with his woman. It was time to gather clams for their evening meal, and now the meal would even be more special, for Gray Fox was going to join them.

Chapter Thirty

Love's not Time's fool,
The rosy lips and cheeks
Within his bending sickle's compassion.
                    —William Shakespeare

Sober, and filled with jealousy of Red Feather that he could not shake, Larry was riding his white stallion, on his way to watch the Chitimacha village from the bluff.

He hoped to catch his brother leaving the village alone. If he did, he would kill his half-brother. Then he would finally rid himself of the man who had always bested him in everything. Troy had been a thorn in Larry's side from the day he finally understood that, even though they were brothers, they were as different as they could be.

Larry had purchased a bow and arrow from a pawn shop in Jamestown for the dirty deed. If he killed his brother with a bow and arrow, would not everyone think that an Indian had done it?

He laughed sardonically, thinking that in a sense they would be thinking right . . . for wasn't he part Indian?

Yes, using the bow and arrow would point the blame away from himself, for he had never owned anything that was Indian; he did not take pride in being a breed.

And although he now believed his father would allow him to inherit everything after all, because his other son had betrayed him, Larry still wanted to see Troy dead!

He had ridden halfway between Jamestown and the Chitimacha village when he suddenly saw a rider in the distance.

His heart skipped a beat when he recognized the horse. Gazing at the rider, he was certain that it was his brother riding his favorite black stallion.

Larry guided his horse hurriedly among some trees growing near the river.

He waited for the black stallion to get closer. Smiling, Larry notched the bowstring with an arrow.

He waited until it would be impossible to miss, then sent the arrow flying from the string.

He laughed to himself when he saw the arrow sink into the back of the rider, then watched as he fell from the horse, landing face down in the river.

He watched as the body began slowly floating away in the current.

Turning to flee, Larry tossed the bow and quiver of arrows into some thick brush, then rode from the shadows of the trees and kicked his horse into a hard gallop in the direction of Jamestown.

His deed was done.

He was finally free of the man he had hated for so long. He tried to remember when those feelings had begun inside his heart. He wasn't sure, but he did know that they had worsened by the year as both his mother and father made a difference in the way they treated their sons. It seemed they idolized Troy.

"Now no one can ever do that again," Larry grumbled to himself.

He was free!

He started to laugh, then instead felt an intense shiver race across his flesh, as though he had just been visited by something unseen.

He swallowed hard, looked cautiously from side to side, then rode even harder across the land.

He was no longer feeling as smug, or as alone, as he had moments before.

He was only now realizing the seriousness of what he had done . . . the evil of it.

Chapter Thirty-one

Beauty is but vain and doubtful good,
A shining gloss that fadeth suddenly;
A flower that dies when first it 'gins to bud.
                    —William Shakespeare

Angela Dawn and Red Feather had gone down-river so far they no longer saw the Chitimacha village. They were alone beneath the beautiful blue sky, the sun warm as it poured its rays down from the heavens.

"This is such fun," Angela Dawn said, standing ankle-deep with Red Feather in a shallow part of the river. She wore a pair of moccasins that

Pretty Moon had loaned her. "What is this basket called that we're using?"

"A *kikiti*," Red Feather said as he swept the large sievelike basket along the riverbed. It held the clams while the water ran out through the bottom. "Father explained to me about the *kikiti* and how to use it."

"It seems you were an astute student. Look at the number of clams we've gathered," Angela Dawn said, pride in her eyes as she gazed at the many clams at the bottom of the basket.

"Just a few more and we should have enough for our supper," Red Feather said. "I look forward to having Gray Fox join us. Before he left for his ride, we had such a good time together in his cabin. I am still amazed by how skilled he is at playing the instrument."

"And you said he never even had any lessons?" Angela Dawn asked as she waded alongside Red Feather down the river.

"No, not any lesson whatsoever," Red Feather said. "He could even play in an orchestra and possibly be chosen as first chair first violin."

"First chair . . . first violin . . . ?" Angela Dawn said, her eyes widening in wonder. "How would you know about such things?"

"Because Father acquainted both me and Larry with music when we were old enough to understand what each instrument of an orchestra is called," Red Feather said. "He took me and Larry to New Orleans many times to hear symphony music."

"Your mother didn't go with you?" Angela Dawn asked softly. She flipped her long braids over her shoulders.

"Father was always very careful where he took my mother," Red Feather explained. "He rarely took her where there might be a crowd. I only now understand why. He did not want to take her where there might be someone who would recognize her, who might report back to Chief Straight Arrow about her. Yes, he guarded his secret very well. No one ever guessed he had abducted a Chitimacha princess."

"It must have come as a shock to you to learn the truth about her abduction," Angela Dawn said.

"Yes, it was certainly a shock," Red Feather said. "But I am proud now to know my true heritage and my true father." He smiled over at her. "Mother prepared me well for this change in my life," he said, then started walking toward shore. "Come. I think we have enough clams."

She nodded and walked beside him, gazing up at him when he began talking again in a voice filled with pride.

"Angela Dawn, I want to teach you everything my mother taught me," he said. "For example, the Chitimacha recognizes a Creator of all things under the name of *Thoume Kene Kimte Cacounche*, or *Cawuche*. This Great Spirit has neither eyes nor ears, but sees, understands, and knows everything. In the beginning he placed the earth under the waters. The fish were the first animals he created. He ordered the crawfish to go and search for earth at the bottom of the water, and to bring a mass of it above the surface. They did so. Immediately he formed many men, whom he called Chitimacha, the same name he bestowed upon the land. . . ."

He laughed softly. "As you see, once I begin, I go on and on," he said. "For now, that is enough. We should concentrate on preparing and cooking the clams for our supper."

"I haven't cooked anything like clams before, but Pretty Moon explained how it should be done. I believe I know enough to prepare a delicious supper out of them," Angela Dawn said, moving ahead of him through the water. She wasn't aware that he'd stopped following her, that he had spied something in the river that had caused the blood to drain from his face.

"Angela Dawn, keep walking and do not turn around until I say it is alright," Red Feather said, the alarm in his voice enough to make Angela Dawn stop. "Go to dry land . . . and wait.

"Keep moving, and do . . . not . . . turn around," Red Feather repeated, his voice solemn.

"What is it?" Angela Dawn asked.

"I will tell you when I am certain myself," Red Feather said as the object floated toward him. "Just know that what I see is gruesome."

He saw out of the corner of his eye that Angela Dawn hurried onto the shore and stood there with her back to him, as he had requested.

Then he focused again on the object in the river. He could see now that it was the body of a man floating face down. He knew by the long black hair and by the buckskin clothes that the man was Indian, surely Chitimacha, since the Chitimacha village was the only one near this part of the river. But which Chitimacha warrior? And why would he be there in the river? Had he accidentally drowned?

All Chitimacha children, boys and girls alike, learned to swim almost as soon as they learned to walk. He knew this because his mother had told him so when she taught him and Larry how to swim.

He gasped when he saw something else, now that the current had carried the body so much closer. There was an arrow in the man's back. It was obvious that he had been murdered.

"Red Feather, how much longer must I wait before you tell me what's going on?" Angela Dawn asked, her back still to him.

Red Feather scarcely heard her voice. Now that the body was lying only inches away from him, he saw the gray streak in the midnight-black hair. There was only one man he knew of who had such gray threads among the black.

He felt as though someone had hit him in the gut.

Red Feather cried out his brother's name, dropped the basket of clams, then gently lifted his brother up out of the water and gathered him into his arms. Crying hard now, he began carrying Gray Fox from the water.

Angela Dawn had heard Red Feather cry out his brother's name, his voice filled with despair, and she could now hear that he was crying.

Eyes wide, and no longer able to keep her back to what was happening, she turned and gasped. Her knees grew weak.

She stared disbelievingly at who Red Feather held so tenderly in his arms.

"He is dead," Red Feather cried. "Do you see the arrow in his back? He was murdered! Murdered!"

Angela Dawn placed a hand to her mouth, tears streaming down her face as she watched Red Feather gently lay his brother on the ground on his stomach. He knelt over him and broke the arrow shaft off so that only the head was still embedded in his brother's body.

"Who would do this?" Angela Dawn asked, sobbing. "It had to have been an Indian, since an arrow was used."

"I am not so sure," Red Feather said thickly.

Still on his knees, he tossed the arrow aside, then slowly turned his brother so that he lay on his back, his thick black hair beneath his head like a black veil. Once again, he swept his brother's body into his arms, then started walking slowly toward the Chitimacha village.

"Who would do this?" Angela Dawn asked.

"I will search until I find the murderer, and when I do, he will wish he had never come near Gray Fox," Red Feather said, then walked onward, Angela Dawn keeping quiet at his side.

As they entered the village and everyone recognized the dead warrior in Red Feather's arms, a loud wailing began.

Red Feather walked onward as the crowd of Chitimacha followed him. Red Feather's eyes were on his father's dwelling, his whole heart crying out to his father. Straight Arrow came to his entranceway to see why his people were suddenly mourning.

When Straight Arrow saw one son carrying the other, he teetered and was stopped from collapsing when a warrior raced to his side and gently held him.

Red Feather was alarmed by the way some of the people were looking at him. Their eyes held deep resentment, even accusation.

What if they thought that he had killed Gray Fox so that he could be the next chief?

When Red Feather reached his father, Straight

Arrow eased himself away from the warrior's grip and stared through tears at Gray Fox, then slowly looked at Red Feather with questioning in his eyes.

Just as Red Feather had feared, someone was wondering if *he* might be responsible, and not just *anyone* . . . his *father*.

"Father, no," he blurted out. "Surely you would not believe that I would do this to my brother. I have grown to love Gray Fox in the short time I have known him. This has to have happened because of mistaken identity. Gray Fox was on my horse when he was shot with an arrow. Whoever killed Gray Fox surely thought he was killing me."

Angela Dawn grew pale at the thought of someone having hated Red Feather enough to want him dead, for surely that was how it had happened.

Soft Flower came from her lodge. She went and stood over Gray Fox. She gazed sadly at him, then gave Red Feather a worried look, for she, also, knew that there would be some who would think he was guilty of the crime.

"Mother, Gray Fox was on my horse when he died," Red Feather explained. "Whoever killed him thought I was the victim. If the killer was not close enough to see Gray Fox's gray streak, he would think he was aiming the arrow at me."

He saw alarm enter her eyes, and wondered at the reason for it.

But his attention was drawn away from her when his father reached his arms out for Gray Fox and received him in his own.

Soft Flower walked slowly beside her husband as he carried Gray Fox out toward the center of the village for everyone to see. But she could not stop worrying about who had done this, her own suspicions making her heartsick.

But, oh, surely not . . . surely Jon Paul hadn't tried to kill Red Feather.

Yes, she had her own idea who might have committed this murder, but she kept silent, hoping she was wrong.

Angela Dawn clung to Red Feather's arm as they walked behind Straight Arrow and Soft Flower.

Red Feather watched, his eyes filled with tears of despair, as his father laid his brother on blankets that warriors quickly spread out for his body.

Everyone formed a wide circle around the fallen warrior and his family.

Straight Arrow turned to Red Feather. He held a hand out for him.

Red Feather took it, and at his father's urging, knelt with him beside Gray Fox. Soft Flower and Angela Dawn stayed back, watching.

Straight Arrow raised his eyes and gazed around him at his people, who still had suspicion in their faces as they glanced occasionally at Red Feather.

"Hear me well, my people, and hear me only this once, because I do not want to be given cause to announce it again: My firstborn son did not kill my secondborn; brother did not kill brother," he said, his voice flat with authority as he held his mourning at bay long enough to clear the name of his only remaining son. "It was not Red Feather who did this thing. It was someone else. It had to have been someone who thought Gray Fox was Red Feather, because he was riding Red Feather's steed."

He frowned from person to person. "Now if any of you wish to challenge this, do it now or forever hold your tongue and speak no ill against my son Red Feather," he commanded.

He waited and watched.

When no one came forward or offered a challenge, he nodded, then turned to Soft Flower and, with an outstretched hand, beckoned for her to come to him. Red Feather beckoned in the same manner toward Angela Dawn.

Both women came forth.

Angela Dawn knelt beside Red Feather as his mother knelt beside her husband.

As though with one voice, the whole village began wailing and mourning the man who would have been their chief.

Angela Dawn was filled with many emotions.

She was sad, yet angry in the same heartbeat, for she was almost certain who had done this terrible deed. It could only be the work of a deranged man, crazed by jealousy. It was the same sort of violent yet cowardly act as the killing of her father.

A man who would shoot a man in the back with an arrow would be the same sort of man who would fire before it was time to shoot his dueling pistol. That man undoubtedly was Larry Ratcliffe!

She felt guilty now for not having revealed what she had learned about Larry sooner.

Chapter Thirty-two

> The little birds that tune
> Their morning's joy,
> Make her moans mad with
> The sweet melody.
> —William Shakespeare

The sound of a soft voice outside his bedroom door awakened Jon Paul.

He licked his lips, cringing when he discovered the dried taste of whiskey there, reminding him why he was in bed at this time of day in the first place. Judging by the slant of the sun splashing through the spaces at the sides of the drawn drapes, he guessed it was past the noon hour.

He had drunk himself almost mindless the night before. Fortunately, he had slept off the worst of it.

All that remained besides the taste on his lips was a slight headache. Other than that, he felt almost human again, until he stopped and thought about what had sent him into such a bout of drinking in the first place.

He had lost a wife and a son. Although he knew they were alright, to him they were the same as dead.

"Massah Ratcliffe," little Hannah said again outside his door, this time louder. "I knows you don' like to be disturbed, but, massah, you needs to know that Massah Troy's horse has came to the plantation without the massah."

"What?" Jon Paul said.

He hurried from the bed, slipped his breeches on, then opened the door and gazed down at the child. "Young lady, what did you just say about Troy's horse?" he asked, raking his fingers through his thick hair.

"It came home without Massah Troy," Hannah said, nervously wringing her tiny hands as she gazed with frightened eyes up at Jon Paul. "I knows you would want to hear. Usually when I sees the horse, I also sees the massah."

Fear grabbed Jon Paul's heart.

The child was right.

If the horse had returned without Troy in its

saddle, that could only mean one thing. Something had happened to his son.

Yes, his son.

He still could not think of Troy as anything but his son. He had adored Troy for too long, not to still love him.

And if anything had happened to him, Jon Paul would truly understand the meaning of loss. It would be worse than losing his son to the Chitimacha people.

"Thank you, child," Jon Paul said, then, barefoot, went past her and rushed down the stairs.

When he stood on the porch, gazing down at the black stallion, and saw how nervous the animal looked, Jon Paul was sure that something had happened to Troy.

He noticed that there was no saddle on the horse. Could someone have ambushed Troy for the expensive Mexican saddle?

When he had bought it for Troy for his last birthday, he had worried that it might tempt someone to steal it.

But Troy was adept at defending himself; Jon Paul had taught him the art of shooting a gun when he was just big enough to hold a weapon in his small hand.

Hannah came out on the porch and stared at the horse, and then up at Jon Paul. "Where is Massah Troy?" she asked. "Does you think he's hurt?"

"I don't know, but I am not going to waste any more time before finding out," he said thickly. "Go and tell the stable boy to saddle my horse, and tell him I said to hurry."

"Yes suh, massah, suh," Hannah said, then rushed down the steps as Jon Paul hurried back into the house.

When he reached his bedroom, he quickly dressed, slid his pearl-handled pistol into the front pocket of his coat, slammed a hat on his head, then hurried out to the stable where his strawberry roan was saddled and ready for riding.

He tipped his hat as a thank you to the young stable hand, nodded a silent thank you to Hannah for alerting him about the horse, then rode off in the direction of the Indian village.

He had to check there first, to find out when Troy was last seen. He would even ask help of the Chitimacha in the search for him.

Perhaps he had only been left wounded, not dead, when the saddle was stolen.

No matter what Troy had done, or had decided to do with his life, Jon Paul couldn't help loving him with all his heart.

And, oh, how he regretted what he had done to his precious Jewel.

But he had been blinded with rage and hurt when he had taken her to the slave quarters. His heart ached even now when he recalled how he had hit her.

No amount of alcohol could erase the look on her face after he'd hit her, or the pleading and the hurt in her eyes when he had taken her to the slave quarters and left her there in shackles.

"And now Troy?" he whispered harshly to himself. "I hope nothing has happened to my son. . . ."

Yes, the only way out for him if he discovered that Troy was dead would be to go home, place a pistol at his temple, and take his own life. That would be the only way he could get away from the misery of having lost his son not once, but twice; first to the Chitimacha, and then to death.

If by chance Troy, or Red Feather as he called himself now, was still alive, Jon Paul wanted to beg his forgiveness for having treated him like a savage the last time they were together.

And he wanted to beg Jewel's forgiveness. Then he would leave them both in peace.

He would begin life anew.

But he wasn't sure what he would do about Larry. That boy always seemed to be in trouble in one way or another. He hated thinking about leaving his wealth to such a man as Larry.

But one thing was for certain. Even though he was ready to accept what his older son and wife had chosen to do with their lives, they could never be included in his will.

He could not completely forgive them for turning their backs on him completely. He was probably the laughingstock of the white community.

He had decided to liquidate all of his assets and move out of the area. In a new town he could hold his head up again.

He had also decided that he would not ask Larry to accompany him. He could not spend the rest of his life bailing Larry out of one scrape after another.

As for the inheritance? In time, Jon Paul would even figure that out.

For now, his main concern was Red Feather.

Yes, Red Feather! Although it was hard to say, and especially to accept, Red Feather was his name now, and would be forevermore.

"If he is still alive, that is," Jon Paul gulped out.

He sank his heels into his steed's flanks and rode at a harder gallop beside the river, which would lead him to the Chitimacha village.

He was not much of a praying man, but today he could not say enough prayers that his son was alive and well.

Chapter Thirty-three

So, either by thy picture or my love,
Thyself away art present still with me.
　　　　　　—William Shakespeare

Even before Jon Paul arrived at the Chitimacha village, he knew that something was wrong there. He knew enough about Indian culture to know that when Indians wailed, it meant someone of their village had died.

His heart ached and his hopes of finding Troy—no, Red Feather—alive dwindled.

Tears burned at the corners of his eyes. He dreaded seeing Red Feather dead. But he had to go on. He had to see Red Feather one last time.

And then he would leave and never interfere in Jewel's life again, nor in the Chitimacha's.

He didn't stop to consider how the Chitimacha might receive him. Only recently they had discovered that he had deceived them through the years by holding one of their women hostage. But he was determined to say a final goodbye to this young man who was so much a part of him; Jon Paul rode on into the village.

His throat constricted as he fought back the urge to cry out in mourning, himself, when he saw how the Chitimacha stood in a wide circle, their wails reaching heavenward, their eyes on something on the ground.

Were they circled around Red Feather? Did he lie on the ground amid them?

When he reached the people, he stiffened when they all turned and stared at him. Their movement made a gap in the crowd, so Jon Paul could see through and view the body stretched out on the ground, lifeless.

He saw the long, flowing hair first.

And then he glimpsed the face and saw enough to be sure that it was Red Feather lying there, the victim of someone's greed.

Forcing himself to hold back his tears, trying to be strong because everyone was still staring at him with resentment and hatred, he dismounted, then hesitated as Jewel broke away from the others and ran to him.

Her eyes swollen from crying told him that, it was indeed their son lying there!

He was not sure what he should do. He so badly wished to reach out for her and hold her.

"Jewel, I'm so sorry . . ." he gulped out, looking past her at the body which he so badly wanted to go and embrace.

But again, he knew that he would be out of place doing that.

The young man who lay there was no blood kin to him. He was the son of a powerful Indian chief!

Just the same, he wanted a last moment with the young man he'd raised.

"May I go to him?" Jon Paul asked. "Jewel, I . . . still . . . love him."

"You never knew him, so how could you have loved him?" Soft Flower said, searching his eyes to try and understand his reaction to the death of someone he'd never even known.

"In a way, no, I guess I didn't, but, Jewel, he . . . was . . . my son for so long," he said, his voice breaking. "I'm sorry for all that I said. I . . . do . . . not truly see him, or you, as savages. Please let me say goodbye to him; then I shall never bother you again."

Red Feather had stood listening, standing where Jon Paul could not have seen him, and he suddenly realized that Jon Paul thought that he was the one lying there dead. From where he stood, Jon Paul could not have a close enough look at the face to know the difference. Just as the one who'd murdered Gray Fox had not known the difference.

"Then it was not you who did this horrible thing?" Soft Flower said, so glad to know that Jon Paul's hatred for her and Red Feather had not caused him to do something so terrible as to kill the man he had thought of as his son for so long.

The humiliation of losing both Red Feather and Soft Flower had not made him mindless enough to kill.

"No. How could you think I could?" Jon Paul asked. He started to reach out for her, but stopped when the old chief stepped into view.

Then Jon Paul saw someone else stepping up beside the chief, and gasped. He stared, then smiled and rushed through the crowd to clasp Red Feather in his arms.

"I thought you were dead," Jon Paul cried. "Your horse. It came home without you. I . . . I . . . thought that was because someone had killed you."

"No, it was not I who was killed, but someone mistaken for me," Red Feather said, feeling Jon Paul's tremendous relief.

Jon Paul hugged Red Feather one last time, then stepped away from him, his eyes filled with questions. "Who *did* die?" he gulped out. "And . . . why?"

"The fallen warrior was on my stallion when he was ambushed," Red Feather said thickly. "Whoever killed him thought he was killing me."

"But . . . why . . . ?" Jon Paul said, his voice drawn. "Who would want you dead?"

Then Jon Paul sighed. "The saddle," he said, slowly shaking his head back and forth. "It was for that expensive Mexican saddle. It was not on your horse when the animal returned to the plantation."

"My saddle is in my lodge," Red Feather said. "Gray Fox enjoyed riding bareback. That is how he was riding when someone shot an arrow into his back."

"An . . . arrow . . . ?" Jon Paul gasped. "This was done by another Indian?"

"We do not know who is responsible, but we shall find out, then make him pay," Red Feather said.

Soft Flower came to Red Feather's side, along with Angela Dawn.

Each woman took one of Red Feather's hands.

"I thought you hated Red Feather and me so much, you might have killed Red Feather out of humiliation and rage," Soft Flower said. "I am so glad I was wrong."

"I could never do anything like that," Jon Paul said, visibly shuddering.

Then Jon Paul stepped closer to Soft Flower. "Since I am here, please let me say a few words to you," he said, then shifted his gaze to Red Feather. "And you."

He gazed into Soft Flower's eyes again. "I want to apologize to you for everything I ever did to hurt you," he said thickly. "I've made a decision. Jewel, I'm going to sell out and leave the area, but I can't unless I first make peace with both you and Red Feather."

"You are calling him Red Feather," Soft Flower said, touched by that mark of acceptance, when she knew that every time he spoke the name, it must be cutting small pieces of his heart away.

"That is his true name, isn't it?" Jon Paul said, smiling at Red Feather. "Yes, I accept that Red Feather is his real name, as I accept that he is where he should have been a long time ago."

"I am so glad that you have had a change of heart," Soft Flower said, but when he reached his arms out for her for a final embrace, she couldn't find it in her heart to completely forgive him.

Those hours in the slave quarters were imbedded in her mind and heart forever, as was the fact that he had denied her her true heritage for so long.

"But you can't forgive me?" Jon Paul asked, his voice drawn.

"You have accepted Red Feather's name; so

must you accept mine as Soft Flower, not Jewel," she said tightly.

Then she said nothing more to him, but instead stared past him, as though he were no longer there.

When he saw that she had said all that she was going to say, that she could truly not forgive him, he turned to Red Feather. He held out a hand. "I won't ask for your forgiveness, but at least give me a handshake as I wish you a good future with your people?" he asked, his eyes pleading. "Red Feather, a father could have never been prouder of a son than I was . . . as I am . . . of you."

Red Feather thought for a minute, then held out his hand and grasped Jon Paul's. "I thank you for all that you gave me, but know that I can never forgive what you denied me," he said, his voice tight.

"I understand," Jon Paul said, swallowing hard.

Then he looked at the fallen warrior. "Who died today?" he asked. "There is such a resemblance . . ."

"That is my brother who lies there," Red Feather said, sighing heavily. "I only knew him for a little while, and now he is gone from me forever. Too often life is unfair."

"Your . . . brother . . . ?" Jon Paul said, his gaze slowly shifting to the old chief, who was kneeling beside his fallen son.

"His name was Gray Fox," Red Feather said.

"I knew him for such a short time but loved him greatly. I shall miss him. And . . . I hope to find the one who robbed me of so much. Now I will never ride side by side with my brother, or join the hunt with him."

"Who could have . . . ?" Jon Paul asked, kneading his chin. "Who could hate you so much that he would want you dead?"

"In time I will discover the killer's identity," Red Feather said tightly. "When I learn who did this, he will pay, and pay dearly."

Jon Paul was shocked to hear such hate and venom in Red Feather's voice. He was known for his kindness and gentleness. But now? It was indeed a new day for Red Feather.

"I will go now," Jon Paul said, glancing momentarily at Angela Dawn, who had stood so quietly beside Red Feather. He tipped his hat to her, gave Soft Flower a lengthy, soft stare, then went to his horse and rode away from the village.

Soft Flower felt nothing but pity for this man who had come today thinking Red Feather was dead. Except for Larry, he was alone in the world.

Her eyebrows rose when she thought of Larry. She had at first thought that Jon Paul might have killed Gray Fox, thinking he was Red Feather. She was relieved to know that she was wrong.

But now that she had more time to think about it, there was someone else who might have hated and resented Red Feather enough to want him dead.

"Larry," she whispered, her face draining of color.

She shuddered at the thought of her other son harboring such hatred in his heart that he might be capable of murder.

Then she felt awash with guilt. She had favored one son too much over the other, because this one was full-blood Chitimacha. Had her unequal treatment of her sons caused one brother to hate the other so much that he wanted him dead?

She gave Red Feather a sideways glance.

She wondered if he, too, was thinking the guilty party might be Larry.

Chapter Thirty-four

On his tongue they pour sweet dew,
And from his mouth flow gentle words.
> —Hesiod

Angela Dawn was touched by the way the Chitimacha buried their dead. The deceased was
placed in an earthen mound, along with many
shells. Soft Flower had explained to Angela Dawn
that this type of clam shell was called *rangia*. The
belief was that the shells ensured that the deceased had food for his or her final journey.

At the burial, Gray Fox's body was placed in
this earthen mound, and in the same mound were

placed some of his favorite possessions, among them his beloved violin.

Angela Dawn had been told that after one year had passed, there would be a ceremony at the grave. Since he was the son of a great chief, and would have been a chief himself one day, Gray Fox's bones would be dug up by the *osh-ba-tchna*, the Chitimacha mortician.

The flesh that remained on the bones would be wrapped in a new cane mat and taken to the ceremonial lodge.

All of the Chitimacha of the village would assemble there, walk six times around a blazing fire, after which the bones would be placed back in the mound.

Then Gray Fox's family, which would include Angela Dawn since she would be Red Feather's wife, would take part in a ceremonial dance.

She would never forget what Chief Straight Arrow had said over his son's grave—that at death, only the body perishes, but the spirit of life never dies.

He had said that when the spirit is separated from the body in death, it visits unknown lands, until returning into the bosom of a woman. Then it is reborn and assumes a new course of life in this world.

That was the first time Angela Dawn had known people who truly believed in rebirth.

She had thought of her mother and father at that time and had wondered if it was true. It gave her a warm feeling, to think that they would live again, somehow, somewhere. . . .

The burial and mourning were now behind the Chitimacha people. Today was the day that the first hunt for Gray Fox's killer would take place.

Little did Red Feather know it, but Angela Dawn was going to be on her own hunt, and she knew *her* destination—Ratcliffe Manor.

She had already placed a ball in the chamber of one of her father's dueling pistols.

Her aim would be as accurate as her father's would have been had he had a fair chance to shoot his firearm on the day of the duel.

Yes, that coward Larry Ratcliffe would finally pay for not only her father's murder, but Gray Fox's, as well, for she was sure that he was the one responsible for that crime, too.

Angela Dawn stood outside the tepee she shared with Red Feather. She was watching the Chitimacha warriors gather on their horses in the center of the village.

She gave Red Feather a weak smile as he walked to her and took her hands in his.

"Angela Dawn, while I'm gone, will you keep an eye on my mother?" Red Feather asked, his eyes searching hers. "She seems strangely withdrawn, and I do not know why. She scarcely knew my brother Gray Fox, yet ever since the day of his murder, I have noticed this strange behavior."

"I'm sure it's only because she knows how much your father is hurting over having lost his son. She hurts for her husband because she loves your father so much," Angela Dawn said, but she did not believe her own words.

She believed that Soft Flower also suspected that Larry Ratcliffe was responsible for the death of Gray Fox. Soft Flower would not ever speak of her suspicions to anyone, because she probably hoped that she was wrong.

Yes, it would be hard to imagine a son who might be guilty of such a crime as murder, a murder that he had committed while thinking he was killing his own brother.

A mother could be tormented by this, for surely no crime could be as horrendous as a brother killing a brother.

"Yes, I have thought that might be the cause of my mother's withdrawal, myself," Red Feather said solemnly. "And I'm sure there is nothing you can do, so don't worry yourself about it. Mother and Father are together, gathering strength from one another."

"Their love will get them through this because they have one another," Angela Dawn said, her voice breaking. "When I lost my mother after so recently losing my father, I was alone. I had no one. It was hard, but I did get through it."

"And now you have me," Red Feather said. He

twined his arms around her waist and drew her close. Their eyes met and held. "Angela Dawn, all morning since breakfast I've noticed something different about you. An uneasiness. Is it because you are concerned about me? You know that I will be safe. Look at the warriors who are accompanying me on the hunt."

"But how can anyone forget that the deadly arrow that claimed your brother's life was meant for you?" Angela Dawn said, swallowing hard. "If the person who did this hears that you are alive, surely he will try again."

"I hope he does, because I am ready for him," Red Feather said in a low growl. "I would enjoy seeing this man take his last breath of life."

Angela Dawn looked past him and saw that the warriors were wearing black streaks of paint on their faces, and were clothed only in loincloths and moccasins.

They carried a various assortment of weapons. Some had bows and arrows, some carried war clubs, and others had rifles in their gunboots at the sides of their horses. All wore sheathed knives at their waists.

Then she stepped away from Red Feather and gazed at him.

He, too, wore only a loincloth with moccasins, which made him truly look like a full-blood Chitimacha.

He wore a beaded headband which held his

hair back from his face, and his face was also streaked with black. He wore his prized red feather in his hair, the one his mother had given to him on the day she revealed many truths.

"You know that whoever sees you will know by the paint on your face that you and the warriors are on the warpath," Angela Dawn murmured. "What if the white authorities see you? Will they feel threatened? Will they possibly try to arrest you?"

"I asked my father the same, and he told me that the white authorities never interfere in the lives of the Chitimacha, especially when my people have the fire of vengeance in their bellies. As long as our vengeance does not interfere with their laws, they will leave us alone," Red Feather said. "So do not concern yourself with that. Just wait patiently for my return. If it is my destiny, I will return victorious."

"Please be careful," Angela Dawn said, placing a gentle hand on his face.

"And you stay here away from all danger," Red Feather said, imploring her with his dark eyes. "I am worried about you today. Are you going to be alright as you await my return?"

For a moment Angela Dawn lowered her eyes, for she felt as though she was betraying Red Feather by not being truthful with him about what she was planning.

But she could not share her plans with anyone,

especially him, because he would stop her from going. And she had to do this.

Yes, she had waited too long to act after learning who her father's killer was.

No one would stop her today. When the sun set on the horizon, she hoped to be free of this ache in her heart that carrying the need for vengeance had caused.

Yes, she had no choice but to lie to her beloved, for she knew that this might be her only opportunity to go alone to the mansion and confront Larry.

Ah, but she had it all planned so well in her mind. Now all she had to do was bring her plans to fruition.

Then she could resume her life with the man she loved with a free mind. She could give her all to him.

"Angela Dawn, do you see what I mean?" Red Feather asked. He placed a finger beneath her chin and lifted it so that he could look directly into her eyes again. "You are acting peculiar."

"I'm just so afraid that I might lose you." She flung herself into his arms, knowing that what she had just said was true, but the full truth could not be told. Her peculiar behavior had mainly to do with Larry Ratcliffe.

"And I will tell you again that nothing is going to happen to me," Red Feather reassured her.

He leaned her away from him. Their eyes met and held.

"I shall be home soon," he said softly. "I shall hold you again. I shall whisper my love for you against your beautiful lips. Just think of that, my darling, until my return, will you?"

"Yes," Angela Dawn gulped out. "Yes, I shall."

"Then I must leave you," Red Feather said. "The warriors are ready. They are as anxious as I to find my brother's killer. I vowed to my father that we would search until he is found. If it cannot be done in one day, then we will proceed a day at a time until we succeed."

"My heart goes with you," Angela Dawn said, swallowing hard. "Now go, Red Feather. You have wasted enough time with this worrisome woman."

He smiled, then turned on a heel and went to mount his steed.

The women, children, the elderly, and those warriors who were staying behind to protect the village stood in clusters, watching as the warriors rode from the village, shouting out war cries which raised goose bumps on Angela Dawn's flesh.

The goose bumps were not only in response to the fearsome war cries, but also in anticipation of her own departure.

She could not help being apprehensive about what she proposed to do. She had never gone after a man with a pistol before. She had never hungered to sink a bullet into a man's gut—not until someone had shot one into her father's back.

"It will soon be over," Angela Dawn whispered as she hurried back into her lodge.

She dressed in a travel skirt, blouse, and boots. Then she left the tepee and went behind the lodges, where the horses were corralled. She readied one of them for riding.

Returning to her lodge, she got her father's dueling pistols, took them to the horse, and slid them into the saddlebag.

Not wanting anyone to see her, she led the horse around the corral into the shadows of the live oaks. She walked the animal far enough away so that when she mounted it, no one would hear the hoofbeats.

When she reached that point, she mounted the white steed, and with a pounding heart rode off in the direction of the mansion.

She had never been as determined to achieve a goal as she was now. She could not fail!

Chapter Thirty-five

> I dream of a red rose tree,
> And which of its roses three
> Is the dearest rose to me?
>   —Robert Browning

As she dismounted in front of Ratcliffe Manor, Angela Dawn was full of fear over what she had planned.

She secured her reins on the hitching rail and stared up at the three-story edifice.

Never had she imagined there could be a house as grand as this, or that she might have had a chance to live in it. If she had chosen Larry over Red Feather, every day of her life would be one of luxury. She would never want for a thing . . . except true love, devotion, and trust.

Larry was not capable of any of those emotions. She would rather be homeless than share a house, or a bed, with that cad.

But she wasn't going to be homeless. She had a home. She had a man who loved her. She was in love with that man. She adored him.

And what she planned to do today was not only for herself, but also for Red Feather.

But . . . could she, in the end, really pull the trigger?

She firmed her jaw.

Yes.

All she had to do was picture her parents' faces and she was flooded with courage to take the life of the man who had destroyed her family.

She knew that she had a choice. She could go to the authorities in Jamestown and tell them about Larry Ratcliffe and what he was guilty of.

But she understood that the name Ratcliffe was well known by everyone in the community. Jon Paul owned much of Jamestown. Surely the authorities were under his thumb.

She sighed heavily as she took one step and then another toward the front door. She paused before knocking. Once she entered the house, there would be no way she could back down.

She reminded herself that by the end of the day, all this ugliness would be behind her. And the authorities would have no idea where to look for the killer.

She would be the last on a list of suspects, for no one knew that she had cause to want the man dead.

She stiffened. The servants! If they were alerted that she had come to see Larry, and that she'd left with him, they could point an accusing finger at her.

So she quickly made a change in her plans. She walked into the house without knocking.

She held her breath, hoping that she would not come face to face with Jon Paul. He alone could foil her plan.

Then she remembered that he had said he was going to leave the area. Undoubtedly, he had much to do in Jamestown, liquidating his assets. She hoped he was there today.

Her pulse racing, Angela Dawn stopped and gazed down the long corridor, then up the winding staircase. She wasn't sure where to look for Larry first, but she needed to act quickly, before any of the servants saw her.

She smelled the scent of a cigar. But who was smoking it? Jon Paul? Or Larry?

She had no choice but to take the chance that it was not Jon Paul.

She followed the scent into the library and found Larry there, alone. He was relaxing, smoking and reading before a slow fire in the fireplace.

A long-stemmed glass of port sat on a table beside his plush, overstuffed chair.

Fortunately, he did not look drunk. She wanted him to have all of his faculties today so that when she made him face up to his sins, he would be very aware of who she truly was . . . who her father was.

"Hello, Larry," she said as she strolled into the room.

She gave him a forced smile when he yanked the cigar from his mouth and looked over his shoulder at her.

"Angela Dawn?" he said, looking thunderstruck. "Why are you here? Why aren't you with the savages?"

He placed his cigar on an ashtray and rose from his chair.

His gaze moved slowly over her. "And where is the savage attire?" he taunted. "Or have you had second thoughts and come to your senses about living with those flea-bitten redskins?"

"I've changed my mind about a lot of things, Larry," Angela Dawn purred, lying. She went to him and placed a gentle hand on his smooth, copper face. "I've decided that I don't want to live like a heathen among the Indians . . . or savages, as you call them. I've decided that I'd rather be with you, not your brother Troy. Do you still want me?"

"Do I?" he said, his eyes gleaming. "You know

that I do—that is, if you're serious. I thought you wanted my brother. What changed your mind?"

"I got a taste of what it was going to be like living at the village," she said, shuddering to make what she was saying more believable. "I want to live here with you, not with a man who has turned himself into a savage."

She stepped away from him and slowly walked around the room, her fingers gliding over pieces of furniture, her gaze stopping on expensive paintings and books.

"This is what I want," she said softly. "It has always been my dream to be rich, to live the life of the affluent in such a house as Ratcliffe Manor."

She turned and smiled devilishly at him. "Can I stay?" she murmured. "Can I, Larry?"

Excited that she had come to him, that she had chosen him over Troy, especially now that he had received word about the killing of Gray Fox and knew he hadn't killed his brother after all, Larry went to her and framed her face between his hands.

"You just don't know how much your coming here means to me," he said huskily.

He couldn't tell her the true extent of his pleasure, for she would then know that he had tried to kill Troy, and he knew that she didn't hate Troy enough to want him dead.

But having her with him was the best way possible now to get back at his brother since his attempt at murdering him had failed.

"Then why don't we get to know each other a little better?" Angela Dawn asked, gazing flirtatiously into his eyes. "In private."

"In private?" Larry asked.

"Why don't we go horseback riding, where we can be alone?" Angela Dawn said. "You could show me the grounds. I've been enthralled by the lagoons and bridges. Surely there are more things that I have not seen."

"Yeah, lots," Larry said. "And if it means being alone with you, hell, yes, let's go. And anyhow, it might be my last chance to see the place myself."

"And why is that?" Angela Dawn asked, acting as though she knew nothing of his father's plans.

"Father is going to sell the place and move elsewhere," Larry said, walking with her from the room. He looked hurriedly at her. "But don't let that alarm you. We will have as grand a home wherever we settle. My father is too accustomed to luxury to give up this grandeur."

"Why is he selling?" Angela Dawn asked, still pretending not to know.

"Because of my damn brother, that's why," Larry said as they went outside. He stopped beside his horse, which he had left saddled and tied at the hitching rail. "Because of Troy, everything's changed. But in the end, moving will be better, anyway. I'm ready for a fresh start somewhere else. I'd like to put as many miles as I can between myself and that brother of mine. If you want to know the truth, I hate him with a passion."

When he came to her, Angela Dawn allowed him to help her mount.

She looked up at the house, then all around her to see if anyone had witnessed their departure. She saw no one.

"It's too bad you hate your brother so much," Angela Dawn murmured as he swung himself into his saddle, and then they rode off together. "You see, I never had a brother or sister. At times I felt so lonely as a child."

"I'll make certain you'll never be lonely again," Larry said, winking at her. "If you know what I mean."

She gave him a forced smile. Then they rode farther away from the house, past the sugarcane and tobacco fields, where fortunately there were no slaves working today. She wondered why, then shrugged and continued riding alongside Larry.

As they rode, he pointed out many beautiful flower gardens, and stopped where a gazebo had been built beside a pond aglow with colorful water lilies.

After they dismounted, Angela Dawn looked cautiously around to see if they were totally alone. The gazebo was completely secluded; there was not another soul in sight.

"I'm glad we've stopped," she said, turning toward her saddlebag. "I've something to show you."

"Oh? What?" Larry asked, walking toward her.

"These," Angela Dawn said, yanking both pistols from the bag.

She turned to Larry and saw his eyebrows rise as he stared at the pistols.

Her heart raced as she came closer to the moment of truth. Could she actually kill a man?

"Larry, do you recognize these pistols?" she asked, holding them both out for him to examine.

"A dueling pistol is a dueling pistol," Larry said, laughing and shrugging. "There is no difference except who uses them."

"Take one," Angela Dawn said, holding one farther out, closer to him.

"Alright," he said, taking one.

Then he smiled crookedly. "Now what?" he said in a teasing fashion. "Are we going to have a duel?"

"That's the general idea when a dueling pistol is offered to a gentleman, isn't it?" Angela Dawn said, her pulse racing.

"Alright, I'm game," Larry said, chuckling. "So you want to have a duel? Alright. I'll walk off the distance that is required for a normal duel, then turn and fire. You know that the one who is the most accurate shot will be the winner."

"Yes, that's right," Angela Dawn said. "I'm glad you are taking me seriously, Larry, for I do want to participate in a duel with you."

Ready to continue with her teasing, Larry turned his back and started walking away from her, then stopped and turned and gave her a strange look.

"You are jesting, aren't you?" he asked.

"If you want to call it that," Angela Dawn said, her eyes flashing as he studied her. "So let's do it, Larry. Turn and continue walking away from me. Then wheel around and face me when you know it's time to fire the pistol."

He chuckled. "I've never met anyone quite like you, but alright, I'll play the game," he said, again placing his back to her and walking away from her. "But tell me when you're finished with your fun. I have other things to show you, things that will be a lot more fun for both of us."

"This is what I call true fun, Larry," Angela Dawn said smoothly. She pulled back the hammer of her pistol, then cocked it and had it ready for firing.

Larry stopped abruptly when he heard the unmistakable click that meant that she had cocked her firearm.

He now realized that she had been playing a game with him, alright, but not a playful one.

Her game was to kill him, though he couldn't imagine why.

He stood still.

He was afraid to turn and face her.

He couldn't take the chance that she would shoot him.

"Alright, enough is enough," he said, trying to find a way to talk sense into her. "What is your game? Why are you doing this?"

"Why?" Angela Dawn said smoothly. "Larry, the other day you threw a lot of things out into the corridor. I saw them. Stop and think about a cane that you stole a few months ago from a dead man . . . a man whom you killed in a duel, a man who never had the chance to draw because you turned before you were supposed to and heartlessly shot him in the back. I found a cane among those belongings that you threw into the corridor in a fit of rage. That cane was my father's. The pistol you are holding now was my father's. So is the one that I'm holding. They were my father's dueling pistols, which were left behind when the killer fled the scene of the crime. You knew their worth, but you left them behind because you were afraid they would eventually lead the authorities to you. You took the cane because you didn't think anyone could identify it as belonging to the man you had killed."

"A cane is a cane," he shouted. "You are wrong. That cane you found in the corridor was mine. Yes, perhaps it looked like your father's. Surely many of the same design were made at the same time. You are wrong, Angela Dawn. I didn't kill your father. You're insane."

"No, I'm not wrong, and I'm far from being insane," Angela Dawn said stiffly. "On the bottom of that cane are my mother's and my name, which my father carved there. They were worn so much from his use of the cane that only those of us who knew they were there would notice them. The cane proved to me that you are the coward who heartlessly murdered my father in cold blood. I purposely tracked you down. I seized the opportunity to travel free to Louisiana in hopes of somehow finding my father's murderer, because my father was killed in Jamestown. There were no witnesses to the duel. The men who found my father's body couldn't tell me he was killed by a half-breed."

She laughed. "Ah, had I known that, I would have known when I met you and learned of your love of gambling that you were the ruthless killer," she said. "I am paying you back today. Turn and face me. I won't shoot you in the back the way you killed Gray Fox with an arrow."

"How do you know that?" he gasped out. "No one saw me—"

"No one had to," Angela Dawn said. "All I had to do was put two and two together. Someone who would shoot my father in such a cowardly way would just as easily and heartlessly kill Gray Fox, thinking it was his brother, a man he was insanely jealous of."

"You won't be able to prove a damn thing, especially when you're dead," Larry growled. "And, yes, I admit to both murders. But I won't let you kill me."

Taken off guard, Angela Dawn gasped as she saw him wheel around, cock his pistol, and aim.

She flinched when she heard the report of the gun before she had a chance to fire her own.

Chapter Thirty-six

Her lips to mine how often hath she joined,
Between each kiss her oaths of true love
   swearing!
How many tales to please me hath she
   coined,
Dreading, my love, the loss thereof still
   fearing.

            —William Shakespeare

Thinking that Larry had fired, Angela Dawn froze and waited for the bullet to enter her body, but instead, to her utter surprise, she saw a bullet slam into Larry's chest.

Still too stunned to move, Angela Dawn

347

watched Larry drop the dueling pistol and grab at his chest as blood seeped out onto his white shirt. He gave her a strange look, fell to his knees, then keeled over, dead. Angela Dawn gazed at him in wonder for a moment longer, then looked at her pistol.

She hadn't fired it.

Then . . . who . . . ?

She turned and saw Red Feather step out from the dark shadow of the trees, a rifle in his right hand.

"Red Feather?" she gasped out. "How . . . ?"

He hurried to her and dropped his rifle to the ground, then drew her into his arms and held her close. "Angela Dawn, I noticed too many signs that something was wrong this morning," he said, his gaze looking past her at his slain brother. "The more I thought about it, the more I became alarmed about your behavior. I circled around and left the hunt to see if you were alright. When I found you gone, I went on a desperate search for you. When I saw you and Larry from a distance, riding together on my father's estate grounds, I followed. Then when I saw you stop and take out the dueling pistols, I came as quickly as I could. I left my horse back in the trees and came the rest of the way on foot so that Larry wouldn't see me. When I got close enough, I stopped and listened to what was being said."

"Then . . . you . . . heard him admit killing two

men?" Angela Dawn asked, stepping away from him to gaze into his eyes. "You know that he is the one who killed my father . . . and . . . Gray Fox?"

"Yes, and I was ready to step out into the open when Larry suddenly turned, ready to kill you," Red Feather said. "I got off the first shot."

Sobbing, she dropped her pistol and flung herself into his arms. "Thank you, thank you," she cried. "Had you not come . . ."

"Do not say it," Red Feather said, his voice drawn. "I still can't believe that you planned this without talking to me about it."

"I had to," Angela Dawn sobbed out. "My father. He . . . killed . . . my father in cold blood. It was my plan all along to find the murderer and shoot him with my father's dueling pistol. I just had not thought ahead, to what might truly happen . . ."

"Well, it didn't, and you are safe now," Red Feather said. "And you no longer have to think of your need of vengeance, nor . . . do . . . I."

"How could two brothers be so different?" Angela Dawn said as she stepped away from him and turned to stare down at Larry. "He had the devil in him." She turned to Red Feather. "You are everything good on this earth."

"All that matters now is that this will soon be behind us," Red Feather said. "I regret so deeply that my brother brought so much heartache to you, as well as to my people. I can't believe that my very own brother plotted to kill me. But I shouldn't be surprised. We *were* two completely different people all of our lives. And I had known for a long time just how jealous Larry was of me."

He paused, swallowed hard, then said, "I regret that. I regret so many things." He stepped away from Angela Dawn and went to kneel beside Larry. "But now is the time to put it all behind us and begin life anew. I will deliver the body of my brother to my father's home. Then I will have the terrible task of telling my mother that she has only one son now."

He laid a gentle hand on his brother's face. "Larry, oh, Larry, I'm so sorry about so many things," he said, his voice breaking. "Most of all, I regret that you felt so left out, so unloved. But now you are at peace. I hope you are happier wherever you are now."

Angela Dawn went and placed a gentle hand on Red Feather's shoulder.

He turned and gazed up at her, then rose to his feet and went to get his horse.

After laying Larry across the back of the horse, Red Feather walked the rest of the way to his home, with Angela Dawn beside him leading her own horse.

His father was just returning in his horse and carriage as they arrived at the house.

Angela Dawn stood back and watched Jon Paul

and Red Feather talking. She felt an ache in her heart when Jon Paul broke down and lifted Larry from the horse, then carried him slowly up the steps and into the house.

Red Feather stared at the door as Jon Paul closed it. Then he turned to Angela Dawn.

"Let's go home," he said, tears shining in his eyes.

"Yes, let's," she murmured.

The ride seemed longer than usual. When they finally reached the Chitimacha village, they went into Soft Flower's lodge.

Angela Dawn stood back as Red Feather explained a son's death to another parent.

Then Soft Flower broke down in tears. She gazed into Red Feather's eyes. "My son, I weep, not because Larry is dead, but because I failed to mold him into a good person," she said, her voice breaking. "I shall carry that guilt in my heart until the day I die."

Red Feather swept her into his arms. "Mother, blaming yourself will not bring Larry back, or change things," he said, his voice breaking. "Please don't. He is to blame, Mother. Only he. He is the one who chose the wrong road in life."

"I loved him," Soft Flower said. "I did love him."

"Yes, I know you did," Red Feather said. "And he loved you in his own strange way. But he did not know how to truly love. There was something born into him that was mean . . . cold. It happens, Mother. It happens."

He stepped away from her. "Mother, I must leave you for a moment and send warriors out to bring home those who are still hunting for a killer," he said thickly. "That killer is dead."

Angela Dawn went to Soft Flower and took her hands. "If you like, I shall stay with you until Red Feather returns," she murmured.

"Yes, I would like that," Soft Flower said, clinging to Angela Dawn's hands.

Angela Dawn turned to Red Feather, nodded, then sat down with Soft Flower beside her lodge fire as Red Feather left. It suddenly came to Angela Dawn that out of three brothers, there was now only one remaining.

And there was only one son left to be chief.

She wondered if Red Feather's father would still refuse to allow Red Feather to be chief because of her.

But she would not think about that. She felt truly free now, for the first time since her parents' deaths, free enough to marry the man she loved, and enjoy life again as she knew she would enjoy it with Red Feather at her side.

Chapter Thirty-seven

At day's brink,
He and his bride were alone—at last.
                    —Robert Browning

"It was so beautiful to see," Angela Dawn murmured as she lay on thick pelts and blankets with Red Feather beside a slow-burning fire. "Your mother and father renewing their vows, the stars in their eyes as they spoke of their love for one another . . . it made tears come to my eyes, tears of happiness, for them and for us."

"My mother deserves all the happiness she will now have with my true father," Red Feather said as he slowly ran a hand across Angela Dawn's bare stomach. "Just as you deserve all the happiness that you shall have. You have had too much heartache in your life. I vow to you that I will protect you forever and ever from any more heartache."

"Being here with you, lying with you, gazing at you, is my happiness," Angela Dawn murmured.

She closed her eyes in ecstasy when Red Feather wove his fingers through the auburn curls at the juncture of her thighs, then slowly began caressing her womanhood.

They had already made maddeningly exciting love once tonight after leaving the celebration.

Angela Dawn felt as though she could continue on and on into the night, her love for her husband was so intense and so true.

"Let me tell you something that my mother taught me when I was old enough to think of one day finding and marrying the woman of my destiny," Red Feather said.

He moved over Angela Dawn, anchoring his knees on both sides of her, his eyes passion-filled as he gazed down into hers.

He still stroked her; he could see in her eyes the bliss that he was stirring within her.

"If your mother told it to you, I'm sure it must be beautiful and meaningful," Angela Dawn said, reaching a hand to his face and gently touching it. "My beautiful Chitimacha warrior, my husband."

She laughed softly. "My warrior husband. That has such a lovely ring to it. I never would have imagined finding anyone like you who would want me . . . who would love me so dearly. I adore you, Red Feather. Absolutely adore you."

He smiled and brushed a soft kiss across her brow, then leaned up away from her.

"My mother told me that the sun and moon were created to be man and wife," Red Feather said, smiling down at Angela Dawn. "The moon was male and intended to vivify and illuminate all things upon the earth, but having neglected to strengthen itself by taking certain baths, it was condemned to remain in the state in which it came from the hands of the Creator. Its light was pale and without vigor, and it lived in ceaseless pursuit of its wife, the sun, without being able to overtake her. The sun, on the contrary, having paid more attention to taking her baths and her *amers*, bitters, was able to project her light on the world and mankind. The sun has always been held in great veneration by my people, and has often stopped in its course to give them time to overcome their enemies, to secure their prey, and attain the other objects of their travels."

"That was a beautiful story," Angela Dawn said softly. "I wish that I had stories to tell you, but my father was not much of a storyteller, nor did my mother spend such time with me. I am proud to say, though, that I am educated. My parents did that for me. But as for knowing much about storytelling? No. And that makes me sad, because I would love to be able to tell our children stories such as the one you just told me."

"You can tell our children this story, and I will tell you others that you can learn, as well," Red Feather said. "Those secret times with my mother were blessed moments. Because of her I am comfortable now in my new life as a Chitimacha."

"You look more handsome, too, in buckskin than in white men's stiff, dark suits," Angela Dawn murmured. She brushed her fingers across his lips. "Do you like me in buckskin, as well?"

"You are an angel in beaded buckskin dresses, even more lovely in doeskin," Red Feather said, then swept her up closer to his hard body, his arms anchoring her against him.

His lips came down upon hers in a meltingly hot kiss, igniting Angela Dawn's senses all over again.

With one insistent thrust, he was inside her, his rhythmic strokes causing her to feel as though she were floating.

When Red Feather reached a hand between them and cupped one of her breasts, rolling the nipple against his palm, Angela Dawn moaned against his lips. She shivered when he groaned out his own pleasure against her lips as he spoke her name, then the words "I love you," as he had so many times this night.

She was flooded with emotion, overcome with the knowledge that tonight was only the beginning.

She was married!

She was married to a wonderful, caring man. She would never be lonely again.

"Let us make a child tonight," she suddenly blurted out, causing him to pause and gaze in wonder into her eyes. "Yes, let's make a child. I have been so alone all my life, and mainly because I had no brother or sister to share things with. I want to have children. I want them to have each other."

"Yes, I want the same," Red Feather said, then gave her a soft, sweet kiss as he renewed his rhythmic strokes within her.

The heat of pleasure soon spread like wildfire within him. He held her tightly as their bodies quaked and shook, dissolving into a delicious tingling heat that spread and seared their very hearts and souls.

And then they lay quietly embracing again, their hearts pounding in unison, their breaths mingling.

"And tonight might have been the night of nights," Red Feather said, rolling away from her.

Breathing hard, yet so content he felt he might

float away, he reached for her hand and held it as he gazed into the flames. "It will never be forgotten," he said.

"Perhaps in fifty years we can renew our vows and be like young lovers all over again?" Angela Dawn murmured as she turned and snuggled next to him. "Fifty years. Can you imagine how we shall look in fifty years?"

"I believe we shall both be gray, and yes, much older, but in my eyes you will always be beautiful. You will always be my morning angel," he said, turning and smiling at her.

She leaned up on an elbow. "Morning angel?" she said, lifting an eyebrow. "Is that how you see me?"

"Is it not morning now as we have spent the entire night talking and loving?" he said, smiling into her eyes. "And ah, I do see you as my angel, so sweet, so good. Yes, I would like to call you by the Indian name Morning Angel. Would you mind if I do?"

"Morning Angel . . ." Angela Dawn said, testing the name on her own lips. "It is so beautiful."

"Then you will accept the Indian name?" Red Feather asked, himself leaning up on an elbow, so as to be eye to eye with her.

"Yes, and with much pride, because it is a name given to me by you," Angela Dawn said. Laughing, feeling giddy with happiness, she flung herself into his arms. "Your Morning Angel loves you."

He cradled her body next to his and kissed her, this time softly, sweetly, and at length.

They only parted when they heard someone outside the lodge.

They gazed questioningly at one another.

"Who could it be at this hour?" Angela Dawn asked. "Who would be up at this hour of the day, except for lovers such as you and me?"

With a concerned look in his eyes, Red Feather rose from the pallet of furs and pulled on his breeches. He handed her a doeskin dress, the one she had worn during the wedding ceremony. "Slip into this."

Angela Dawn slipped on the dress, then went with Red Feather to the entrance flap.

As he opened it, her eyes widened.

There was enough light from the fire to see Chief Straight Arrow standing there with Soft Flower. In Straight Arrow's arms was the headdress, the headdress that Straight Arrow wore as chief.

Red Feather gazed in wonder at the headdress, then turned slow eyes to his father. "Father, why . . ."

He didn't get the chance to finish. Straight Arrow handed the headdress toward him and said, "It is only right that you, my only remaining son, carry on as chief of our people when my body or mind is too worn out to continue myself."

Straight Arrow laid the beautiful headdress of feathers across his son's outstretched arms.

Too touched to say anything, Red Feather gazed at the headdress, and then at his father again.

"My son, I was wrong to deny you what should have been rightfully yours all along," Straight Arrow said. His gaze slid over to Angela Dawn. "And as for you? I was wrong to see you as anything but my son's wife. You are no more a commoner than I am. Everything about you speaks of nobility. You will sit at my son's side as his princess, admired and loved by all of our people."

"I don't know what to say," Angela Dawn replied, her pulse racing. "Except . . . thank you. I hope I don't disappoint you."

"You never could do that," Soft Flower said, smiling at Angela Dawn. "I have spent enough time with you to know exactly why my son loves you. You are a special woman. You will sit at my son's side, glowing and sweet. You will be called princess by our people."

Red Feather turned to Angela Dawn. "She is already my princess," he said, smiling at her. "As I was given a special name to use when I rejoined my people, so has my wife been given a new name. She is now called Morning Angel."

"That is so beautiful," Soft Flower murmured. She stepped forward and took Angela Dawn into her arms. "Your name fits you well."

Angela Dawn . . . Morning Angel . . . beamed with a pure joy she had never thought possible only a few weeks before when her life was nothing but sorrow and loneliness.

Now?

She had everything that any woman could ever want.

She gazed heavenward and said a quiet "thank you" to the One who had brought such blessings to her life.

She had read somewhere that in Him all things were possible. Now she knew that to be true!

Chapter Thirty-eight

Grow old along with me!
The best is yet to be!
      —Robert Browning

It had been two years since that wonderful night of vows and promises. Angela Dawn, now proudly called Morning Angel, lay on her bed, a newborn baby wrapped in a soft blanket in her left arm, while her ten-month-old son cuddled on her right side, asleep.

Red Feather came into the cabin they had built and knelt beside the bed, a bed that he had brought from Ratcliffe Manor. He had taken many luxuries for his wife from the mansion before Jon Paul sold everything to strangers.

Jon Paul had come to Red Feather and had made peace with him and Angela Dawn.

He had even been forgiven by Chief Straight Arrow, because he had brought a considerable amount of money to the Chitimacha people, so that they would not want for anything for a long time.

That had been the only way he could think of to make up for all the wrong he had done the Chitimacha, especially Soft Flower, Red Feather, and Chief Straight Arrow.

Jon Paul had left that day with his head held high, his offering accepted, his misdeeds forgiven.

The money had been accepted only at the urging of Soft Flower. She had felt that she had earned it by living so many years with Jon Paul against her will.

"And so one son sleeps and the other lies awake, his green eyes taking in everything around him," Red Feather said, scooting a chair over beside the bed. His smile was broad as he gazed down at the newborn, who did seem too curious about the world to sleep. He had seen how uncomfortable the small spaces of a tepee had made his wife. He had built her a three-room cabin . . . a place filled with love and devotion.

"While their chieftain father sat in council, working out details of the upcoming New Moon

Ceremony celebration, our son Gray Fox played with his building blocks on the floor until he was exhausted, while his brother Red Beaver filled his tummy with his mommy's milk," Morning Angel said, laughing softly. "I would think Red Beaver would be so full and content, he would also want to take a nap. But, Red Feather, he is such a curious child. His eyes are forever exploring everything around him."

"If you recall, our firstborn son, Gray Fox, did that, as well," Red Feather said, reaching over to gently touch his newest son's copper brow. "One day they will each want the headdress and what goes with it—the chieftainship. But only one can be chief."

"I am sure the right one will follow in your footsteps," Morning Angel said, gazing over at Gray Fox, who had been named after Red Feather's slain brother. "Gray Fox has such a gentle spirit, yet I'm sure that in time he will become as willful as the next young brave."

She shifted her gaze to Red Beaver. "His eyes are finally closed," she said, sighing. "And look, he's smiling. He must be dreaming of angels."

"Father and Mother are doing better," Red Feather said on a serious note. "With both having a fever at the same time, I was afraid . . ."

"They both are strong enough in spirit to ward off this sickness," Morning Angel murmured. She took one of Red Feather's hands. "They will be fine. You will see. Then we shall all celebrate the birth of our secondborn."

"Mother and Father have so looked forward to the New Moon Ceremony," Red Feather said. "I hope they will be able to attend. There will be much worshiping and dancing."

"Has the huge cone of dry reeds been erected yet?" Morning Angel asked.

"Yes, and today at noon it will be set afire," Red Feather said. "The dancing will begin then and will continue around the fire until it is consumed."

"It sounds so exciting," Morning Angel said. "I hope I'm strong enough to attend and watch."

"I shall carry you there," Red Feather said. "You *will* watch. So will Mother and Father. I shall see that you are all comfortable beside the fire."

"Life is good," Morning Angel said, gazing at her sleeping children. "How could it not be? Look at our sons."

Red Feather smiled at Morning Angel. "We do have two sons," Red Feather said. "But there is no daughter yet. Shall we see about that soon, my wife?"

"I told you long ago that I want a big family, so, yes, I do want to try again, especially for a daughter, so that I might have a little girl to play dolls with," Morning Angel said. "I shall enjoy that so much."

"As I will enjoy seeing it," Red Feather said. He took one of her hands in his. "Your contentment shows in your eyes and I can hear it in your voice. This Chitimacha chief is proud to have had something to do with that contentment."

"You have had everything to do with it," Angela Dawn murmured. "And you? You are content? You are enjoying your title of chief?"

"More than words can say," Red Feather said, then reached over and gave her a soft, sweet kiss. "You have made quite a wonderful mail-order bride."

She giggled.

Afterword

Like an old oak tree, the Chitimacha tribe teeters in the winds of change. All that is left of what was once the tribe's vast lands are 2,607 acres.

But despite all odds, the Chitimacha's will to survive gains strength as younger tribesmen carry energy and hope into the future.

True glimpses of Chitimacha culture can be seen on the Bayou Teche side of the reservation. Oak trees stand tall and encircle old houses that hold generations of memories. Families fish and swim in the bayou. In the nearby lakes, commercial fishermen fill their seine nets with fish.

An elder once said, "Where we live, it is peace-

ful and quiet. It has always felt good to be here
among my people."

By many, the Chitimacha are called Lords of
the Land.

And so shall they be until the end of time.

Letter to The Reader

Dear Reader:

I hope you enjoyed reading *Savage Destiny*. The next book in my Savage series, which I am writing exclusively for Leisure Books, is *Savage Hero*, about the Crow Indians. *Savage Hero* is filled with much excitement, romance, and adventure. This book will be in the stores in August 2003.

Many of you say that you are collecting my Indian romances. For my entire backlist of books, and for information about my new fan club, you can send for my latest newsletter, bookmark, and autographed photograph. For an assured reply, please send a stamped, self-addressed, legal-sized envelope to:

Cassie Edwards

Cassie Edwards
6709 North Country Club Road
Mattoon, IL, 61938

You can also visit my website at:
www.cassieedwards.com

Thank you for your support of my Indian series. I love researching and writing about our country's beloved Native Americans.

SAVAGE LOVE

CASSIE EDWARDS

Monster bones are the stuff of Indian legend, which warns that they must not be disturbed. But Dayanara and her father are on a mission to uncover the bones. Not even her father's untimely death or a disapproving Indian chief can prevent Dayanara from proving her worth as an archaeologist.

Any relationship between a Cree chief and a white woman is prohibited by both their peoples, but the golden woman of Quick Fox's dreams is more glorious than the setting sun. Not even her interest in the sacred burial grounds of his people can prevent him from discovering the delights they will know together and proving his savage love.

Night after night she sees a warrior in her dreams, his body golden bronze, his hair raven black. And she knows he is the one destined to make her a woman. As a child, Misshi Bradley watched as one by one her family died on the trail west, until she herself was stolen by renegade Indians. But now she is ready to start a family of her own, and Soaring Hawk is searching for a wife. In his eyes, she reads promises of a passion that will never end, but can she trust him when his own father is the renegade who destroyed her life once before? As Soaring Hawk holds her to his heart, Misshi vows the tragedies of the past will not come between them, or keep her from finding fulfillment beneath the savage moon.

Savage Honor
Cassie Edwards

Shawndee Sibley longs for satin ribbons, fancy dresses, and a man who will take her away from her miserable life in Silver Creek. But the only men she ever encounters are the drunks who frequent her mother's tavern. And even then, Shawndee's mother makes her disguise herself as a boy for her own protection.

Shadow Hawk bitterly resents the Sibleys for corrupting his warriors with their whiskey. Capturing their "son" is a surefire way to force them to listen to him. But he quickly becomes the captive—of Shawndee's shy smile, iron will, and her shimmering golden hair.

___4889-2 $5.99 US/$6.99 CAN